THE WIDOW

VALERIE KEOGH

Boldwood

First published in Great Britain in 2022 by Boldwood Books Ltd.

Copyright © Valerie Keogh, 2022

Cover Design by Head Design

Cover Photography: Shutterstock

The moral right of Valerie Keogh to be identified as the author of this work has been asserted in accordance with the Copyright, Designs and Patents Act 1988.

A CIP catalogue record for this book is available from the British Library.

Paperback ISBN 978-1-80415-463-2

Large Print ISBN 978-1-80415-462-5

Hardback ISBN 978-1-80415-461-8

Ebook ISBN 978-1-80415-464-9

Kindle ISBN 978-1-80415-465-6

Audio CD ISBN 978-1-80415-456-4

MP3 CD ISBN 978-1-80415-457-1

Digital audio download ISBN 978-1-80415-460-1

Boldwood Books Ltd
23 Bowerdean Street
London SW6 3TN
www.boldwoodbooks.com

For my niece
Niamh Elliot
with love

PART I

1

My parents loved each other. They were always hugging, holding hands, touching. If separated in a crowd, they'd exchange passionately adoring glances. Parted by distance, they'd pine and make frequent phone calls. They rarely used their given names, the plain John and Eve everyone else used; instead it was 'darling', 'honey', 'sweetheart' and other various nick-names, the most nauseating of which was 'sex bomb' for her, 'stud' for him, these last only used in the privacy of their home.

Where I lived.

Their love was exclusive, inward-looking, nothing remaining for anyone else, not even the children these self-obsessed people had brought into the world. The children they'd named Allison, Beth and Cassie but dismissively referred to as A, B and C or, as I overheard my mother calling us once... the 'alphabet sprogs'.

We weren't mistreated, not really. Hard to mistreat someone you barely acknowledged being alive. We offspring of these two were fed, and clothed, but little money was spent on procuring either.

Our eyes were opened when we went to school and, as the eldest of the three sprogs, I was first to suffer for the sin of being 'different'.

I was the child the other children laughed at; my thin, spindly body clothed in well-worn, badly fitting, charity-shop clothes. The child who from self-preservation became a skilled, believable liar.

Lies to save face – the ones when I insisted I wasn't hungry as classmates unwrapped their lunchtime sandwiches, my mother's attitude being if I didn't want to eat the meagre bread and jam provided free by the school, I could do without. Jam sandwiches, no butter so that the bread was soggy, the resultant mess unappetising. Maybe I'd have eaten it, hungry as I was, if taking one of those vile offerings hadn't pushed me further down in the already low estimation of my classmates.

Lies to protect me from my mother's ire when a teacher asked if I'd eaten breakfast the morning I fainted. Even at a young age I was aware that although my parents didn't care about their children, they did care about how they were perceived by authority.

Lies to cover my petty thieving, the bars of chocolate, packets of crisps, anything I could slip into my pockets or my scuffed, raggedy schoolbag.

I was the child other children laughed at.

The child who gazed about her and wondered why her life was so incredibly sad.

2

Allison met Peter at a party given by Lorraine, a work colleague she wasn't particularly friendly with. The invitation was unexpected and Allison, who wasn't keen on social gatherings of any sort and work ones in particular, desperately searched for an acceptable excuse to avoid an event where she'd have to make small talk with people she wasn't keen on.

'It's my fortieth. Do come, it'll be fun.' Lorraine, clipboard in one hand, a pen in the other with its point pressed to the space beside Allison's name, gave an impatient huff as she waited for an answer.

Guessing she'd been invited to make up the numbers rather than any real desire to have her company, Allison wanted to say an unvarnished no. She didn't owe Lorraine anything. They weren't friends. But, unable to think of a good enough excuse, she found herself nodding and spouting lies. 'Of course, thank you, I'd love to come.'

For the remainder of the day, all kinds of acceptable reasons to refuse popped into her head. Too late, as these things usually were. It was a week to the party, and she promised herself she'd find an opportunity to tell Lorraine she couldn't, after all, make it, that something unexpected had come up and how genuinely sorry she was. But the week had flown by and a chance to tell her, even if Allison could have found the words, never occurred.

The night of the party, she took out a dress she'd bought months before and never worn. It had been in the window of an expensive boutique she regularly passed on her way to work. Her social life being non-existent, there was no requirement for fancier clothes than the rather dull suits she bought in M&S, so she'd never gone inside.

But on a particularly grey morning, the colour of the dress had caught her eye... a shade of turquoise she associated with the tantalising seascapes on the covers of holiday brochures. She'd stood staring at it as busy commuters surged by, then turned to join the flow, trying to put it from her mind. It was a busy day with little time for daydreaming but now and then, just for a few seconds, she allowed her mind to drift to the dress. A woman wearing such a divine garment couldn't be dull; she'd be dazzling, oozing charm; her conversation would be sparkling and witty. She'd be everything Allison wasn't, everything she longed to be.

It was a Thursday night. Late-night shopping. When she left the office for home that evening, the streets were heaving with shoppers who ploughed onward, laden carrier bags bumping into others willy-nilly as they passed. Allison slowed as she approached the boutique, half-afraid the dress would be gone, half-hoping it would be. If it was still there... she might go inside, try it on. Not buy it, of course, she'd nowhere to wear a dress so elegant.

It *was* there. She stood with her nose almost pressed to the traffic-dusty glass of the shop window. The dress was more lovely than she remembered and absolute longing consumed her. There was no harm in going inside to look at it, was there?

The interior of the shop was large and lavishly decorated with gold trimmings. The only assistant, a short, attractive woman who moved about on towering stilettos as if floating, was busy with a customer who was holding up a dress in two different shades as if trying to decide which to purchase.

Conscious the suit she was wearing had seen better days, Allison resisted the temptation to hug the large satchel she carried to her chest like a shield. Instead, overcompensating, she swung it in what she hoped was nonchalance, praying it didn't look as odd as she feared.

When neither the assistant nor the other customer as much as glanced in her direction, she relaxed and looked around. Dresses were hanging on a rail on the far side of the shop. As she crossed, her footsteps on the polished wooden floor seeming over-loud, she scanned the collection, hoping the dress in the window wasn't the only one.

No, there it was! She reached out to touch it, fingers skimming over the fabric. The colours were more vibrant up close, the material soft and light. She held the skirt of the dress out, picturing herself in it, the fabric swishing sound her legs. With a sigh, she let it drop. She didn't need such a dress, but it didn't stop her searching for the price tag. Perhaps if it weren't too expensive...

But it was. Ludicrously expensive, in fact. The assistant was still busy; Allison could simply leave and put this nonsense behind her. Her fingers, however, had other ideas and reached out to touch the dress again. Then, suddenly, she had the hanger off the rail, and she was crossing the shop floor with it in her hand.

After all, it cost nothing to try it on, did it?

But when Allison tried it on, when she twirled and admired her reflection in the triad of mirrors that formed the back walls of the small changing room, when she saw how the dress transformed her from dull to scintillating, she knew she had to have it.

'How is it?' the assistant asked through the thin curtain of the changing room.

Allison nodded at her reflection. 'It's perfect. I'll take it.'

* * *

The dress had sat in her wardrobe, unworn, in the months since she'd bought it. Now and then, she'd take it out, getting pleasure from the sheer gorgeousness of it. Reluctant as she was to attend Lorraine's birthday celebrations, it was an opportunity to wear it.

On the night of the party, Allison hung the dress on the outside of the wardrobe door. An unexpected excitement edged away any lingering reluctance and pushed her into making more of an effort. Normally, she pinned her long brown hair up... a tight chignon for work, a low ponytail at the weekend. That night, she allowed it to dry naturally rather than blow-drying it, and gentle waves framed her face before falling to her shoulders. Against the turquoise fabric of the dress, her hair looked more auburn than mousy brown.

Reaching for her usual make-up, she hesitated. For years, she'd applied the same heavy foundation, eyeshadow, lipstick. It had become as much part of her work uniform as her M&S suits. She ran her fingers over the smattering of freckles on her cheeks. Perhaps that night, she'd go au natural with maybe just a flick of mascara and a touch of lipstick. She stared at herself in the mirror, pleased with the results.

She looked like someone else. Even better, she *felt* like someone else. The woman from her imagination... the one who dazzled. The woman she could have been had she made different choices all those years before.

3

The party was held in the small upstairs function room of a pub near King's Cross station. Allison had been inside it years before, not long after she'd joined McPherson Accountancy and had been eager to fit in. It had been a work night out to celebrate something or other; the reason had long since slipped her memory. The group had quickly descended into drunken bawdiness, and she'd made her exit as quickly as possible, swearing never again. She hadn't socialised with her colleagues again, and the memory of the previous debacle swamped the excitement of her dress.

It would be better to go home, and perhaps she would have done if the door of the pub hadn't suddenly opened and a laughing group surged out. Their laughter released some of the tension that had gripped her. What harm could it do to go in for one drink?

Inside, it was busy and groups of raucous drinkers with brimming pint glasses stood between her and the door to the narrow stairway that led to the upstairs venue. She dodged around them, one hand holding the skirt of her dress tightly to her body. Her *whew* of relief was lost in the din as she pushed the door open and went through.

The stairway was dimly lit. From the bottom, she could see the startlingly bright lights of the landing, and as if lured, she climbed slowly. At the top, she stopped, taking stock. *Girding her loins.* She smiled at the thought. It was a party, not a battle; it was supposed to be fun.

Through double doors, she saw a crowd of people milling about laughing and talking. They were obviously enjoying themselves. She could walk over, crack a joke, smile, laugh, be just like them. They were no different to her, were they? Not on the surface, anyway. She slipped past the doors and followed a sign on the wall to the ladies', relieved on reaching it to find she had it to herself. The facilities were surprisingly generous. An ornately framed mirror hung over each of the three wash-hand basins with a matching full-length one fixed to the wall at the end. On one side of this sat two velvet-covered chairs angled to face each other. They offered a comfortable place to sit. Perhaps she could simply stay there. Lorraine was bound to come in at some stage during the evening. Allison could sit on one of the chairs, wait till she did, say hello, wish her a happy birthday and make her exit.

She could. The lighting in the room was flattering. Allison smoothed a hand down the fabric of her dress and walked towards the full-length mirror. It was exactly as she'd imagined she'd look. It hadn't transformed her into the life and soul of the party but she looked glamorous, attractive and like other women she'd admired who were dressed up for a night of excitement. Not a woman who came to a party to hide in the toilets. Allison was a grown woman, an accountant, not a child. Plus, it was a bloody expensive dress; showing it off would go somewhere toward justifying the ridiculous amount of money she'd paid for it.

When she returned to the landing, there was a group of people heading into the venue. She didn't recognise anyone but tagged along with the laughing group until they were inside, where the noise was slightly louder than it had been downstairs in the pub. A few people were gyrating on the small dance floor, hands pumping the air with enthusiasm in time to the beat of a song Allison didn't recognise.

She looked around for the birthday girl but couldn't see her in the crowd. When her eyes adjusted to the dimmer light inside the room, she recognised a couple of people from the office; they raised their hands in greeting when they saw her but made no effort to invite her to join them.

A rising tide of red crept over her cheeks, her eyes flicking to the doorway as panic's icy fingers gripped and squeezed. There were so many people between her and the exit, she wasn't sure she could make it.

'Allison!' Lorraine appeared at her side, a drink in one hand, a party horn in the other. She blew it next to Allison's ear, almost deafening her. 'I really didn't think you'd come.' Alcohol slurred the edges of her words. 'You didn't come to the Christmas party, so I'm honoured.' She waved an arm around the room, swaying alarmingly. 'You know everyone; grab a drink.' Another expansive wave pointed towards where a table was set up with glasses and bottles. 'It's free till it runs out' – she giggled drunkenly – 'which won't be long at the rate everyone is drinking, so grab a glass while you can.'

Another blow on the party horn and she left. Allison's panic had faded. Her duty had been done; the birthday girl had seen her. She didn't want a drink; she could leave.

The music changed to a song she liked, a George Michael one she hadn't heard for a while. With a shrug, she headed to the drinks table, humming along to 'Faith'. She might as well stay for one drink.

The white-linen-covered table was festooned with birthday banners and helium balloons. It had probably looked jaunty and festive at the beginning of the night but now, only an hour into the party, it was looking bedraggled. The biggest of the banners was torn in two; two of the balloons had been untied and were bouncing lazily along the ceiling. To add a touch of Gothic horror, red wine dripped ghoulishly down one side of the white linen.

A waiter stood behind a table. The uniform waistcoat he wore had obviously been purchased many years... and a couple of stone... before. The small metal buttons that fastened it strained against the buttonholes and looked ready to pop at any moment. She imagined them firing into the crowd, making the drunks bleed.

He looked and sounded bored. 'What can I get you?'

The choice seemed limited to white, red or beer. 'A glass of white wine, please.'

Maybe he was in a hurry to finish the free drinks or perhaps he didn't know any better because the glass he handed her was filled to the brim. Wine trickled down the outside as he passed it to her. As she hesitated, she caught him looking, a smile hovering just out of reach. He probably thought she was too precious to take it. She wasn't, but she was conscious of her dress. 'You can put it down, thanks.'

When he did, she used an edge of the table covering to dry the glass before lifting it carefully to take a mouthful. Only then did she move away with it in her hand, searching for a place where she could stand without looking conspicuously alone. Lorraine was wrong: she didn't know everyone. In fact, apart from the few people from the office she'd already seen, nobody looked familiar. Or maybe, like her, they'd taken off their work masks.

Maybe if she downed a few glasses of this bloody awful cheap plonk, she'd be able to relax. Let go. Maybe join the group on the dance floor and sway in time to the music playing now, a song she remembered from her university days but couldn't put a name to. She hadn't liked parties then any more than she did now, but back then she and her equally nerdy friends would dance anywhere. The words came to her, and she sang along under her breath, shimmying in time to the music. Lost in the moment, she wasn't aware of the man who appeared at her shoulder until she felt the warmth of his breath on her cheek as he leaned closer to be heard above the surrounding noise.

'I've always liked this song too.'

Startled, she jerked around, her lips suddenly within kissing distance of a handsome stranger who was looking at her with an admiring glint in his eyes.

Allison took a step away and lifted her glass to her mouth, taking a gulp rather than a sip, her mouth dry. She hoped he'd think the colour in her cheeks was the result of alcohol, not embarrassment... or if she was being completely honest, the unaccustomed, overwhelming dart of desire. Small talk wasn't her forte; she was great with numbers, above averagely useless with words. 'How do you know Lorraine?' An open question, she'd read, was better at promoting interaction.

'I don't.'

As a conversation ender, it was perfect. She stared at him, willing her brain to come up with something scintillating to say. It didn't, but it wouldn't have mattered; her tongue was suddenly large and clumsy in her mouth, refusing to work.

'I don't know anyone here.' He put a warm hand on her elbow and led her away as they were crushed by a huddle of people attempting to reach the drinks table. 'I suppose you'd call me a gate-crasher.'

A drunken roar from the dance floor drew their attention. Allison felt the heat of his hand on her elbow. She should pull away, glare at him for taking liberties, but she wanted him to stay, to keep his hand exactly where it was. It was times like this she wished for a Cyrano to slip her the right words, a quick, sassy comment to make this incredibly handsome man look at her in admiration. Be enthralled by her. Want to stay.

By the time the noise level had dropped again, she hadn't thought of anything better to say than a very lame, and not very complimentary, 'Why on earth would you want to gate crash this party?' She pulled her arm away from his hand. The patch of skin he'd touched was instantly chilled; she rubbed her hand over it. It was time to leave. This man... with his well-cut suit, a glint of gold in the cuffs of his shirt, his tie undone just enough... he was out of her league. Previous boyfriends, and there had been many, had been those who, like her, lurked on the edges of whatever was going on. This man belonged centre stage.

'I was in the bar downstairs with some work colleagues when I saw you come in.' He reached forward and before she could stop him, he'd gathered a fold of her dress in his hand. 'You stood out in this amidst all the dull suits and black dresses.' He dropped the material and raised his hand to her hair. 'Your hair caught the light. I was curious about you, so I followed.'

She wanted to laugh, to dismiss him as an opportunist, a scam artist, one of those men who preyed on desperate or vulnerable women. Perhaps she would have done, if he hadn't taken her hand and looked into her eyes with such intensity, she felt weak. She'd sneered at women who fell for such obvious tricks. How desperate they must have been.

'Why don't we get out of here and go somewhere we can talk?'

She wasn't desperate, or vulnerable, she was an intelligent, mature woman who had no desire to become a statistic, but when he reached for her hand, she laid hers in his and went with him like a lamb to the sacrificial altar.

4

I learnt to read when I was very young and quickly discovered a fantasy world where everything was bright and cheerful. Where children were loved and cosseted by adoring parents. I would read the words, greedy for this imaginary world, reluctant to leave it, rereading my favourite stories, finishing the last page, turning immediately to the first page again, reliving a life so unlike mine.

Perhaps stories would have been sufficient if a new student hadn't joined our class when I was almost nine. She was small, mousy, nothing special, although she was adopted, which caused a few minutes of staring as if being such meant she had to look different in some way. When she didn't, we went back to ignoring her. Things wouldn't have changed if I hadn't walked out after school that first day to see her mother waiting for her with open arms. There was a beaming smile and a look of love on her face as she folded the mousy girl in her embrace as if she was the most precious thing in the world. Jealousy was a new emotion for me; it brought me to a halt, my eyes fixed on the scene, wanting desperately to be that girl, to have that woman as my mother, to have the life I knew I should have been born into.

The girl, Monica, became my obsession. Never a friend, though;

losers like me, girls who didn't have lunch, who never invited classmates to birthday parties, who were dressed in charity-shop cast-offs, who were obviously 'different', didn't have friends. Even then, I knew my place. But I watched. I followed Monica and her mother home, stood outside their house for hours at a time and followed their comings and goings. Perhaps I wanted to see that the reality of their life was no different to mine, that the school greeting was merely for show, but no, they appeared happy, content, loved-up, every single time I saw them.

My envy grew. Especially when I had to go home after seeing them together, when I was forced to contrast their idyllic life with mine.

Why couldn't I have been adopted into a loving family? That thought began to obsess me until finally I realised that I could be.

If my parents were to die.

5

Peter took Allison to a wine bar a short distance away. The clientele older, smarter, *richer.* The décor sumptuous. Damask chairs, polished wood, the light dim and flattering.

'This is better.' He brushed away the menu the waiter held out to him. 'A bottle of Dom Perignon, please.'

'Certainly.'

Allison bit back a sigh of pleasure as she sat on a chair so comfortable it was like being hugged. She was being swept along; it wasn't a sensation she was used to. 'You didn't ask if I liked champagne.'

'Do you?'

'Yes, but that isn't the point.' She tried to put a little steel in her voice. 'I don't even know your name.'

He laughed then, the confident, self-assured sound of a man who always got his own way. 'Peter... Peter Fellowes. Are you happier drinking champagne with me now?'

Once again, she wanted to dazzle him with her witty repartee. 'Safer, perhaps.' *Safer, perhaps.* That was the best she could come up with?

It may not have been scintillating, but it made him laugh anyway. 'You think knowing my name makes it safer; I could be lying to you.'

'Are you?'

Instead of answering, he reached into the inside pocket of his jacket. 'Here you go.' He handed a business card across.

The card was thick, matt black, the writing in gold script. *Peter Fellowes, Attorney at Law.*

'I'm not sure this makes me feel safer.'

This drew another laugh. Perhaps she wasn't that bad at snappy retorts after all. The arrival of the champagne, and the palaver of opening it, gave Allison time to assess the man sitting opposite with a more objective eye. He was certainly handsome, reminding her a little of a young Paul Newman. Brown eyes, though, not blue. Lighter brown hair, cut a little too short for her taste. Large hands with slightly stubby fingers. No wedding band, no indent to say one had been there recently. All almost too perfect.

A discreet pop brought her eyes back to the waiter, who performed the ritual opening and poured with a minimum of fuss. When he left, Peter picked up his glass and held it forward. 'Here's to auspicious beginnings.'

Beginnings. The bubbles ticked her nose as she sipped. Then, throwing caution to the winds that were whirling around her... ones filled with dazzling opportunities... she took a large mouthful. She didn't drink much. Wine if she was out for dinner. The occasional glass at home in the evening. Maybe the unaccustomed alcohol was responsible for the feeling of lightness, the huge sense of expectation.

'I want to know all about you,' Peter said, putting his glass down. 'Starting with your name.'

It would have been nice to have talked of some fascinating life spent in various parts of the world, a childhood in India, teenage years in South Africa, university in Boston. She could have invented a believable past if she'd had warning; without it, it was easier to go with a version of the truth. 'There's not much to say. My name's Allison. I'm from Oxford. Went to university in Southampton, then studied to be an accountant here in London.'

'And you still work here?'

She was tempted to say *yes* and name one of the more reputable accountancy firms, any of the ones who'd considered her not good enough. Not her qualifications... *her*. Each of the rejection letters had contained a variation on *you're not quite what we were looking for*. She still brooded over those rejections, worried that they'd seen something in her that wasn't quite *right*.

It was dangerous to lie about where she worked, though. London could be a small city when it came to certain professions. 'Yes.' She waited for him to ask who she worked for, preparing herself for his disdainful expression when she mentioned the bargain-basement company McPherson Accountancy.

He didn't ask. Instead, he rubbed his hand across his forehead in pantomime relief, adding a *whew*, in case she might have misunderstood, or perhaps he doubted his acting skills. 'Good, I was afraid maybe you were here for a conference or something and would vanish to some far-flung part of the country.'

Relief that he didn't ask where she worked vied with irritation that he hadn't been interested enough to do so. She brushed aside both and smiled. 'Only as far as Tottenham.'

'You weren't tempted to commute from Oxford to be near your family?'

Allison longed for the day when that one word, *family*, didn't send a frisson of fear and loathing down her spine. For what she'd done, for what she was. She finished the champagne to wash the sensation away. 'I don't have anyone there any more.' The waiter, as if pulled by an invisible string, appeared and topped up her glass. Not Peter's, she noticed. He'd barely touched his. She should have stopped when she noticed his abstinence, certainly shouldn't have drunk the second glass even faster. Whether it was the bubbles or the intense regard of the man sitting opposite, she became unusually talkative. 'My parents died in an accident several years ago.'

He leaned towards her, his expression suddenly sombre. 'I'm so sorry, that must have been tough. Do you have siblings?'

She lifted her glass and took a large mouthful. He was waiting for her answer. She shrugged. 'No. I'm an only child.'

'Tough... and lonely.' He sat back but his eyes never left her face.

'I think only children are more resilient and become self-contained from necessity. I've always been content with my own company.' She dropped her eyes to her glass, watching as the bubbles rose and vanished. 'I have friends, of course.' A lie... she had one friend, Portia, who Allison had met only recently. Otherwise, there were a few acquaintances who invited her to the occasional party to make up the numbers, or who rang when they were bored and nobody else was free.

'Another bottle?' The waiter looked at Peter as he emptied the last of the champagne into her glass.

Allison wanted to take umbrage at the waiter's deference to Peter. Wanted to raise a hand and say with cool disdain that yes, they'd have another bottle. But she'd drunk most of the champagne and was afraid the words would come out slurred, perhaps even garbled rather than firm and authoritative. So she said nothing, relieved when Peter shook his head.

When the bill came, presented to him on a silver salver, she made a half-hearted objection. 'I should pay; I think I drank most of it.'

'Don't be silly, you're here at my invitation.'

Dom Perignon... in a place like this... she was slightly annoyed by his *don't be silly* but more than happy to be spared the cost. 'Thank you.' She picked up her handbag. 'I should be getting home.'

'I have my car parked close by; I'll drop you back.'

Strangely relieved to have his abstinence explained, she shook her head. 'No, that's fine, thank you, I can call a taxi.'

'Nonsense.'

She should have been irritated at his dismissal of her decision but when she got to her feet and felt the floor swaying under her, she was inordinately grateful. If she hoped he wouldn't notice, she was enlightened when he laughed and put a hand on her waist. 'You're a lightweight,' he said, pulling her closer to him.

He was solid, his hand warm through the fabric of her dress. It was the excess alcohol that made her melt into him, that allowed her to be led along, and once again she thought of the sacrificial lamb being led to the slaughter.

But who was leading whom? Because suddenly she thought Peter could be exactly what she needed.

6

It had been her friend, Portia, who'd inadvertently given Allison the idea. They'd met at yoga, quickly discovering they had a similar dismissive, cynical attitude towards those for whom the perfect bird of paradise pose was a raison d'être.

Allison was between boyfriends. *Boyfriends.* She called them that although they were rarely more than one-night stands. It wasn't that men didn't like her... they did, but they were such hard work and she bored easily.

She was feeling more than a little... untethered. 'Lonely' wasn't a word she allowed into her vocabulary. Perhaps it was why she allowed herself to drop her guard a little and agreed to join Portia for coffee after the class. She was far older. Sixty, Allison decided when she was being kind, nearer to seventy when she'd had a bad day and wasn't feeling generous. Despite the age difference – thirty or forty years – and although they had little in common apart from their shared dislike of pomposity, the coffee became a weekly habit and they became friends.

Allison didn't have any others. Circumstances had meant she'd made none in school and those she'd made in university had dispersed to other cities, other countries. Despite vocal and usually drunken promises to stay in touch, they hadn't. Eventually she could barely remember their names and wasn't sure she'd recognise them in a crowd.

Portia, with her vividly bright red lipstick, sky-blue eyeshadow and dramatically arched eyebrows, was amusing, eccentric and, if her designer clothes, bags and expensive jewellery were any indication, also very wealthy.

After coffee the following week, they left the café together, Portia chatting away, Allison nodding now and then to indicate she was listening. When a car pulled up in the car park, Portia was still talking. It was only when the car blasted its horn that she turned, her words cut off mid-sentence.

Allison was surprised by the change in her friend's expression. From excitedly animated, it had become tight and almost fearful.

'There's my darling,' Portia said, waving towards the Porsche.

The words were at such odds with the tone of her voice that Allison was tempted to ask Portia if there was something wrong, if perhaps she and her husband had had a row, but before she could get the words out, Portia looked towards the car again. 'I'd better dash; he hates to be kept waiting.'

Without another word, she was gone, leaving Allison standing staring after the car in bemusement.

* * *

The following week, Portia surprised Allison with an invitation to dinner. 'Do come,' she said. 'We'd love to have you.'

Caught by surprise, Allison felt obliged to say yes. Anyway, she was curious about her new friend's home and husband. The following evening, she followed the directions she'd been given and reached Portia's Kensington home. It was breathtakingly beautiful.

Inside, it was equally so. 'Come in,' Portia said, throwing the front door open wide. 'I hope you don't mind, but we wear slippers inside to protect the wooden floors.' She pointed to a pair of pink slippers sitting on the polished wooden floor. 'They're new, so don't worry. Or you can go barefooted, if you'd prefer.'

'Barefooted is fine.' Allison kicked off her shoes.

'Great, come on, I'll open a bottle and we can chat while I finish cooking.' Portia pushed the door open into the biggest kitchen Allison had ever seen. It was also probably the coldest. All white shiny cupboards, white tiled floor, white walls. Portia opened the door of the huge American-style fridge and took out a bottle of Prosecco. 'This okay?'

Allison nodded and perched on a bar stool as Portia peeled the foil from the neck of the bottle and removed the cork with a satisfying pop. She poured into the waiting glasses. 'Cheers,' she said, tipping her glass against Allison's. 'Stuart has some emails to send. He'll join us when he's done.'

'Cheers.' Allison sipped her drink and put the glass down. 'You have a lovely home.'

'It's fabulous, isn't it?' Portia waved a hand around the room. 'The décor mightn't exactly be to my taste, but I do love the space, and living in Kensington is amazing.'

Portia was so exotic, and the décor so incredibly bland, Allison was puzzled. Perhaps the house was rented. 'Oh, I see, it's not your place then?'

'No.' Portia's smile was forced. 'It's Stuart's house. He likes minimalism.' She drained her glass and reached for the bottle. 'Some more?'

Allison, who had barely touched hers, shook her head.

Portia filled her own glass and took a mouthful. 'When I met

Stuart, I was young, poor, aimless. He was older, wiser, and introduced me to a different world.' She waved her hand around the
room again. 'I got all this and more. Accepting we had different
taste seemed a small price to pay.'

Allison thought she understood. Portia had said 'older' and
'wiser'; she'd left out 'richer'. When Stuart came through the door
moments later, she was convinced she was right. He was perhaps
twenty years older than Portia, maybe in his eighties.

Portia leapt to her feet and laid a hand on Allison's shoulder.
'Stuart, this is Allison.'

For a second, Allison felt on display. Stuart's eyes, cold and
hard in an unattractively piggy face, slid over her with unpleasant
intensity. He crossed to her with his hand extended. 'Welcome to
our home.'

'Nice to meet you,' she said, feeling her hand engulfed in his
unusually large one. He held it a fraction too long for her liking as
he continued to weigh her up. She must have passed whatever
internal criteria he used to judge people because suddenly his
expression became welcoming.

Portia fluttered around with a smile on her face. 'Bring Allison
through to the dining room, Stuart. I'll bring the food in a mo.'

'Certainly, my dear.' He smiled and waved Allison to a doorway
on the far side of the room.

It opened into another large cold room. A huge table was
surrounded by eight chairs. One painting hung on the far wall.
There was no other furniture. None of the knick-knacks that
turned a house into a home.

Stuart held a chair out for her, only taking his hands away after
she'd sat. Allison thought she'd felt his fingers brush her neck and
jerked, startled. But when she looked at him, his expression was
one of innocence. Perhaps she'd imagined the touch. It was this
house: it was strangely creepy.

When Stuart took the seat opposite, she searched for something to say. 'You have a lovely home.' It was a whopper of a lie but it worked and Stuart smiled and sat back.

'Minimalism suits me.' He waved a hand around the room. 'Clean lines, cool colours, no clutter.'

Portia came bustling through with plates and dishes a moment later and the room was filled with the aroma of good food. Wine flowed a little too freely for Allison's liking. She left hers untouched when it was refilled and sipped from her water glass instead.

As Portia and Stuart imbibed several glasses of wine, the conversation became a little risqué. Perhaps if Allison had drunk as much, she'd have found it entertaining instead of boring and verging on the unacceptable. She sat back with a forced smile and nodded when appropriate. When Stuart began to put his wife down with subtle cutting comments as the night progressed, and Portia, normally chatty and effusive, became restless, almost on edge, Allison was glad to escape.

'Stay over,' Portia insisted at the end of the night. 'We've plenty of space after all and Amy's room is always kept made up in case she should arrive home unexpectedly.'

There was a hint of longing in the words. Allison knew about Amy, Portia's daughter who'd left home the year before to attend university abroad. She obviously missed her. Was that why she pushed the friendship with Allison – was she a substitute daughter?

'No, thanks,' she said. 'Actually, I ordered a taxi earlier, it should be here...' She checked her phone for the time. 'Any moment now.'

'Oh, that's a shame.' Portia looked so genuinely disappointed that Allison felt a moment's regret until she looked at Stuart, whose expression had reverted back to the coldly assessing one.

'Next time, perhaps,' he said, getting to his feet.

'Perhaps.' She smiled non-committedly and followed the couple to the hallway, where she slipped her feet into her shoes and took her jacket from Portia. 'It's been lovely, thank you so much.'

'A pleasure, my dear.' Portia gave her a quick hug. 'We'll do it again soon. And I'll see you in class next week.'

Allison held a hand out to Stuart and offered yet another of her collection of social lies. 'It was lovely to meet you.'

He took her hand but instead of shaking it as convention dictated, he pulled her into his arms and a lingering embrace. His body was soft; she felt herself sinking into it. 'I look forward to seeing you again,' he said before releasing her.

As the taxi negotiated London streets to her home, Allison thought about the couple. Portia, she guessed, had married for money, not love, and it had got her what she obviously wanted.

Allison rested her head back and shut her eyes. And as she relaxed on the journey home, an idea flickered.

Marry for money. Could she do the same?

7

The idea burrowed itself into her head, but it would probably have died without germinating had she not met Peter less than two weeks later. Then it suddenly sprouted. If he was as wealthy as he appeared, could she make it work? Could she really marry for money? She read enough gossip columns to know it was done far more frequently than people liked to admit.

As Allison allowed Peter to guide her along the pavement, the idea became more appealing. Portia had done it, and it had worked out okay for her. Allison shivered when she thought of Stuart. No, that was a step too far. Peter, however, seemed charming and he was undeniably handsome.

When they reached the underground garage, she half-expected the car to be something flashy. Something that went with Peter's confident swagger... a Porsche, maybe even a Lamborghini... but when he clicked his remote, she had to bite back the snort of disbelief when the lights of a Ford Fiesta flicked once.

Such a reliable, sensible, mundane car. She was amused at her disappointment. It also made her regard Peter with renewed inter-est. In her limited experience, it was unusual and refreshing to meet a man who didn't need a big, showy car to confirm his masculinity.

He opened the door for her, and she slid inside.

'Okay. Where to?'

She gave him her address. 'It's kind of you to drop me home. I hope it's not too much out of your way.'

'I have a place in Islington.' He reversed the car from the space and headed toward the exit. 'I don't normally drive but I had to visit a housebound client who lives in Watford, so it was easier.'

'I don't keep a car myself.' No point in telling him she couldn't afford to. Living in London was crazily expensive, and she hadn't been one of the lucky ones who'd been able to combine college with a part-time job. It had taken every hour of study to get her through and enable her to finish in the top five per cent of her class. She'd hoped it would pay off, that she'd have her pick of positions when she'd finished. It hadn't quite worked out that way.

With her salary adequate rather than good, it had taken far longer than she'd hoped to pay off her student loans. She had hoped to buy her own place but, fast as she saved, property prices continued to rise out of her grasp. Even using a help-to-buy scheme she would only have been able to afford a tiny apartment somewhere she didn't want to live.

The car swayed as Peter negotiated the winding exit from the multi-storey car park. Allison had had a tiring day and the unaccustomed alcohol was taking its toll. Her eyelids drifted shut and flew open again only to slowly shut again seconds later. How embarrassing it would be to fall asleep! She shuffled to a more upright position, determined to stay alert, and rattled her brain for something to say.

'You're a very restful woman to be with.' Peter glanced her way as his window slid open at the exit. He pushed the parking card into the slot and the barrier rose. Before he drove forward, he took his hand from the steering wheel and rested it briefly on her thigh. 'Most women fill the silence with chattering about nothing.'

Most women! Allison bridled and would have made a sarcastic comment if the alcohol hadn't dimmed her ability to formulate a sentence.

Luckily for him, she could no longer fight against the soporific effect of the car's motion and fell asleep. When she woke, she was outside her apartment block, his hand gently shaking her shoulder. She looked at him, struggling to remember why she felt momentary irritation. Hadn't he said something to annoy her?

Then he leaned forward and kissed her gently on the lips and she thought she must have imagined it.

'I'll walk you to your door,' he said, reaching to undo her seat belt. He waited till they reached her apartment on the fourth floor, took her keys from her and inserted them into the lock, pushing the door open and handing the keys back. 'Will you be okay?'

She smiled sleepily... drunkenly. 'Yes, thank you.'

'I'd like to see you again.' He leaned forward and, this time, planted a soft kiss on her cheek. 'You have my card. Ring me.'

She waited till she saw him vanish into the lift before she shut the door.

Ring me.

There was no doubt of it.

8

The following day, Allison took out Peter's business card and flicked it against her nail as she wondered whether to ring him or not. He'd seemed the perfect choice, or had she been affected by the glow of alcohol? The crippling hangover she'd woken with eased after a couple of paracetamols and several glasses of water. She was wrapped in a robe, curled up on her living room sofa with a mug of coffee. To ring or not to ring, that was the question.

There were definite pros... he was handsome, entertaining, wealthy. Single – maybe, it was always hard to tell. She did a quick internet search. Armed with his business card, it was easy. He had a plain, no-nonsense website with business information, addressing his qualifications, condensed into a few lines. His speciality was commercial law. Apart from contact details, that was it. No personal details whatsoever. A check on various social media platforms proved to be a waste of time. In his line of work, she wasn't surprised he favoured privacy, but it was irritating.

Tossing her phone to one side, she cupped her fingers around the almost empty mug. She'd been flattered – what woman wouldn't be – but wasn't it a bit stalkerish for him to have followed her upstairs from the pub, gate-crashing the party in order to do so?

More concerning was his controlling behaviour coupled with a definite tendency to override her wishes. Perhaps it was a hangover from his chosen profession, but even his final *ring me* was somewhat dictatorial. Allison lifted the mug and drained it. If she was serious about this blossoming idea to marry for money, wasn't she being overly fussy? With her social life a non-starter, it was hard to meet men. Harder to meet decent ones. Peter seemed both decent and suitable and, as such, was worth considering. Tossing the card onto the table, she got to her feet. Time to get on with daily living.

* * *

She decided to call him but left it until the Monday afternoon. No point in looking too keen. She'd half-expected to have to leave a message, surprised into silence when her call was answered after one ring. 'Hi,' she said on a long exhale, grasping for the correct words. 'It's Allison. I'm having a hell of a day and wondered if you'd like to meet after work for a drink?' After work. She would get away with going as she was and had chosen to wear the best she had for that very reason.

'Allison, how lovely to hear from you. Yes, that sounds like a wonderful idea. Where were you thinking?'

They agreed on a rendezvous spot, and she hung up, satisfied.

* * *

When she walked into their chosen venue – a quiet pub Allison had heard one of her colleagues recommend – he was already there, seated in a corner booth with a clear view of the entrance.

She saw him immediately and felt her colour rise as she lifted a hand in greeting.

He stood to greet her; they exchanged the usual social kiss to each cheek, his lips lingering longer than they should.

'A glass of wine,' he said as he stepped away. It didn't sound like a question.

'I'll get them.' She smiled and nodded towards the bar. 'What'll you have?'

'No, I'll get them, I insist,' he said, pressing her into a seat with a firm hand on her shoulder.

There didn't seem any point in arguing. She watched him as he stood waiting at the bar to be served. His suit was sharp, well-cut. He held himself like a man who was used to getting what he wanted.

He returned with a bottle of wine and two glasses. 'I'm not driving tonight.' He gave her a wink and poured wine into both glasses. 'Tell me about your day. It's good to talk.'

It sounded like a mental health slogan. She hadn't had a bad morning at all, but she'd had enough in her day to enable her to spin a tale. She was amused, admiring even, when he held a hand up in the middle of her litany of complaints to reach into his inside jacket pocket for his phone. 'I have it on vibrate,' he said, giving her a nod of apology before indicating the exit and walking away with the mobile clasped to his ear.

'A new client,' he explained when he returned almost ten minutes later. No further apology, as if she must understand the role of an important solicitor.

She slipped on the mantle of an understanding, undemanding, uncomplaining girlfriend, biting her tongue to stop the sarcastic remarks she wanted to make when, as happened during their next date three days later, he left her alone in the restaurant for almost twenty minutes while he took an 'urgent call'. As she tried to ignore the curious glances from other diners, she understood why Peter was still single. He'd already given her a clue as to the kind of woman he wanted – a compliant one. A woman who never questioned him, didn't talk too much, never argued, never contradicted, happy to allow him to choose where they met, to be in control. For Allison to defer to him at all times.

It was a boring role, and she wasn't sure she could play it for long. She wasn't Portia.

On the positive side, he was charming and treated her as if she were precious, fragile. If she spoke out, if she questioned his archaic attitude, she probably wouldn't hear from him again. And if he found out about her past... what then? Would he back away, regard her with horror, disgust, maybe even fear? And keep going?

Probably.

But he was never going to find out.

Anyway, the gloss had worn off her crazy idea to marry for money and she was getting tired of being compliant.

9

Allison had almost decided to give up both her idea to marry for money, and Peter. Despite his many advantages, she had to hide too much of her personality to suit him. When he rang on Friday and invited her to his home for dinner the following evening, *no* hovered on the tip of her tongue. She hesitated. It had been so long since she'd had a Saturday night date, it was too good to pass. To his home, though... he'd been increasingly passionate the last couple of dates; was he expecting more? Maybe even that she'd stay over?

Would spending the night watching TV be preferable? She wasn't entirely sure.

'I'm a pretty good cook, if I do say so myself,' he said. 'I won't poison you. And I know what you like.'

How? Allison wanted to ask. He'd never asked her, taking her tastes for granted. That she wasn't the slightest bit fussy and would eat virtually anything – apart from tripe, which she had tried once and thought it as disgusting as it looked – wasn't the point. She was tempted to come up with a list of things she didn't eat, then sighed instead. It was the way he was; she wasn't going to change him, or even try. 'Yes, I'd love to come for dinner.' If he did expect payment for the meal, she'd handle that when the time came.

The last few dates had been, at her request, after-work affairs. It was easier as, apart from her work clothes, she had nothing much else to wear. Certainly nothing glamorous enough to come remotely close to the dress he'd seen her in that first night. It was why, on the Saturday evening, she decided to wear it again. It might be her last opportunity to wear it for a while. She certainly wasn't going to waste money buying something new when she might not be seeing him again.

She gave the taxi driver the address and sank back in the seat. The dinner would be a final attempt to see if Peter was worth pursuing. When the taxi pulled up outside his home on Union Square, her eyes widened. She assumed he, like her, would live in a small apartment, not an impressively elegant Victorian end-of-terrace home. The house of her dreams. Painted white below the first-floor windows, the upper part was mellow, old brick. Some of the houses along the terrace were missing the wrought-iron rail on the upper windowsills. Not Peter's house. It was all simply perfect.

When the taxi pulled away – with a far bigger tip than she'd planned to give, merely because she was so entranced with the house – she stood on the footpath and stared for a moment before slowly climbing the steps to the front door.

There was a doorbell and a brass knocker. Tempted to use the latter, she shook her head at her foolishness and pressed the bell, hearing it chime within, a sonorous *ding dong* that made her smile.

It was opened almost immediately. 'Allison! Wow, you look stunning.'

'I know you like this dress,' she said, as if she'd looked through her vast wardrobe of clothes and chosen to wear it to please him.

'I like *you* in that dress.' He leaned forward and pressed his lips briefly to hers. 'I have an odd feeling I'd like you in anything.'

She smiled. He really could be so charming. How could the owner of such a beautiful house not be?

A door to the right gave her a glimpse into a beautiful room. Trying to take it all in, she was left with the impression of elegant comfort and hoped he'd bring her inside, allowing her to examine the details.

Instead, he led the way to the back of the house. Allison followed, her heels click-clicking on the beautiful tiles, her eyes glued to their geometric design in shades of brown and orange.

'I'm lucky,' Peter said, drawing her eyes up. 'The tiles are original.' He pushed open the door in front of him. 'I've changed some of the house but unfortunately, it's a work in progress. This' – he indicated the interior of the galley kitchen – 'is next on the list.'

Allison looked into the narrow, cluttered room and searched for words that weren't critical. Luckily, since she couldn't find any, Peter slapped the wall with the flat of his hand. 'My plan is to knock this wall down and have a big kitchen-diner. It would be much better. I was always telling Mum she should do it.'

It was the first time he'd mentioned his family. Had she been remiss in not asking? Possibly. Family dynamics were something she tried to avoid. 'Your mum?'

'Yes, didn't I say? This was my parents' house. They died a few years ago. Mum first, then my father simply faded away and followed her a few months later.'

Allison, who hadn't mourned the loss of her parents, heard genuine sadness in his voice and reached for the convenient conventional words of sympathy. 'How terribly sad; you must have been devastated to lose them both.'

He smiled sadly at her. 'Not as traumatic as losing both together in an accident as you did, but yes, it was a difficult time.' He lifted the lid from a pot on the cooker, picked up a wooden spoon and gave the contents a stir. 'I inherited the house, of course.'

He'd inherited this amazing house. All Allison had inherited had been bad memories, frightening dreams, a desperate need that she'd never managed to satisfy. Maybe this time...

Peter opened the fridge, took out a bottle of wine and poured them both a glass. 'Cheers!'

She tipped his glass with hers. 'Cheers.'

'Right,' he said. 'There's not much room. You can stand in the doorway while I work my magic.'

She did as he suggested and stood leaning against the door frame, sipping the wine and watching him cook.

'Mum was forty when she discovered she was pregnant,' he said, using his teeth to open a packet. 'She used to call me her surprise child.' He grinned at Allison. 'I think "shock child" might have been closer to the truth. She was never particularly interested in having children and when they didn't come along, she wasn't bothered.'

Allison sipped her wine and listened to him talk. She was impressed with his cooking skills; he seemed to know exactly what to do – stirring, adding ingredients with dramatic flair. Not a cookery book in sight. He was proving to be a very interesting man. And handsome; her eyes drifted over his muscular upper arms, the soft hairs on his forearms, his dexterous fingers. A slight belly rather than the six-pack she preferred was more than counterbalanced by those melting brown eyes.

She felt the first stirrings of desire and struggled to concentrate on what he was saying.

He lifted a lid, gave the contents a stir, turned the heat down and turned to pick up his glass. 'They made space for me, though. We were a tight threesome while I was growing up. When I decided to get my own place, I didn't go far and when Mum died suddenly, I moved back home to be with Dad, who was lost without her.' He took a mouthful of wine, his expression softening with memories. 'Totally lost. I watched him fade away, almost day by day.' He tilted his head to the door. 'We'd sit at the dining table every night and pore over photographs. Mum at the beach, walking along the canal, on various holidays. And he'd tell a story of things she did, the funny things she'd say. Although I was devastated when he died, I wasn't really surprised. He wanted to be with her.'

Allison was fascinated by the glisten of tears in his eyes. She wasn't sure she'd met anyone like him before. She refused to entertain the idea that she was finding him far more interesting now that she'd seen his home. 'There must be a lot of memories in this house.'

'Yes.' He put his glass down and returned to his pots, stirring one after the other, gusts of steam rising as he lifted each lid. 'I wasn't sure if I could stay at first, but the house is full of happy memories. It was a comfort.' He put a lid on the pot and switched off the heat. 'Right.' He picked up the bottle of wine. 'Come through and get seated; this is almost ready.'

He pushed open a door into a room stuck firmly in the seventies. Burgundy flocked wallpaper clashed with the swirling waves of red-and-gold-patterned carpet covering the floor. Luckily, most of this horror was obscured by an ugly mahogany table and chairs, and a matching oversized dresser. A single lightshade cast a curious glow over everything. She shivered. Had Peter lied? He'd said the house was filled with happy memories, so why did she feel menace in the air? A curious foreboding. It made her reluctant to enter.

Peter didn't notice her hesitation. He'd set two places at the table, one at the end, one at a right angle to it. He pulled a chair out and smiled across the room to where she still hovered in the doorway.

She was being silly. Returning his smile, she took the offered chair and sat. 'Thank you.'

There were chunky, squat candles grouped in a low, circular dish in the centre of the table, tall, slim ones in candlesticks on the dresser. Peter struck a match and lit them, then switched out the main light. Although possibly a little too dim, it was preferable to the odd glow from the overhead light and almost, almost made the atmosphere romantic rather than creepy.

Peter refilled her wine glass. 'Right, I'll go and dish up. Back in a tick.'

She'd have preferred to go with him rather than sit there alone in the unsettling half-light. Luckily, before she embarrassed herself by following, he returned with their meal. 'I hope you enjoy it,' he said, placing the plate on the table in front of her.

'I'm sure I will.' It certainly smelt delicious, and she was delighted to find it tasted equally as good.

They laughed and chatted as they ate, the level in the wine bottle quickly lowering until Peter went to the kitchen and returned with another.

Finally, she pushed her empty plate away. 'That was absolutely delicious.'

He grinned at her. 'Have I found the way to your heart?'

'Good food always helps.'

He got to his feet and reached a hand to her. 'Why don't I show you the rest of the house?'

There was no missing the implication in his words. She smiled. Did it matter that she was finding him suddenly more sexually attractive thanks to his home? He had odd notions and perhaps the role of perfect girlfriend would have proved to be boring and impossible to maintain. It would be easier now. She might even see this crazy plan through.

As she took his hand and followed him up the stairs, she expected the night to be exciting and satisfying.

But she'd also expected him to drive a Porsche or Lamborghini.

Like his Ford Fiesta, he was surprisingly dull in bed.

10

Once Allison had decided what she wanted, it was easier to make sure she got it. It wasn't difficult. All she needed to do was to give Peter what he wanted, to get what she needed.

The Thursday following their first night together, she headed back into the boutique where she'd bought the dress. This time, she spent money on smart-casual clothes. Well-cut trousers, silk shirts, a couple of dresses. She spent more than she'd spent for years, but she handed over her credit card without a twinge. This was investment dressing.

It also gave her something to post on her seldom-used Instagram page. And she began to enjoy this new version of herself. Along with the photographs of her new clothes, the designer handbags and the dinners out with Peter, she posted shots of five-star hotels and exotic beaches, blending truth with reality as she always did.

The clothes helped maintain the illusion of being an understanding, undemanding, uncomplaining girlfriend. And if it ever crossed her mind that she couldn't follow through with her plan, moments when Peter was being too Victorian, she'd think of the house on Union Square and sigh as she swallowed her ire.

A house this beautiful she could make into the home she'd always been looking for.

Walking home from a nearby restaurant the following week, he stopped suddenly and turned to her. 'You're such a restful woman.'

'You have a stressful enough life without me adding to it,' she said, lifting a hand to push a lock of hair back from his forehead. 'I like to provide a calm environment for you.' She hoped she hadn't gone overboard; the words had come out more nauseating than she'd planned. She needn't have worried. He might be a brilliant barrister, top of his field, but when it came to women, he was a D student.

She was soon staying at his house most nights. He gave her a key, happy for her to come and go as she pleased. 'I like having you here,' he said. 'You're good for me.'

Of course she was... she played her part well. If she wavered, if she felt the burden of the act too onerous, she made her excuses and stayed a few nights in her tiny, claustrophobic apartment. It was enough to reset her priorities.

When he asked her to marry him, only two months after meeting, she was stunned and relieved in equal portions. She was beginning to wonder if she could keep up the act. 'Yes,' she said in answer to his proposal, her eyes widening as he slid a plain gold band with the tiniest diamond she'd ever seen onto her finger.

'It's dainty and restful.' He kissed her. 'Like you.'

It was boring, like him, which didn't surprise her, but it was also cheap, which did. Perhaps she should have listened to the warning bell that was tinkling quietly, listened to it before it became a loud clang. 'It's beautiful,' she lied.

He pulled her into a hug. 'You've made me the happiest man.

There's no point in hanging around, is there? You don't want a big wedding, I'm guessing.'

It was almost tempting to say she did. A big wedding, in a cathedral, with a reception for a couple of hundred guests in a nice hotel. Bridesmaids, flower girls. Flowers everywhere. The whole shebang. 'You're right, as usual. I'd be happy with a register office do.'

'I knew you would be. Well, we can give notice tomorrow, then we'll be able to marry within the month.' He stood back, holding her upper arms, looking into her eyes. 'Then you'll be Mrs Fellowes and I'll be the happiest man alive.'

And for the first time, basking in his love, she wondered if perhaps, after all, marriage to him wouldn't suit her very well.

PART II

11

Peter leaned against the breakfast bar, an almost empty pint glass in his hand. 'Who's this woman you're meeting tomorrow?'

Allison fitted the last dinner plate into the dishwasher before turning to answer him. 'I told you already: Jo Kirby, a woman I met in a Facebook book group. She commented on a few of my posts, then she sent me a DM. I don't normally respond to private messages but when she mentioned she was an accountant too, I decided why not.' She reached for a dishwasher tablet, popped it into the slot and pressed the buttons to start the cycle.

He swirled the remnant of beer around the glass before taking a sip. 'You sure it's safe? She could be an axe murderer; there's a lot of dodgy types on social media.'

'This from a man who doesn't use anything apart from LinkedIn.' She patted him gently on the cheek. 'Don't worry. We've been exchanging messages for months so when she mentioned she was coming to London, it was my idea we meet up for lunch. It's almost funny how much we have in common. Apart from our jobs, we're both originally from Oxford and went to university in Southampton. That was odd enough but then she mentioned in the book group that E.F. Benson's Mapp and Lucia series was a favourite of hers. I was stunned. You know how much I love those books.'

'You've been trying to get me to read them since we met, so that would be a yes.' He grinned.

She swatted him with the tea towel she held. 'I'm not giving up.' She folded the towel in half and slipped it onto the towel rail, straightening it until it hung neatly in the middle. 'To add to the list of coincidences, both you and her husband are solicitors.'

He gave this a slight smile. 'You'll be telling me next that tomorrow is their three-month wedding anniversary.'

'That would have been one coincidence too far.' Allison shivered. 'And verging into creepy territory. Anyway, no, she's been married for years. Has a grown-up son in university. And she's thirty-nine, so ten years older than me.'

'Not a secret alien clone of you, then.' He drained the glass and dropped it into the sink. Left it there for Allison to deal with. God forbid he should do anything that was considered housework. In the short time they'd been married, she'd never seen him as much as rinse a cup. He hadn't said as much, but she knew he considered the domestic sphere to be her domain. As if she was home all day with nothing else to do. It shouldn't have surprised her. She'd noticed his Victorian attitude the very first day. It didn't surprise, but it annoyed, grated, ground her down.

When she had suggested that she give up her job – which she was desperate to do – she'd expected him to agree and had pictured herself joining the *ladies who lunch* brigade. She had been stunned by his sharply worded response.

'Give up your job? What would you do all day?'

'I thought you'd like me to concentrate on looking after you?'

He'd pulled her into his arms and held her tight. 'Aren't we doing fine as we are?'

There was little to say to that. Without another word, he'd kissed her on the cheek and vanished upstairs to his home office.

He did the same now, jerking his thumb towards the ceiling. 'I've an email I need to send; I'll be down in a few minutes.'

Allison bit back the comment she wanted to make, a sarcastic one about how many minutes were in a *few* because she knew she wouldn't see him again that night.

It didn't matter. During one of those long, lonely nights while he'd worked upstairs, she'd made a decision. She wasn't going to be like Portia.

She wasn't in the mood to watch TV, instead curling up on the sofa with a book she'd started the previous day. A few pages later, she dropped it on the seat beside her and thought about the following day. It was going to be busy. Jo hadn't mentioned where her meeting was being held and Allison hadn't thought to ask. She assumed her choice was suitable for the other woman, as she didn't demur when Allison suggested a restaurant in Covent Garden convenient to her office.

She planned to arrive early the following morning. Even an extra hour would allow her to get through all she needed to do before she left for lunch. She didn't plan on returning. Although it wasn't unusual for staff to leave early on a Friday, it was for her, and no doubt would cause raised eyebrows and quizzical glances.

Jo's visit to London the following day was unfortunate timing. It was three months to the day since Allison and Peter had married.

'We should celebrate,' he'd said a few days before.

'We should. I'll book somewhere special.'

'Perfect, I'll leave it to you then.'

'Do, it'll be a lovely surprise for you.' It would be. Perfect timing. She made careful plans.

She could have said she wasn't free when Jo mentioned she was coming to London for a meeting, but Allison was reluctant to say she wasn't available. She'd developed a connection with the other woman, a rare enough event in her life; it would be good to see if it survived meeting face to face. Over the next few weeks, she might be in need of a friend. Anyway, it didn't matter, there was plenty of time to fit in everything she'd planned.

12

The following morning went as smoothly as Allison had hoped. After reminding Peter once again to leave his office on the dot of five, she hurried from their home and walked the ten minutes to the nearby train station.

The fifth floor, where most of the offices of McPherson Accounting were situated, was blissfully quiet. There'd be none of the annoying, often-endless interruptions that punctuated her usual workday. It would be an hour before most of her colleagues and the support staff arrived. Sixty minutes where she hoped to get the bulk of her more pressing issues sorted.

Her office, like all the others on this floor, was compact. Tiny but hers: hard-won with long hours, lunch at her desk, pandering to those who made the decisions, never complaining when more work was assigned than she could cope with, spending longer hours, working from home at the weekends. The small window, grimy with pollution on the outside, looked onto the grey-bricked building next door a mere two or three feet away. If she pressed her cheek to the glass and strained to look upward, it was possible to get a glimpse of the sky. Sometimes, desperate for a glimpse of the world that was whizzing by, weeks, months, years where she seemed to be standing still, she did press her cheek to the glass, her make-up leaving a strange pattern that she struggled to remove with paper tissue and spit.

That day, she didn't. She wasn't standing still any more.

* * *

The Covent Café, where Allison had arranged to meet Jo at one, was a short walk from her office. At a quarter to the hour, with two emails still to send, she blew a frustrated sigh, tapped out a few more words, grunting in annoyance when she made errors, deleting and correcting with her teeth clenched. It was a minute to the hour when she switched off, grabbed her bag and jacket and raced through the door.

The lift in the badly maintained old building was always slow. She took the stairs instead, feet clattering on the stone steps as she raced downward. Too fast. Almost at the bottom, her leather soles slipped on the smooth, worn surface. An awkward twist to grab the handrail failed and with a cry of pain she tumbled down the remainder of the steps and landed in an ungainly heap of legs and rucked shirt.

Stunned, she didn't move for a few seconds. It was tempting to stay there. Cry at her stupidity, curse her clumsiness. Instead, tentatively she moved each limb, relieved to find everything still in working order. Nothing damaged apart from her dignity, which luckily hadn't been witnessed, and – she groaned – a rip in her almost-black tights. 'Damn it to hell.' Getting to her feet, she kicked off her shoe and tried to manoeuvre the ladder to the inside of her leg. It wasn't a vast improvement, but it would have to do. There was a spare pair in her office drawer, but it would take too long, and she was already late. With a tug, she pulled her skirt straight and brushed dust from the black fabric with her hand.

Picking up her bag, she pushed open the bar of the emergency door and exited onto the street, moving as swiftly as she could along the busy pavement. She'd wanted to make a good impression on this first meeting with Jo; now here she was, twenty minutes late, a ladder in her tights, and bedraggled from having to rush.

13

Jo Kirby had found Allison years before after a long and frustrating search. The first time she saw her she wasn't sure – Allison had changed so much – then she saw her eyes. They hadn't changed. Still cold and hard. For years she'd followed her in person, ducking and diving, lurking. The switch to social media was a natural progression. Jo was surprised to see Allison's life was as dull and boring as hers.

It was almost a relief to see they had so much in common, despite everything, and perhaps Jo would have got bored after a while looking at someone who was a reflection of herself if the next time she looked hadn't made her weak with jealousy.

At first, Jo assumed she'd made a mistake, that she'd stupidly opened the wrong Facebook page, realisation coming slowly, painfully. *Married!* It took a third can of beer before she could bring herself to open Allison's Instagram account and see the truth in full, glorious, over-the-top colour. The dress, the flowers, the handsome... gorgeous... husband. Everything so beautiful, so larger than life, so fucking unfair.

Jo drained the can and flung it across the room, white flecks of foam flying from it, peppering the air like confetti.

Her fixation with Allison's social media output started that night. Suddenly the life she'd almost discounted as being, like hers, boring and dull, was filled with promise and colour, expensive clothes, designer handbags and shoes, glamorous hotels. Jo examined every photograph, pored over every word of every boasting post.

Annoyed with herself for her lapse, for having missed the lead-up to the wedding, she increased her vigilance, checking all Allison's socials as often as she could, easier now she was unemployed.

When Jo had first searched for Allison, the plan had been to get revenge for what she'd done. Only seeing a life as miserable as Jo's own had deflected that idea. When that changed, when there were honeymoon photos, shots of sumptuous meals in glamorous restaurants, photographs of the two of them, Allison looking surprisingly glamorous, her husband handsome and sexy, bitterness burst to the surface, pushing the plan for revenge ahead of it with a gleeful cackle. Jo should never have let it slide.

It was important to allow the relationship to develop organically. She went through Allison's contact list and sent each a friend request. Most ignored it. Of the several who accepted, she went through their friend list, sent more requests and so on. It took time. She wasn't in a hurry. She'd been waiting a long time for this. Within a few weeks, she'd sufficient friends in common to move on to the next step. She began to like comments Allison made in various groups. Nothing too obvious, a simple thumbs up, no heart emojis. She waited for the right post before making a comment, keeping it short and simple, taking her tone from other comments, fitting in.

It was weeks later before someone in one of the Facebook

groups asked how everyone's week was going. Jo didn't answer immediately, waiting to see if Allison did. When she did, it couldn't have been better.

Exhausted, having a gruelling week.

It was exactly the kind of comment Jo had been waiting for. She gave it a sad face emoji, then waited until a couple more members posted about their week before adding a comment.

It's been one of those weeks when I wonder if accountancy is really for me.

To her satisfaction, Allison gave her a heart emoji. A big step up.

But her big breakthrough came the following week. In one of the book club groups, someone posted to ask what everyone's all-time favourite book was. Jo didn't wait; she dashed off a comment to say the Mapp and Lucia series was her favourite. It was over an hour before she saw what she'd hoped for. Not just a heart emoji this time; Allison replied to her comment.

Me too – I love them!!

Of course she did. She bloody well mentioned them enough. She was even in a Facebook page dedicated to the series – Jo had tried to join but there was a list of questions about the series of books and she'd no idea of the answers.

It didn't matter; knowing about the books was enough. Hopefully, she'd never have to read them. Jo never read, couldn't see the point. She'd looked at the Mapp and Lucia books on Amazon. The blurbs seemed interesting enough, but she still wasn't tempted. When she saw there was a TV series based on the books, she searched for it and watched it, surprised to find it rather amusing and certainly entertaining. Now, she could hold her own if the series came up in conversation when she and Allison met.

That they would meet someday was never in doubt.

Pleased with how things were going, she wasn't tempted to rush. 'Softly softly catchee monkey' was a motto she lived by.

A week later, in a different Facebook group, someone asked where everyone was from. Jo waited for a few members of the group to post a comment before adding *Oxford* and sitting back, chewing on her thumbnail until the corners bled.

Several comments were added before she saw Allison's *Oxford*, then, afraid Allison mightn't have seen her answer, she dared to reply.

We both like Mapp and Lucia and we're both from Oxford!

When Allison gave her a laughing emoji, Jo punched the air. This was it: she was in. She waited a few minutes and sent her a friend request. It was an excruciating five hours before it was accepted, hours Jo spent alternating between pacing the living room of her tiny bedsit or sitting on the fold-up bed, chewing her fingernails, spitting bits of flesh onto the coffee table where they gathered like blood-tinged maggots.

When her friend request was accepted, she celebrated with a beer. She popped the tab and sucked up the foam that oozed before tilting the can back and gulping a few mouthfuls. One can. A minor celebration. Now wasn't the time to rush in all guns blazing, and ruin all her hard work.

Slow and cautious, she waited for the right opportunity to

develop the relationship, continued her observations and added to her notebook. Sometimes, she stared at Allison's photo, clicking on the enlarge icon till it couldn't get any bigger. Jo would search for wrinkles on the enviably perfect skin, for any blemish. She was ridiculously pleased to see the furrow between Allison's eyes increasing over the years since she'd first started to watch her.

A frown. Maybe Allison's life wasn't as hunky-dory as social media indicated. Jo wasn't a fool; she knew how it could be manipulated. When she met her, face to face, she'd know the truth.

Face to face.

Jo wasn't impatient but she'd waited a long time for a meeting. It was time to be proactive. Since discovering Allison was an accountant, Jo had made a point of checking out the various accounting bodies. When she saw there was an annual general meeting of management accountants in Birmingham the following month, she decided it was the perfect opportunity. She'd no idea what type of accountant Allison was, but it didn't matter.

It was the ideal opening to send Allison a message.

It took several tries and two mugs of strong coffee before she was happy with what she wrote.

Hi, I hope you don't mind my contacting you this way, but I wondered if you were attending the CIMA AGM in Birmingham next week? I'm stupidly shy about events like this so it would be great to know someone else who was going.

She sent it and stared at her phone for several minutes, willing Allison to reply, knowing she was being stupid, that she was unlikely to do so for a few hours yet. Over time, Jo had noted a pattern – Allison didn't post often in any of the Facebook groups and when she did it was within a small window bracketing the day. It wasn't hard to understand it was during her commute to and from her office. Instagram posts were always done at the weekend.

When there was no reply that evening, fear simmered. Had Jo blown it? Another beer from her meagre supply didn't make the waiting any easier. Nor did the sleepless night.

The following day, tired and restless, she railed against the unfairness of it all. She'd worked so hard, been so patient; her plan should have worked. So much time wasted. The thought of having to start again from the beginning made her stomach cramp and her head thump.

Her phone had been glued to her hand. In frustration she threw it to one side, minutes later picking it up again, checking every Facebook group Allison was in to see if she'd posted or commented. Seeing nothing gave her enough relief to curl up on the fold-up bed and switch on the TV. A movie she'd not seen before helped pass the time and relaxed her enough to make her eyelids droop over itchy-tired eyes.

But when her phone pinged to say she had a message, she was instantly alert. Nobody sent her messages. It had to be Allison. Her hand was trembling when she picked it up and tapped the message icon.

Hi, Jo. I don't normally communicate via messenger with people I don't know but since you're also an accountant and have such good taste in books 😊, I'm making an exception. Unfortunately, no, I won't be going to that Birmingham meeting. I'm a chartered accountant, not management.

Management or chartered. Jo guessed it was a chalk and cheese scenario. Who knew? Who gave a fuck? She'd have liked to have waited till the next day to reply, show that she was a busy woman with too much on her mind to be answering messages at that hour of the evening. She'd have liked to, but she didn't and tapped out a short, friendly answer.

Shame, it would have been nice to have met up.

She sat watching her phone, willing Allison to respond. When she did... Jo laughed out loud. Bingo! So bloody gullible.

If you're ever in London, I'd love to meet you.

14

Jo had Allison hooked and over the next few weeks she reeled her in. Longer replies to her Facebook posts. Admiring comments on her frequent Instagram contributions. Adding some of her own. Photographs of posh meals she borrowed from a variety of restaurant websites, beautiful bedrooms taken from hotel websites, hinting at gloriously luxurious and decadent weekends away with her fictional husband, Ethan.

Finally, it was time to go for it. She debated telling Allison she was going to London on a shopping trip. Too risky. She might have suggested accompanying her or have expected Jo to arrive with carrier bags from upmarket London boutiques. Much more sensible to invent a meeting. This had a downside... she had to fix a day rather than leaving it open.

Hi, Allison. I'm in London next Friday for an early morning meeting. Would you be free to meet up for lunch?

For sixty minutes, Jo barely moved, her eyes fixed on her mobile. Perhaps Allison's alleged interest in meeting had been a polite social lie. She'd either answer with an excuse, or not bother to answer at all.

Jo's lips were pressed together painfully by the time her phone buzzed. She was almost afraid to look at it and read the brush-off. It had taken so much work to get to this moment. On a shuddering inward breath, her hand sneaked across to pick up the phone, the breath coming out in a whoosh as she read Allison's reply.

Sounds good. Let me know where and when. Look forward to meeting x

A kiss... Jo grinned. She knew it meant nothing, but she still saw it as a step upward. She gave careful consideration to her reply.

I don't know London that well, where would you suggest? The meeting finishes at midday so I'm free from then.

Another minute passed before she saw the three dots indicate a reply was being written. She barely blinked as she waited to see what it said.

The Covent Café on Langley Street is good, if that's convenient for you?

Langley Street was certainly convenient for Allison, whose office was nearby on Floral Street. She hadn't asked where Jo's business meeting was being held. It showed a selfish streak that hadn't come across in her social media posts. Jo smiled. Something else to add to her notebook.

It didn't matter; after all, there was no meeting for Jo to attend. Still, she wasn't letting it slide that easily.

I'm not sure where that is. I'll do an internet search and find it. If I'm late it's because I got lost. Lol x

It was a lie. Jo knew London well. Knew exactly where the Covent Café was, knew where Allison's office was too. She'd hung around outside it, trying to catch a glimpse of her years before. Giving up after the fifth or maybe it had been the sixth visit. It was then she'd come up with the idea to find her on social media, get to know her before facing her.

After such a long time, she was finally going to meet the woman who'd destroyed her life.

15

On Friday, nervous anticipation had made Jo arrive far too early for the lunch meeting. To pass the time, she wandered around Covent Garden, admiring items she couldn't afford to buy. When a jewellery stall caught her eye, she spent several minutes trying on silver bracelets, asking the assistant to take one after the other from the display cabinet.

'So gorgeous,' she said, holding her wrist out to catch the light outside the rather low parasol roof of the stall. 'Such beautiful designs, so intricate. And each so different.' She asked to try on several different styles, comparing one to the other, holding each out to catch the sun. Tilting her head in deep consideration.

So many pieces tried and discarded willy-nilly, one on top of the other. 'I can't decide.' She held her wrist up again, twisting it to and fro, frowning in concentration, as if deciding which to buy was a serious life-or-death decision. She pulled the bracelet off and dropped it on top of the others.

Finally, she huffed in feigned frustration. 'I simply can't decide which I prefer. I'll have a think and come back.'

A lie, of course. One of the twisted silver bangles had caught her eye from the first. There was an art to shoplifting – don't look suspicious was the key. In her smart, stylish, *borrowed* suit, she looked able to afford whatever she wanted. As she'd held her wrist up to the sun to admire a different bracelet, she'd taken the eye of the sales assistant with it. It was a simple sleight of hand to slip the desired bracelet into her jacket pocket.

With a smile for the resigned sales assistant, she left holding her bag over her pocket to hide the circular bulge in the fabric. She waited until she'd left Covent Garden behind before slipping it on.

The Covent Café, close enough to legitimately use the name, was still a few minutes' walk away. Still too early, Jo walked slowly, window shopping, feeling nervous anticipation build as the time ticked toward the hour of meeting.

It was still ten minutes to the appointed hour when she pushed open the door of the restaurant. A black-garbed waiter standing behind a dais looked up as she approached, a sycophantic smile barely moving his thin lips.

'I'm meeting a friend. She's made a reservation. Fellowes.'

'Fellowes,' he muttered. 'Just one moment.'

It seemed to take an unnecessarily long time for him to check. Irritation segued to fear. Maybe it was the wrong place or the wrong time. Or worse, the wrong day. Or maybe – Jo swallowed the lump that lodged in her throat – maybe she'd been made a fool of, and Allison had never really planned to meet up.

So many emotions shot through Jo, she couldn't pin one down. Unable to decide whether to laugh at herself for being a fool, or howl at the anguish of disappointment, she stood with her lips pressed together and tried not to cry. All the years of waiting. The desperate need to face her nemesis. It had come to nothing.

She was about to laugh it off and say she'd got the time mixed up, muster a little dignity and make her escape, when the waiter lifted his face and nodded. 'I'll show you to your table.'

16

The table Jo was taken to was set in a corner, two chairs tucked underneath, tall, leafy potted plants acting as a screen to separate it from the tables on either side. Both seats giving a good view over the restaurant, she was happy to take the one the waiter pulled out for her. Once she was seated, he placed menus on the table in front of her. 'Would you like to order a drink while you wait?'

Jo would have liked a gin and tonic to settle her nerves, but she was aware she might end up paying for some if not all of this lunch and a G&T in this upmarket establishment wouldn't be cheap. 'No, thank you, I'll wait till my friend arrives.' He was about to move off when she stopped him with a raised hand. 'But...'

'Yes, madam?'

'If you could bring some water... tap,' she added hurriedly. She was damned if she'd waste money on fancy mineral water.

'Certainly.'

A different waiter brought a carafe to the table moments later. 'I'll be back to take your order when the other party arrives,' he said and left her.

She sipped the water, catching a faint hint of mint. It was pleasant and she drank it thirstily as she looked around. The restaurant was perhaps half full. Suited types mostly, probably having business-expense-account lunches. She picked up a menu and opened it, feeling an instant acid burn at the prices. Even skipping a starter and going for the cheapest main was going to make this a ridiculously expensive meal. Next time, she'd suggest coffee, not lunch.

Shutting the menu, she checked the time. Allison was late. Jo took out her phone and checked her socials, wondering whether to take a photo of the restaurant for Instagram, deciding against, scrolling through some posts, checking the time, a nervous cycle she repeated several times before putting her phone down on the table with a snap loud enough to draw attention from two nearby tables. Jo shot them a glare and they hastily looked away.

It looked like she wouldn't have to worry about the cost of lunch after all. The earlier surge of emotions returned and she felt the quick sting of tears. She'd been stood up. It was time to leave. She looked around for the waiter, hoping it would be the second more friendly one who would appear, not the supercilious first one. Because she'd had enough and might be tempted to pick up the shiny fork from the table in front of her, stick it into his eyeball and pop it out to serve to those irritating people at the next table as an hors d'oeuvre.

Luckily for all concerned, it was the second waiter who responded to her raised hand.

He was almost at her table when she was distracted by movement nearer the door. Looking over the waiter's shoulder, she saw Allison frantically waving. Half an hour late. A dart of anger pressed Jo's mouth into a tight line, her expression grim enough to startle the waiter into a step backward. Angry eyes swept over the approaching woman, lingering on the dirt mark on the skirt, the ripped tights, the genuine remorse on her face. Something had obviously happened, an accident of some sort.

Before Allison reached her, Jo had decided to forgive. Not forget, perhaps, but for the moment to forgive.

She stood to greet her new friend.

A woman who'd caused her such pain.

17

Allison wasn't surprised Jo's expression was less than welcoming. It was unforgivable to be late to their first meeting. She greeted her, kissing the air each side of her face with a loudly vocalised *mwah*, then stood back with a self-deprecatory laugh. 'As you can see from my shockingly ragged appearance, I've had an accident, which is why I'm so embarrassingly late.' In search of forgiveness, and sympathy, she twisted her leg to show off the ladder in her tights. 'I fell as I was coming down the stairs.'

She brushed a hand over her skirt and sank onto the seat with a dramatic sigh as she assessed the woman opposite. Older than Allison had expected; she'd have put her at least twenty years older than she was, not ten. She didn't like to stare but she guessed Jo had had cosmetic surgery... not by someone good, though; her face was stretched a tad too tight. And her hair was decidedly suspect. Too uniformly thick, it covered her head like an old-fashioned floor mop.

Trying to put her critical thoughts aside, she was relieved to see Jo's initial forbidding expression soften.

'You poor thing! Are you sure you're okay?'

Allison shuffled on the seat and dropped her bag at her feet. 'I had a bit of a shock and I'll no doubt be multi-coloured later, but I didn't break anything, so I suppose I'm lucky.' She rested her hands on the table in front of her. 'Never mind me and my clumsiness – it's so great to meet you in the flesh at last.'

'It is!' Jo reached out and laid her hand briefly on top of Allison's. 'I was telling my husband how much we had in common.' She took her hand away, picked up the menus and pushed one across the table. 'Let's order, then we can set the world to rights.'

'I'm not terribly hungry.' Allison glanced briefly at the menu before shutting it. 'A Caesar salad will do for me.'

The cheapest item on the menu. Jo laughed in feigned disbelief. 'Exactly what I was going to order! Seriously, we could be twins.'

'And a glass of Pinot to wash it down?'

'Sounds perfect.'

Allison gave the order when the waiter appeared. 'Large glasses,' she added when he'd taken note of their order. When he'd gone, she held a hand up in apology. 'I'm sorry, I should have asked, is large okay with you?'

'Of course. You read my mind.'

When the glasses of wine were placed before them only moments later, Allison raised hers in a toast. 'To new friends!' Expecting a smile in return, she was surprised by the odd expression that flickered across Jo's face but before she could comment to ask if everything was okay, the expected smile appeared.

'To new friends!' Jo tipped her glass against Allison's a little too hard. Wine lapped over the side and dripped to the pristine white tablecloth. 'Oops.'

'Seems to be a day for accidents.' Allison took a napkin and dabbed the liquid. 'Luckily we weren't drinking red.' She tossed the napkin to one side. 'How'd your meeting go?'

Jo took a miniscule sip of her wine and put the glass down. 'I work for a school. They're keen on reducing their carbon footprint so that's what the conference was on.'

'Interesting?'

'Yes, to my surprise, it was.' She shrugged. 'I've come away with lots of plans, few of which will be instigated.'

'That's always the way: we're sent on these wonderful box-ticking courses and that's as far as it goes!' Allison took a large mouthful of her wine.

'Always the way,' Jo agreed. 'How was your morning?'

'Busy!'

Allison was going to launch into a description of her morning but stopped when she saw the waiter approach with their lunch. A few minutes later, she took up the thread of the conversation again. 'I needed to get into work early this morning to get everything done before taking the afternoon off—'

'You're not going back to work after lunch?'

'No, we're three months married today so we're going to celebrate.' She twirled her fork in the air. 'I've warned Peter to leave the office on time for a change. Five on the dot. Then, he should be in Charing Cross station at ten past, and home by six. He'll have time to shower and change and get into relaxation mode before we head out.' She grinned. 'It's taken me the full three months to get him trained!'

'Lucky you, I'm still struggling with Ethan. Three months married, how lovely – so you're still in the honeymoon phase.'

Honeymoon phase? Allison kept a vacuous smile pinned in place as she tried to think of a suitable reply. 'I don't think we'll ever leave that.' A little nauseating but it appeared to be the correct reply if Jo's expression was anything to go by.

'Have you known each other long?'

Allison laughed and then, because why not, she told Jo about meeting Peter and how quickly they'd decided to spend the rest of their lives together. With the slant she put on it, it sounded quite romantic.

'He sounds lovely,' Jo said.

'Yes, he is.'

The conversation slowed. When they had to resort to talking about the quality of the Caesar salad they were eating, Allison decided what they had in common was superficial; there was no real rapport. Searching for an acceptable topic, she told Jo about a problem she'd had earlier in the week with a junior member of staff. 'Hazel came into my office and sat for almost an hour, professing to being confused about the company's policy on inclusivity; it isn't that complicated.'

'Hmmm.' Jo's eyes narrowed in thought. 'She's new, you said?'

'Yes, a little over a month.'

'I bet, if you ask the other senior accountants, you'll find she's been to each with a similar problem. She's sizing you all up.'

An anchovy hung perilously from the end of the tines as Allison stopped with her fork halfway to her mouth. She put it down and nodded. 'I think you have something there. Hazel struck me as the ambitious type, and I noticed the way she looked around my office as if assessing the size and suitability.' She speared the anchovy more securely and put it into her mouth, chewing slowly as she thought. It made sense. She'd known from the beginning that Hazel was a woman to watch. Looks like she'd have to be more careful.

Maybe more careful with her new acquaintance too. Allison seemed to have been doing all the talking. 'It must be nice working in a school.'

Jo tilted her head from side to side. 'I love it, but the salary isn't great, and the workload is longer than the hours I'm paid for. Ethan keeps telling me I should quit and get something easier.'

She finished the last of her salad, put the cutlery down and sat back with the glass in her hand. 'Perhaps I should have done when Sam was younger, but now he's gone to university, I'd just be rattling around the house on my own. Ethan works long hours.'

'Like Peter! Another thing we have in common.'

'We'll have to get our husbands together some day; sounds like they're two of a kind.' Jo checked her watch. 'I'm going to have to get going, I'm afraid.'

Allison looked at the time on her phone. 'Goodness, where have those two hours gone! Yes, I'd better get going too. I've things to do before getting home to make myself look like the woman Peter married only a few months ago.'

'Wait till you're married twenty years like me!'

Allison laughed as she turned to scan the restaurant for the waiter, raising a hand when she caught his eyes, writing in the air as she mouthed, *Bill, please.*

'This is on me,' Jo said. 'It was my idea after all.'

Allison shook her head. 'My city, my restaurant choice, so I insist on paying. When I come to Swindon, you can treat me.' She handed her credit card to the waiter, adding a generous tip to the final figure. 'Great, thank you,' she said, taking the receipt and tucking it into her purse with the card.

They gathered their belongings. 'That was an enjoyable lunch,' Allison said as they walked from the restaurant.

Jo was looking around, her eyes puzzled. 'I've to get to Charing Cross station. I thought I knew which way to go but now, I'm not sure.'

Allison checked her watch. 'I'll walk there with you; I've time to spare.'

'If you're sure, that would be great.' Jo linked her arm through Allison's again. 'Do you think in future we could chat on the phone? It'd be so much easier than tapping out messages.'

Allison hoped her hesitation wasn't obvious. For her, messaging was preferable. They were quick, she could knock them out in seconds anywhere... on her daily commute, waiting in the queue in the supermarket, even while sitting on the loo. Calls, however, meant more time. Commitment. Jo suddenly appeared rather needy. A quiver of irritation swept over Allison. She felt cornered: if she said no, she'd be causing offence, no doubt about it; if she said yes, it would be hard to back out.

Carefully squeezing from between the rock and the hard place, she pressed the arm linked in hers in a gesture that was neither assent nor refusal. 'We'd better walk faster if you're going to make your train.'

'I feel like we've known each other for years.' Jo returned the pressure on her arm. 'It looks as if these business meetings of mine are going to be a regular event so we should be able to meet up more often.'

A group of tourists heading towards them forced Jo to release Allison's arm and step behind. The huge gaggle of visitors, their eyes on stalks, cameras held high to capture details they wouldn't later recognise, took a few seconds to flow by. Not long, but enough that Allison felt able to ignore Jo's last comment because she wasn't sure she wanted to meet again at all... never mind on a regular basis.

There was no need to say anything. It would be easier to simply make an excuse the next time Jo contacted her. It was a coward's way out; Allison had to hope the other woman would eventually get the hint.

18

Jo had been worried in case the conversation over lunch drifted to work and became too technical. She was inordinately relieved when the only problem Allison had was an easy one to advise on. Her colleague, Hazel, was obviously set on climbing the ranks and happy to climb over whoever got in the way. Jo, who understood and admired the focus and determination to get where you wanted to be, guessed they'd have a lot in common.

A shiver of pleasure had slid over her when Allison had raised her glass in a toast to new friends, pleasure combining with a shot of relief when she'd insisted on paying the lunch bill. Jo hadn't been sure how it would work, whether they'd split the bill in a spirit of fairness or whether, as it had been her suggestion, she'd be expected to pay. She'd calculated she could have done although it would have meant penny-pinching till her unemployment benefit came through at the end of the month. When Allison asked for large glasses of wine rather than the cheaper standard, it took every ounce of control to appear perfectly happy with the order.

When the waiter came with the bill, Allison's *my city, my*

restaurant choice, so I insist on paying sent a shiver of relief through her.

When she asked if they could chat on the phone rather than tapping out messages, Jo took the squeeze on her arm as assent and sighed, speeding up when requested, appreciating Allison's concern that she didn't miss her train. It was all going so much better than Jo had anticipated. At the station, they exchanged goodbyes and she stretched her neck for the obligatory cheek-kissing, echoing Allison's *mwah, mwah* as if she'd been doing it all her life, as if she hadn't spent the previous days practising with a pillow so she wouldn't bump heads. 'Have a great night tonight.'

'Have a safe journey. I'll message you soon.'

With a wave, Jo joined the moving throng of travellers heading towards the elevator. She looked back at the last minute, using the hand she'd raised for a final farewell to push the hair back from her face when Allison was no longer in view. Jo stepped back and scanned the area, spotting the figure hurrying away. Was she so desperate to get away? Perhaps Jo had got it wrong and Allison hadn't enjoyed the lunch after all, hadn't intended to meet her again. She'd also never replied to Jo's comment about ringing rather than messaging. Anger and disappointment pirouetted in tandem. Stupid woman, if she thought she was getting away that easily.

Jo's plans were dynamic, ready to respond when the perfect opportunity arose.

As she watched Allison vanish into the crowd, she smiled.

19

Allison pulled her arm free from Jo's rather clingy grip and accepted the kiss on both cheeks, trying not to grimace as she felt wet lips brush her skin. 'Have a safe journey. I'll message you soon.' She hoped her emphasis on *message* wasn't too obvious... or too subtle. A final hug and a wave, and they separated.

She could have taken a Tube from Charing Cross to King's Cross, and maybe she was being foolish, but it seemed important to follow her original plan. It was only a ten-minute walk to Leicester Square. She'd plenty of time, and once there she'd be back on schedule. A light rain began to fall as she walked. It suited her. The light mac she had packed neatly in her bag would cover her stained skirt and was long enough to help hide her laddered tights. She unfolded it and slipped it on as she walked.

* * *

Two hours later, she looked even more dishevelled as she pushed open her front door and almost fell inside. She felt numb and stood staring, her eyes unfocused, until the *beep beep* of the house alarm warned her to move. With the alarm off, she rested a shoulder against the wall before knocking her head against it, the clunk loud in the silence. Again and again, she banged her head, wanting the pain, desperate to drive away the dullness of shock. It was all she could do. Once again, she couldn't change the past or what she'd done. Now, as it had been then, it was a case of damage limitation. Pulling away from the wall, she dragged herself up the stairs.

The master bedroom was to the front of the house, overlooking the street, triple glazing keeping road noise down to a low background rumble. A small box room, also to the front, had been converted into an en suite and a walk-in wardrobe. When she'd moved in, a scant two weeks after that first night together, Peter had insisted she have this for herself, moving his clothes into one of the two spare bedrooms.

Three months married. She would be expected to be wearing something stunning for dinner. Her wardrobe had changed dramatically since she'd met Peter and she'd plenty of choice. The final decision came down to a choice between a little black dress she'd only worn once before, and a red one she knew Peter loved. Under the circumstances, black seemed to be the better option.

Laying it on the bed, she took off her clothes, left her hair tied up and went for a shower. She stayed with the hot spray beating down on her shoulders for a long time, but when she switched it off and stepped out into the steam-filled room, she was still as tense. Wrapped in a towel, she reached up and pulled the grips from her dark hair and ruffled the copper-highlighted strands. Loosened, it fell about her shoulders.

Peter liked it loose. He'd run his hands through it. The copper highlights had been his idea. He'd been right. They looked good. Allison pulled on fresh underwear and slipped the black dress over her head. It was the perfect choice. A pair of strappy black stilettos and she was ready.

At six fifteen, she opened the expensive bottle of wine she'd been saving for a special occasion and carried it and two glasses through to the living room. Leaving the bottle and glasses on the coffee table, she crossed to the window. A solitary pedestrian strolled by, eyes down, lost in thought. One car passed, slowed and squeezed into a parking space a few metres away. Nothing else claimed her attention.

Unable to relax, she checked the slim gold watch that circled her wrist again. Six thirty. *Damage limitation.* She picked up her phone and pressed to ring. It went directly to voicemail. She waited for the beep, and spoke: 'Peter, where are you? I've the wine opened, waiting for you to join me in an anniversary toast. You'd better get home quickly before I pour a glass and start without you.'

Tossing the phone on the sofa, she sat and switched on the TV to pass the time. A few minutes later, she picked up the wine bottle and half-filled each glass. It looked good; the stage was set to fool all onlookers. Seconds later, she gave in to temptation and picked up one to take a sip. As she watched the news, raising her eyes to hear yet another scandal engulfing the current government, her eyes flicked continuously towards her mobile. It didn't ring.

When it did, she pounced on it and answered without checking, immediately regretting it when she heard Jo's voice.

'Hi, I wasn't expecting you to answer!' An irritating laugh tinkled, grating on Allison's already sensitive nerves. 'I assumed you'd be out celebrating your anniversary and was going to leave a voicemail to say how much I enjoyed our lunch and to tell you I'd reached home safely.'

Ringing her, not sending a message. Allison had obviously failed to make it clear she preferred the latter. 'Great. We've not left yet. Peter has been delayed. Work. You know how it is with these driven solicitors.'

'Oh yes, but what a nuisance. I hope he's home soon.' A laugh rumbled down the line. 'Luckily you had lunch otherwise you'd be chewing those beautifully manicured nails.'

'Oh, here he is now. Thanks for ringing, Jo, I'll be in touch.' Allison hung up on the two lies... there was, of course, no sign of Peter, and she doubted she'd be in touch with Jo. Meeting her had been a bad idea. Sometimes, superficial social media relationships were best not being developed further.

She switched off the TV and picked up her wine glass. The wine she'd poured was almost gone when the doorbell pealed almost an hour later. The sound, falling into the silence, startled Allison into crying out; a laugh at her foolishness verged on hysteria. When the doorbell rang again, the sound echoing through the house, she got to her feet.

She put on a welcoming smile as she pulled open the door. 'I was getting worried.'

It wasn't Peter who stood on the doorstep.

But she knew it couldn't have been.

20

Neither of the two men who stood on the doorstep were familiar to Allison. Backlit by the street light behind, they were intimidatingly large. Her hand tightened on the door, the smile she'd pasted on freezing in place, twisting into a grimace as one of the men held a card forward as he identified himself.

His words became a whoosh of sound, darkness creeping around the edges of her vision. She staggered backwards, flailing hands grabbing onto the wooden spindles of the banisters. That the oak was surprisingly rough under her fingers was her final bizarre thought.

It was sound that came back first. Male voices rumbling over her head. Words that made no sense. She didn't want to open her eyes. Reality wasn't all it was cracked up to be after all. Perhaps she'd have stayed there in the darkness if one of the men hadn't gently shaken her arm.

She opened her eyes, shutting them immediately against the glare of the overhead light she and Peter rarely used. When she opened them again, it wasn't the concerned face of the man leaning over her she noticed, but the fine, lacy cobweb hanging between the arms of the light fitting as it swayed gently in the draught from the door. Something so strangely mundane managed to calm her sufficiently to turn and meet the eyes of the frowning man who continued to loom over her.

'Mrs Fellowes?'

'I fainted.'

'Yes.' He straightened and moved away to take a seat opposite.

The other man came through the door with a glass of water in his hand. He stood uncertainly before placing it on the coffee table and crossing to sit in the leather bucket chair. Unfortunately, this wasn't designed for people of his size. For a second, he balanced on the arms of the chair before standing again with an air of nonchalance that fooled nobody and moved across to take the vacant seat on the sofa.

Allison pushed herself into a sitting position and swung her legs to the floor. She reached a trembling hand for the glass of water and took a sip.

'I'm Detective Inspector Stephen Doyle,' the first man said before tilting his head to his colleague. 'And this is Detective Sergeant Long.'

They'd make good poker players; it was impossible to read their expressions. She gripped the glass tighter. 'Something's happened to Peter?'

'There was an incident in King's Cross station just after five.' His voice was a flat monotone. 'Your husband fell onto the track as a Tube was arriving. The driver, despite his best efforts, was unable to stop in time.'

The glass Allison was holding so firmly slipped from her hands. It clattered to the floor, water splashing in all directions.

'There was a protest outside the station earlier, which stopped people from entering. When it was cleared, there was a sudden rush of people piling in and onto the platforms. A lot of pushing and shoving. Chaos that the transport police should have prevented.' The detective obviously realised this wasn't something he should be saying because he hurriedly added, 'I think it was unexpected. Anyway, because of the crush of people on the platform, it isn't clear what happened.' He hesitated, his eyes locked unwavering onto Allison's. 'There will be a full investigation. We'll be analysing CCTV footage to see if we can get a clear view of what happened.'

Allison smoothed a hand over the black fabric of her dress. It had been an opportune choice. But then, of course, she'd known it was going to be. 'You're sure it's Peter?'

'We recovered his wallet, Mrs Fellowes. It would help if you could do a formal identification but if you don't feel able, we can use dental records.'

She shivered as she imagined his dreadful injuries. Could she bear to see him that way, for the last memory of her handsome husband to be a broken, battered body? But if she didn't... 'I need to see him to believe it's true.' She brushed the tears from her eyes. 'We've been married three months today. We were going out for dinner tonight to celebrate.' She looked at the two glasses, red lipstick smudges on the empty one, Peter's sitting untouched.

DS Long, who hadn't yet spoken, raised a hand to attract her attention. 'Because of the crowded platform, most people didn't notice what had happened until it was too late. One of the women we interviewed...' He held a hand up as if in anticipation of her objection. 'She thought he might have jumped.'

When the implication of what he was saying cut through the fog of confusion, Allison wanted to leap to her feet and tear his eyes out. Tears were running down her cheeks. She brushed them away. 'Suicide! There's absolutely no way. Peter was a great husband, a brilliant and successful solicitor. He didn't suffer from dark moods; in fact, he was irritatingly happy-go-lucky.'

She waved a hand around the room. 'A nice house, no mortgage or money worries. Absolutely no reason for him to want to throw it all away.' She pointed to the wine glasses, her voice rising, shrill, strident, echoing around the room. 'We were going to celebrate.'

DS Long held both hands up, palms out. 'We have to look into every aspect, Mrs Fellowes.'

DI Doyle nudged him with a shoulder. 'Now's probably not the time. Is there someone you can ring to be with you, Mrs Fellowes?'

Allison threw DS Long a final withering glare before answering. 'I'll ring my friend, Portia; she doesn't live far away.'

'Good.' The detective got to his feet. 'A police liaison officer will be in touch with you tomorrow to organise the visit to identify your husband. They'll be your point of contact throughout the investigation.' He stood looking down at her. 'I'm sorry for your loss, Mrs Fellowes.'

She shut her eyes, rested her head back and listened to the sounds of their departure. Their footsteps on the wooden floor of the hall, the opening and shutting of the front door, the faint squeak of the gate, the unnecessarily loud crash as they banged it shut after them. Normal everyday sounds in her suddenly strange, alien world.

Tears squeezed from between her eyelids. They trickled down her cheeks, silent, unstoppable, liquid sadness. When she opened her eyes, the day had drifted into night, the day her husband had died already almost over. She reached for her phone and scrolled through for her friend's number.

It rang several times before being answered. 'Allison? For goodness' sake, what're you doing ringing so late?' Murmurs in the background combined with loud rustling before the sounds faded.

'Portia?'

'Hang on, I'm taking you into the spare room.' She didn't hide her irritation. 'Hopefully Stuart will go back to sleep otherwise he'll be unbearable tomorrow.'

'I'm sorry.'

'Yes, well, I'm assuming it's something important.'

'Something life or death, you mean?'

'Well, that's maybe a little overly dramatic. Let's say something important enough to wake us at almost midnight.'

Almost midnight. Soon Peter would have died yesterday, time marching on regardless of his loss. 'Death.'

'What did you say?' Portia's voice was crisp with irritation. 'Have you been drinking?'

'Portia, can you come over?'

'Now?' The voice jumped an octave in surprise. 'Allison, are you okay? Have you and Peter had a row?'

'Worse.' Saying the words, didn't that make it real? 'Peter is dead.' The silence that followed her stark announcement was broken by her friend's loud, nervous laugh.

'That's not funny, Allison.' The indrawn breath was loud. 'Hell, you're serious! What happened? No, wait, don't tell me, I'll get a taxi and be over as soon as it can get me there.' She hung up without another word, leaving Allison with a dead phone pressed to her ear. There were other people she should ring. Peter's friends. A cousin in Essex. The phone was still pressed to her cheek, tears running down the edge. She pulled it away, wiped it on her sleeve and dropped it on the sofa. Phoning family and friends could wait till the morning.

Her friend was true to her word. Less than an hour later, Allison was startled from the chilling numbness by the chiming of the doorbell. It sounded again and again, her friend's usual impatience ratcheted to extremes by the news she'd heard. Allison struggled to her feet and walked unsteadily to the door. She'd barely opened it when it was pushed inwards. Portia, her face devoid of make-up, enveloped her in a hug of such ferocity Allison gasped and winced as her friend's holdall walloped her bruised thigh. That fall down the stairs. She'd almost forgotten it. The spillage of wine at lunch. Didn't accidents come in threes?

Portia spoke into her hair, her breath tickling. 'I don't know what to say.'

And true to her word, the normally loudly vocal Portia remained silent in the hug until Allison took a calming breath and pushed her away. 'Thanks for coming. I needed someone.' She linked her arm through her friend's and led her into the living room. 'I didn't want to drink alone. Now you're here, I'm going to get plastered. Is white okay?'

'Sure.' Portia was still holding the small holdall. She lifted it, shrugged, then dropped it at her feet and kicked it into the corner of the room. 'I threw some stuff together. I'm going to stay for a while.'

Allison filled the glass she'd been using, then reached for the other. She pressed her trembling lips together as she picked it up. Peter would have drained a glass, restless to get going. He'd probably have missed lunch. *Keeping my appetite*, he'd have said. Always determined to get his money's worth when they went for a meal, determined to finish every bite. He'd have bundled her out the door, draping a heavy arm across her shoulder as they walked the short distance to their favourite restaurant. A place they went to frequently; she wondered vaguely if they were surprised at the no-show... or if they'd even noticed, if they'd cared.

Her fingers closed around the bowl of the glass. 'Damn him for leaving me.' The glass went flying, hitting the wall with a crash, shards of broken glass tinkling to the floor.

Portia's startled yelp was loud. She stepped away, her eyes wide and fearful before reaching to take the bottle from Allison's hand. 'Sit. I'll go and get another glass.'

When she returned, she poured a small amount of wine into her glass.

Allison raised hers towards Portia. 'Peter and I should be here toasting our first three months together. I'm not supposed to be drinking to my widowhood.' She gulped a few mouthfuls before sitting.

Portia took the sofa opposite and sipped her wine. 'I'll understand if you don't want to talk about it, but can you at least tell me what happened?'

'He fell. In King's Cross. In front of a Tube.'

'Shit!' Obviously thinking this deserved more than a sip, Portia swallowed a quarter of the glass in one long mouthful. 'He fell?' Her face twisted in confusion. 'How, for goodness' sake? Or was he pushed, was that it? Was he involved with some dodgy client?' She swirled the rest of her wine around the glass before emptying it in another long gulp.

Allison reached for the bottle and filled both glasses again. 'The police are investigating. They said the platform was busier than usual because an earlier protest had delayed trains. Maybe he simply lost his balance.' She didn't mention what that horrible detective had said. That witness had been wrong. Peter wouldn't have jumped. 'Whatever the reason, Peter fell in front of the approaching train. The driver didn't have a chance to stop.'

'You don't think…' Portia stared into her wine before lifting her eyes to meet Allison's quizzical gaze. 'Did Peter know you weren't happy?'

21

My obsession with Monica and her mother faded as a more dangerous one took over. If I could be adopted... if I had a mother like Monica's, a life like hers... I'd be happy. My life would be perfect. It was all I wanted. It wasn't much to ask for, was it? Happiness. Weren't we all entitled to it? Wasn't every child?

The more I thought of it, the more convinced I was that I'd been robbed of something that was rightfully mine. And the more convinced I became, the more I was determined to alter my fate.

Because it wasn't written in stone. It could be changed. I could have the life I wanted.

I would have.

My plan was simple.

I'd wait till it was late, my parents asleep, and I'd kill them.

And then, I, and my siblings, would be adopted and live the life we deserved.

I wasn't quite ten; my plans were airy-fairy constructions born of watching too many action movies, and the fire I lit that should have sent my parents to the hell they had earned wasn't so easily contained and took more lives than my silly idea had considered.

A mistake I paid for, was still paying for.
Worse, it didn't get me the life I'd desperately wanted.

22

Portia's question, *Did Peter know you weren't happy?*, floated in a speech bubble between them as Allison stared at her friend.

Portia filled her days not only with long hours in the gym but also in taking Open University courses. Having taken several in psychology, she considered herself to be somewhat of an authority and was only too happy to indulge in a little psychoanalysis if given half a chance.

But on that day, of all days, Allison didn't need any dubious expert analysis. 'I never said I was unhappy.'

'You didn't have to. I'm your friend; I could tell.'

'Nonsense! For goodness' sake, I thought you came here to support me, not to make ridiculous unfounded claims. We were perfectly happy. I was perfectly happy. Peter never had reason to doubt me. And I can tell you, if you're trying to infer he was suicidal... that he deliberately jumped... you couldn't be more wrong.'

'Right, okay, I'm sorry.' Portia reached out to take her hand. 'You rushed into this marriage; I'd always wondered if you repented at leisure.'

Allison wrenched her hand away. 'I don't know what you're

talking about, and I don't think you do either. There was no rushing, no repenting. You look at something that's clearly black and white and see shades of grey, Portia. It's all those psychology courses you do, they addle your head.' Allison reached for the wine bottle, resting her hand on it for a moment before getting to her feet. 'Maybe getting drunk isn't the best idea. D'you want a cuppa?'

She didn't wait for a reply. When her stiletto heels click clicked on the tiles of the hallway, she stopped to kick them off and sent them skittering across the floor. Everything seemed disconnected. It was some other woman who filled the kettle and switched it on. A stranger who opened the cupboard and took down two mugs.

Somewhere, as if at a distance, she heard Portia's heavy, slow steps approaching. Allison was sorry now she'd asked her to come. She was consumed with unexpected, bitter grief, and grieving was a lonely personal journey; it would have been better to have travelled alone.

The kettle seemed to take forever to boil, or had everything in her life ground to a halt? Her gaze drifted from it to the sash window behind. Dark outside, the window was a mirror, her reflection oddly deformed by the crossbar, the black dress she wore vanishing into the darkness as if part of her was invisible.

Portia's face appeared alongside, and even in the glass Allison could see frown lines concertinaing her brow.

'I'm sorry, I didn't mean to infer Peter...' Even over the sound of the kettle finally coming to the boil, Portia's gulp was loud. 'You know... committed suicide.'

Allison turned from the strange alternative reality in the window to the pathetic sight of her friend. That was exactly what she'd been inferring. So yes, she should be sorry, the stupid, stupid, stupid cow. If she'd let the words out, all the angry, bitter, twisted words she wanted to spew, her friend would have run from the house in horror. When she saw colour smear Portia's cheeks, she realised she didn't need to say a word.

'I'm sorry,' Portia repeated, an unattractive puce spreading in a rash down her neck. 'Put it down to shock at the news. I like to think everything can be explained away.'

The click of the kettle switching off removed the need to reply. In silence, Allison heated the teapot, dropped in a teabag and poured the boiling water. 'Tea always seems oddly appropriate, doesn't it?' She was aware her words were anything but... too calm, too *normal*. Putting the pot on the table, she returned for the mugs and a jug of milk, ignoring the eyes that followed her every move.

There were no words exchanged as they sat drinking tea. Allison stared into her mug, watching the level drop as she sipped, only reaching for the teapot to top it up when it neared the bottom. When she tilted the pot and a single drip wobbled from the spout, she sighed and put the teapot down so heavily the lid rattled. 'Only three months married and only a few weeks before that—'

'Eight,' Portia interrupted.

'What?'

'You only knew him eight weeks before you were married. I remember we thought you were crazy.'

We. Portia and Stuart with their boring, small-minded attitude to anything outside the narrow, wealthy social chink they inhabited. Allison struggled to contain her anger. 'We knew we wanted to be together; there didn't seem any point in waiting. And, despite what you think, we were happy. Incredibly happy.' Her voice hitched on the last two words.

'I'm so sorry.' Portia shook her head. 'I'm not being much support, am I?'

Allison drew a shuddering breath and let the anger out on the exhaled sigh. There was no point in being mad with Portia. Her wealth had removed her from what was, at times, the grim, grating, utter crassness of life. Unlike her, Allison had been forced to make her own luck. 'We may not have had much of a past, but we should have had a wonderful future.'

There were only so many ways to apologise. Wisely, Portia didn't attempt any one of the euphemisms or clichés that were waiting to spill from her all-too-often loose lips. That she was finding it difficult to stay quiet would at any other time have made Allison smile. She wasn't sure she was ever going to smile again. 'I'm going to the morgue tomorrow to identify his body.'

'Is that really necessary?'

'The detectives said it wasn't because they found his wallet. They said they'd have used dental records to confirm if I didn't feel up to seeing him.' Allison used her thumb and first finger to wipe the tears from her eyes and wiped her fingers on the sleeve of her dress. 'I have to see him... I need to see him.'

'To believe?'

'Yes.' She shot Portia a grateful glance. 'That's it exactly. There's a tiny part of me that hopes they've made a mistake.' She shrugged. 'It's possible, isn't it?' It wasn't, of course, she knew that. Peter's wallet held his driving licence. The photograph on it was clear. Such a good image of him she'd laughed when she'd seen it, teasing him about how good he looked when it was standard in such photographs to look hideous. 'I have to see for myself.'

'I'll go with you.'

'No, that's okay, it's not necessary. There'll be someone... a liaison officer of some sort... who'll be with me.'

Portia looked appalled. 'You need more than a stranger to be with you, Allison.' She held her hand up to stop any argument. 'How about we do it this way. The liaison officer can go in with you to identify poor Peter and I'll be there waiting for you when you come out. We'll go for lunch somewhere, drink cocktails and celebrate Peter's life.'

Allison knew her friend meant well. It was probably something she'd read in one of her damn psychology books. Something banal about focusing on the positive. *Celebrate Peter's life.* She wanted to scream at her, but the weight of loss was smothering her, blinding her, rendering her numb. Nothing made sense. Not even the answer she finally managed to squeeze through tight lips. 'Thank you. I knew I called you for a reason.'

'Yes, and I'm going to be with you through this, and for as long afterwards as you need me.' Portia got to her feet and picked up the holdall she'd kicked into a corner hours before. She stood holding it and frowned. 'Maybe it would be better if you came back to ours? You could stay for as long as you wanted. We'd both love to have you, you know that, don't you?'

'Yes, I do.' Allison smiled sadly. 'And that's really kind of you.' She ran a hand over her hair. She remembered Peter running his fingers through it once when they'd returned from a restaurant, full of good food and wine. A hand on her shoulder startled her back to the present. She wanted to slap it away, to tell Portia she needed to stay in the past a little longer.

'We'd better get some sleep.'

Portia was right, of course, but Allison wasn't in the mood to be sensible. She'd have preferred to have stayed there and, despite earlier reservations, get senselessly, stinkingly drunk and stay that way for a long, long time. Certainly, until these next few days were over. It was one way of dealing with the unthinkable.

Maybe her intention was clearly written on her face because Portia grasped her elbow in a firm grip and led her from the room. She didn't let go when they reached Allison's bedroom, leading her inside and, without a word, turning her around and undoing the zip of her black dress.

Portia didn't stop then, helping Allison out of her underwear, opening the drawers of the dresser in search of something appropriate, finally helping her into a T-shirt. Allison didn't resist, even as the garment was slipped over her head and she realised, despite being laundered, it still smelt of Peter.

It was easier to give in to Portia's ministrations. Easier to go where she was led, do as she was directed.

'Try and get some sleep,' Portia said, tucking the duvet around Allison's shoulders and bending to place a light kiss on her cheek. 'Call if you need me.'

Allison waited until she heard the spare bedroom door click shut before throwing the covers back and swinging her feet to the floor. She sat on the edge of the bed and wrapped her arms around herself, bringing her T-shirt-clad shoulder to her nose and inhaling deeply, crying out when instead of Peter's scent she smelt Portia's rather overpowering perfume. Nothing was staying the same.

Getting to her feet, she crossed to the window and looked out at the empty street below. It had started to rain, the light from the street light reflected in the raindrops, softening the hard edges of the houses opposite, blurring the boundaries of the footpaths and road. Making it all surreal. Like her life.

The sash window was locked. She reached up and slid the catch across before pushing the cross bar up as far as it would go. Bending to lean out, she gasped a mouthful of night air mixed with raindrops, and as she did the lines of a poem she'd read many years before came to her. *All changed, changed utterly: A terrible beauty is born.*

This lovely house was hers, but without Peter, was it really a home? Had she once again made a terrible mistake?

23

Jo tapped her mobile against the palm of her other hand. Allison had sounded pathetically grateful for her call. A slight smile twisted her mouth as she replayed the conversation in her head, weighing up the words used, the tone of voice. She'd heard the lie, of course; it wasn't difficult – Peter hadn't turned up, obviously – but it was a lie easy to forgive.

Until that day, she'd assumed everything in Allison's life was rosy... every post and photograph on Instagram supported that belief. Now she knew the truth.

Allison hadn't changed from the girl Jo had known all those years before after all.

She reached for the remote and switched on the TV, her small studio apartment flooding with the voice of the presenter of one of the self-improvement programmes she liked to watch. Thanks to one, she'd had her teeth straightened and whitened, had spent a ridiculous amount of money on a plastic surgeon and had finally given up trying to grow her hair and bought a wig. She ran a hand over it. It had been expensive but worth it; nobody would guess it wasn't her natural hair. It had taken every penny she had, and a few she didn't. It had been hard work to make up the difference. Sordid, mind-numbing, soul-destroying work. Picking up men in city bars, offering whatever they wanted, charging extra for the more degrading acts they'd asked her to perform. But she'd done it. Made the money she needed, become the woman she'd wanted to be.

The first stop to getting the life she deserved, the one she should have had... would have had if it hadn't been for Allison.

Jo looked around the miniscule studio apartment. The inadequate kitchen with its two-ring hob and tiny oven. The uncomfortable sofa that opened out into an even more uncomfortable bed. And the ludicrous wet room where the shower head sat immediately over the toilet seat. It was *that* small, but she was still struggling to afford the rent.

When she'd taken it, she'd been working in an insurance company earning a fairly decent salary. She'd still be there if her obsession hadn't taken over.

'You need help,' the human resources manager had said, trying to sound sympathetic, the attempt ruined as she glanced rather obviously at her watch as if measuring the time she was wasting by talking to Jo. When she spoke again there was more than a hint of impatience in her voice. 'We were able to ignore your fixation with social media while you were on your official breaks as it's not our policy to dictate how people pass their free time, but you've been caught numerous times using your mobile to check your accounts while you were supposed to be working and that is not acceptable. You were warned on multiple occasions by your direct line manager before she reported you to us. We've followed procedure with verbal and written warnings as per company policy, to no avail. I'm sorry, we're going to have to let you go.'

Jo had wanted to shout at her. To explain about Allison and the need to keep a close eye on her; to tell her the job was drudgery and only frequent glimpses into richer, better, more glamorous lives helped her get through each day. Instead, she shrugged, collected her belongings and left without a word.

In a city as big as London, there was always another position on a lower rung of the job chain. Her next, a minimum-wage zero-hour contract in the kitchen of an upmarket restaurant, was physically exhausting and mind-numbingly boring. Only by checking her socials every moment she could did she get through each horrendously long, spirit-stealing day. Facebook, Instagram, Pinterest... every bloody place she could go to escape from reality.

Less money required her to work more hours, the searing constant weariness grinding her down and escalating her need for escape into the parallel universe of social media. She took more risks, found hiding places in the storeroom, behind shelves, in the staff toilet, any-bloody-where to whip out her phone and scroll through the images and respond to posts.

The job lasted a week. The restaurant manager didn't bother being polite. 'Get your bag and coat and get the fuck out of here.' A fistful of cash shoved into Jo's chest nearly knocked her off her feet. She'd liked to have been able to tell him to stuff his money and his crappy job, to have had the freedom to be that stupidly careless.

One day, not then, when the rent on her tiny studio apartment in Bermondsey was due.

One day, though... she had plans.

24

As she hid under the duvet, an acrid, nose-crinkling stink of smoke made her gag then choke, her eyes burn and water. Lost in her own nightmare, she heard the stomach-churning scream of terror and agony... was it her or someone else?

As she dropped to the floor, gasping for breath, there were more shrieks, ones that begged for help, for rescue, ones that grew shriller and more desperate before stopping suddenly.

And through it all was the smell. Thick, throat-choking, eye-burning. Smoke... stinking of burning wood and furniture, of the gauzy, grimy curtains that did nothing to keep the light out or heat in yet burnt so readily, of the cheap nylon carpet that allowed the flames to lick along the floor.

A stink that grew worse... nauseatingly, skin-crawlingly worse... a smell recognised from summer barbeques drifting across the wall from neighbours' gardens.

The smell of roasted meat.

25

Jo tossed her mobile on the seat beside her and stretched her arms above her head, the wide sleeves of her robe sliding down to puddle around her shoulders. She'd changed out of the suit she'd worn that day to meet Allison for lunch as soon as she'd returned. It was hanging on the wardrobe door. Later, she'd use the steam setting on her iron to remove any obvious creases and check over it for any damage. But she'd been careful, she always was. Tomorrow, she'd take it back to the department store where she'd bought it only the previous day and explain she'd made a mistake. Or maybe she'd use the old my husband/partner/boyfriend didn't like it. In the twenty-first century, it was amazing how easily such a lame excuse still worked.

For her next meeting with Allison, Jo would choose a different department store. Rotating was the easiest way to avoid suspicion. It was easy; she kept a spreadsheet on her computer, carefully logging details of what she bought and where. It wasn't stealing. Not precisely. The clothes were always returned in perfect condition. When she wore these borrowed clothes, she avoided fragrance and used non-perfumed deodorant to ensure they retained their shop-fresh smell.

Only once had she had an issue.

* * *

It had been almost three months before. She'd seen an advert for an exhibition of an up-and-coming artist in a gallery in Chelsea. It would, she knew, attract an interesting attendance. And she wanted to be among them. Wanting to fit in, she'd planned to find something in one of the department stores she frequented but had been foolishly lured into a small boutique by a dress in the window. Dramatic, colourful, arty. It was perfect. The price wasn't, but she hadn't planned to keep it.

The exhibition was boring. The crowd attending equally so. All little cliques huddled together. Impossible to breach. She'd tried and failed, keeping her bright smile in place with difficulty at each snub, each raised eyebrow, each snigger sent in her direction. The voluminous, multi-coloured dress that had looked so suitable in the shop window, the one she'd thought made her look so right, was all wrong. Most of the women were wearing trousers, one or two wearing long skirts, a few wearing the little black dress that was saved for events like this. Jo's dress, rather than screaming *arty*, shouted *trying too hard*.

It was tempting to run from the exhibition hall, or at least walk as fast as her stiletto heels would allow... instead she stayed to the very bitter end. Only then did she turn with a swirl of multi-coloured fabric and walk slowly from the room.

It had been a failure of a night. At home, she'd have liked to have torn off the dress and dump it out the window to watch it float from the fourteenth floor and sail into oblivion. She didn't have that luxury. Instead, she took it off and hung it on the wardrobe door. Only when that was done and she was swathed in her robe did she open a beer and guzzle it straight from the can, gulping it down in a desperate attempt to rid her mind of the memory of the horrendous night.

The one beer and a good night's sleep helped restore her equilibrium. She even managed to shake her head in amusement when she looked at the dress. Seriously, what had she been thinking? After a quick check to ensure it was in shop-shape, she wrapped it back in the same tissue paper the assistant had so carefully folded it in two days before and brought it back to the boutique.

Deciding to go with *my partner doesn't like it*, she'd placed the smart, shop-logoed carrier bag on the sales desk and smiled at the same assistant she'd dealt with on her previous visit.

'Such a shame, I think it's fabulous.'

'It looked so good on you too.'

'Yes, but if Emmet doesn't like it, there's no point in keeping it really.' Emmet, a nice strong name for a man. The kind of man she'd have thought would attend exhibitions of up-and-coming artists. Her sigh was heavy.

'A shame.' The assistant unfolded the tissue paper and held the dress up. Shaking it slightly, she frowned. 'Oh dear!'

Oh dear? Jo felt a dart of worry. Had she missed a spillage? There were quite a few people floating around the exhibition with drinks in their hands... had they slopped some on the dress? She usually checked so carefully before she wrapped a garment up. 'Is everything okay?'

'I'm afraid not.' The dress was folded and placed on the counter.

Jo stared at her, then down at the dress. It had cost three hundred and seventy-five pounds. She had to have the money back. 'I don't understand. What's the problem?'

The wooden counter was topped with glass. Various notices

and business cards had been slid underneath. Instead of answering, the assistant tapped a long, bizarrely embellished fingernail on the glass over one of the cards.

Realisation hit with a lick of horror as Jo peered at the words. 'That's ridiculous! I never saw that notice.'

The assistant folded her arms. 'There's one in the dressing room too and I put a copy with the receipt when I gave it to you.'

Jo had a vague recollection of taking the receipt out and putting it carefully to one side before tossing the other bits of paper into the bin.

'It's one of our rules, I'm afraid.' The assistant looked genuinely apologetic. 'All garments must have their original labels attached in order to be returned. I think there was an issue at one stage of people buying dresses, wearing them and then returning them.' Her expression was suitably horrified. 'Not that I'm accusing you of any such nefarious act, you understand, I'm simply explaining why we have this rule.'

'But surely you can make an exception in this case.' Jo used her best wheedling voice. 'It was you I bought it from. Only the day before yesterday!' The sympathy creeping into the assistant's eyes made her change tack. 'This isn't good enough. I'd like to speak to someone more senior please.'

'I'll get Mrs Simmonds.' The speed at which the assistant left indicated her relief at passing a difficult situation over to someone else. Seconds later, voices drifted from the office behind.

Jo eyed the till. If this were a movie, she could reach across, open it, grab a wad of cash and scarper. A blinking light in the corner of the ceiling dragged her eyes upwards. She wondered if the assistant and Mrs Simmonds, whoever she was, were sitting back there assessing her. Perhaps they'd decide she looked reliable, dependable. Not the kind of woman who would dream of wearing an outfit only to return it the following day. Not the kind of woman who would do… what was it the assistant had said… ah yes, such a nefarious act.

To appear chilled, as if the outcome of their discussion didn't really matter, she turned to admire some jewellery in a cabinet. Perhaps they'd refund the money if they imagined she was going to spend it on other items in the shop. *Three hundred and seventy-five pounds.* She could only think of one way to make up that loss. She'd sworn never again after the last time. A chill ran through her as she remembered the pain. No, she wasn't doing that again.

'Good morning.'

The sharpness of the words didn't augur well for a good outcome. Determined not to give up, Jo turned and nodded in a manner she hoped was seen as regal… not desperate. 'Good morning.' She indicated the jewellery cabinet with another nod. 'You've some lovely jewellery. My friend's birthday is coming up soon; I'll have to consider getting her a piece.'

If Mrs Simmonds was impressed, she gave no indication. 'Dorothea tells me you desire a refund for this dress.' She rested a hand lightly on the swathe of colourful material on the counter. 'As she explained, our returns policy is strict. The sales tickets have been removed, which unfortunately makes a refund impossible. However…'

Relief… Jo uncurled her fists and began to relax.

Mrs Simmonds continued, '… we would be willing, in this case, to allow store credit.' She pointed towards the cabinet. 'Since you've professed an interest in the jewellery, it seems a sensible and convenient option.'

Jo wanted to kick herself for being so stupid. Even if she did have a friend, she wouldn't be buying her ridiculously expensive jewellery in this poxy little pretentious boutique. She felt anger flare and fought to keep it under control. 'No, that doesn't suit. I'd like a refund, please.'

'I understand. Unfortunately, as both I and my assistant have explained, that isn't possible.' She plucked a fold of the material. 'Dorothea tells me the dress looked good on you, that it was a partner who expressed dislike. Since women tend to dress to impress other women rather than men; I'd suggest you hang on to it.'

Three hundred and seventy-five pounds. For a dress Jo now hated. There was nothing to do except retreat and lick her wounds. 'Good idea.'

With an expression that could only be called smug, Mrs Simmonds wrapped the dress in the tissue paper and slid it into the bag. 'Excellent decision.' She handed the bag across. 'We'll look forward to seeing you again when you're shopping for your friend.'

Jo left with the bag swinging from her hand and a weight of despair in her chest. She tried to sell it on eBay. When that failed, when she didn't get one damn offer, and despite her protestations of never again, she did what she had to do. Shutting her eyes to the depravity of it, to the nauseating, vomit-inducing horror as men pawed and pushed into her body with their stinking appendages.

Never again. And this time she meant it.

It was then, when she was at her lowest, that Jo discovered Allison had married.

26

Allison didn't sleep. She didn't even shut her eyes because she knew Peter's face would be there smiling at her with the promise of all the years he'd assumed would be ahead of them. Mostly, she lay staring at the ceiling with tired, gritty eyes.

It was quiet. The old house with its own language of creaks and rattles had settled down for the night. Usually, if she was awake, she'd listen to the rhythmic sound of Peter's breathing, taking comfort from his nearness. The faint growl drifting from the spare bedroom didn't have quite the same effect. Allison was sorry her friend had stayed. This was the first day without Peter, the beginning of the next part of her life.

She'd have liked to have wandered around the house. *Her house*. It would take time to adapt to that way of thinking.

The day ahead of her wasn't going to be easy and she wasn't sure if having Portia with her was going to be a hindrance or a help. Allison groaned and stretched her arms over her head. Grief was an easy blanket to drape around herself. She knew the part she was expected to play. Most of it was easy. Peter's death had hit her with a sadness she hadn't expected. Despite his old-fashioned nonsense about anything domestic being her responsibility, his habit of vanishing into his office for hours, abandoning her, even despite his rather dreary conversation about nothing citing confidentiality when she asked about his clients, when she probed for something – anything – interesting to talk about, despite it all, hadn't it been good? And looking back, hadn't she been happy?

He'd never spoken to her in anger, never offered her violence of any sort. Bored her with his insistence they were deliciously happy, annoyed her with his obsession with having a family, bored her rigid with his clumsy lovemaking. Poor man. She'd tried to make him happy but hadn't it all been as fake as the photographs she posted on her socials, most of which were acquired from free photo sites? Once or twice, when she let the mask of the good wife slip, she'd seen Peter look at her with a puzzled expression on his handsome face and she'd had to hurry to reassure him.

Gullible as he'd been, it had been easy.

She would miss the good bits… the pleasure of walking into a restaurant with a handsome man, the unaccustomed delight in strolling hand in hand, Peter's obvious affection. *Peter.*

She pushed him from her head. *Concentrate on the positives.* She was now a wealthy widow, a homeowner, and she could finally have the life she wanted.

27

Despite the triple glazing, Allison could hear the twittering of the hedge sparrows in the holly bush outside and knew the day had dawned. She pulled on a robe and opened her bedroom door quietly. On the landing, the growl from the spare bedroom was louder. Portia, thank goodness, was still asleep.

It wasn't an easy house to move around quietly. Several of the steps on the stairway creaked loudly. Allison skipped over the ones she could and hoped the rest would be drowned by Portia's snore. The plumbing was another matter. As soon as she turned on the tap in the kitchen, a gurgle travelled along what appeared to be every pipe in the house. Enough water for a pot of coffee and silence was restored. Luckily, it was warm enough not to need the heating on because the pipes would whistle, and the floorboards over them would creak – a noisy duet that would disturb even the heaviest sleeper.

She needed peace to have a coffee, wanted the silence to settle her thoughts. Time enough to have to act. To don the widow's weeds.

Taking the mug of coffee through to the dining room, she put it on the table and pulled the curtains. There'd been frost, the garden a sugar-coated wonderland. She opened the double door into the garden and stepped outside. The air was crisp; she took a deep breath and watched the plumes she expelled float away with a smile before pulling up the neck of her robe and stepping back inside.

The cold had been an effective chisel; it cut through the rather maudlin thoughts she'd been having of Peter to the nitty-gritty underneath. She cupped her cold hands around the mug of coffee and sipped it slowly as she thought.

She'd already done some research. Peter had rewritten his will when they married. Everything had been left to her. All she needed to do was play the grieving widow for a few months till his estate was settled and she would live comfortably ever after.

Then? She looked at the wall separating her from the kitchen. Although Peter had admitted trying to persuade his mother to have it knocked down, when it came to it, he was ridiculously insistent they wait.

'I was thinking we should extend out into the garden. Plan for the future.' He'd snaked an arm around her shoulder and pulled her close. 'For when we have a gaggle of kids.'

He'd probably assumed her shiver in response was agreement, maybe even an erotic reaction to his closeness. It was neither. She wanted to pull away from him but was afraid he'd see the look of loathing on her face. A gaggle of children. Not in her worst nightmare. Not even one. There was no point in telling him and bursting his little bubble of happiness. Let him believe whatever he wanted.

Poor Peter. At least he'd never had to see his dreams flutter in the wind around him, sailing up, up and away before falling spent to the ground. He'd never had to face reality.

Not everyone could.

Reality. She'd considered whether it would be better to sell up and move into something more modern. For what she'd get for the house, she could buy a very nice apartment. One with a balcony, a decent view, gym, concierge. Maybe even a pool.

It was tempting.

It was the thought of so many people living in close proximation that made her decide to stay put. Not the danger of seeing them – she guessed people would keep to themselves – no, it was simply being aware they were there. Surrounding her. Above, below. Too close.

The thought sent a shiver through her.

No, she'd stay in Peter's house. Make it hers.

She looked around at the hideous wallpaper, the ugly, dark furniture, that glaringly bad carpet. All would go. With the wall down and a new, top-of-the-range kitchen, the place would be transformed. She stood and did a circle of the room. In her mind's eye, the French doors were replaced with bifold, the walls a pale cream, the floor... oak, maybe.

She felt a thrill of excitement and barely managed to get her widow's expression in place when the door opened, and Portia sailed into view. 'Good morning.'

The mug Allison raised in front of her face gave her the seconds needed to compose herself, to force the corners of her mouth downward. Lack of sleep would make her look pale; it always did. That too would work in her favour. 'Hi, can I get you a coffee?'

Portia closed the distance between them and reached out to lay her hands over Allison's. 'You look wretched, you poor thing. Sit. There's no need to wait on me, I can help myself.'

Allison was happy to do as she was bid. She sat and continued her redesign of the room, vaguely aware of the sound of Portia pottering in the kitchen. Lost in mental colour charts, it wasn't until Portia's puzzled face appeared around the edge of the doorway that she realised her mobile was ringing.

'Would you like me to answer it?'

'No.' The word was baldly abrupt. Allison pushed the corners of her mouth down again, managing a slight quiver of her lower lip as she did so. 'Sorry. I was lost in thoughts of Peter.' The phone continued to ring. She reached for it. A number she didn't recognise. 'Hello?'

'Mrs Fellowes?'

'Yes?'

'My name is Sally Bennet. I'm your police liaison officer. I'm so sorry for your loss and want to assure you I'll help you as much as I can to negotiate the various official channels.'

'Thank you.' Allison felt Portia's eyes on her and slid her hand over the mouthpiece. 'It's the police liaison.' With a nod, as if to say she'd guessed, Portia vanished back into the kitchen. 'So what happens now?'

'Your husband's body is in the mortuary of the Royal on Whitechapel Road. I can pick you up, if you'd like, or if not, I can meet you there.'

Only a day in and Allison was already growing weary of the enforced pretence. Bad enough having Portia constantly assessing her, slotting her into some predestined psychological category and possibly wondering why Allison didn't quite fit. The police liaison, more used than Portia to seeing grief, might be more difficult to fool. The less time spent with her the better. 'Thank you, I have a friend with me. We'll get a taxi.'

Afterwards, as Portia had suggested, Allison would knock back a few glasses of champagne. In memory of Peter... and to toast her future.

28

The identification process was as hideous as Allison had expected and she had no difficulty in portraying a devastated widow. Peter's poor face, despite their best efforts, was a mess. Her cringe at the sight was obviously, and conveniently, seen as sorrow. He really had been such a handsome man.

'Yes, that's my husband, Peter.' Allison swayed slightly and hitched a few sobs.

The liaison officer moved in with a comforting arm. 'Would you like a few moments alone to say goodbye?'

Allison leaned into the arm, feeling the officer steady herself to bear the extra weight. 'Sorry,' she said, straightening. 'Yes, please, I'd like that very much.'

Her moment of weakness had obviously been enough to convince the liaison officer, who pulled over a chair and hovered solicitously as Allison lowered herself onto it and gripped the sides of the seat as if she was going to keel over and fall off.

'I'll wait outside. Take as long as you want.'

Allison waited till she heard the door shutting behind the officer before getting to her feet and approaching Peter's body again. Her nose crinkled at the smell. Not unpleasant but not the Hugo Boss cologne she was used to recognising. 'Poor Peter.' She leaned down and pressed her lips to the small triangle of skin on his forehead not criss-crossed with evidence of his catastrophic end. The icy chill of the touch made her shiver and pull away.

He wouldn't have felt a thing. She took consolation from that. He'd been good to her; she wouldn't have wanted him to suffer. Despite his end, he'd died with the bubble of his fantasy intact. 'I did that much for you, Peter.'

A click behind her alerted her to the return of the liaison officer. Allison had enough time to throw herself across Peter's body, shaking her shoulders in what she hoped was a good impression of someone in the deepest throes of sorrow. Luckily, this close, the smell emanating from his body was acrid enough to make her eyes water. When she stood, a convenient tear was displaced to run elegantly down her cheek.

'If you need to stay longer...?'

'No.' Allison pressed her trembling lips together. Oscar-worthy material. She leaned down once more and pressed a final kiss to the same spot she'd chosen earlier. 'Goodbye, my darling, I will miss you forever.' With her head down, one hand grasping the other, she walked shakily to the door, along the corridors and up the short stairway to the reception area.

She turned to the liaison officer. 'Thank you, you've been very kind.'

'There will be an inquest, of course. I'm afraid there's rather a backlog so it could be a few months. Not usually more than six, though.'

The liaison officer said this as if it was a consolation. It wasn't. *Six months.* 'Oh my goodness, it's going to be so stressful to have to wait that long before I'm able to lay poor Peter to rest.' She couldn't get a damn death certificate until after the inquest. Without it, she couldn't apply for probate. Couldn't get access to the money. Couldn't start the rest of her life.

Bennet shook her head. 'I'm sorry. Sometimes, if the cause of death is clear—'

'Isn't it?' Allison's voice was sharp. She saw Bennet's eyebrows rise in surprise and lifted her hand over her face, hiding behind them for a few seconds to re-establish control. She dragged them down her face. 'I'm sorry. It's all so hard.'

'Of course,' Bennet said, her voice carefully controlled. 'Unfortunately, and I know this is hard, but the police have to investigate whether your husband fell, was pushed—'

'Or he jumped, is that what they think?' Allison had told them – had insisted – Peter had no reason to jump. No reason at all.

'They don't think anything; they're simply doing their job.'

Allison couldn't bring herself to speak.

'It simply means a bit of a delay, Mrs Fellowes.'

It was an effort to sound unconcerned. 'So how long are we talking about?'

'They have various CCTV footage to look through, witness statements to collate, the train driver's testimony to consider. It all takes time. Only when this is done will the inquest take place.'

Perhaps she should have expected this, but she hadn't. Allison struggled to keep her expression neutral. She guessed she was failing, and anger was leaking around the edges of her mask when she saw Bennet's eyes narrowing slightly. A sob seemed in order. She managed a creditable one, relieved to see a softening in the liaison officer's taut expression. Holding her hand clasped to her mouth for a few seconds, Allison shook her head and took it away. 'I'm sorry. It's all so impossibly hard. The funeral is going to be such a difficult time; I'm not sure I can bear to wait for so long, thinking about it every day.'

'Of course. The funeral is all part of the grieving process. It's important to get through these steps as soon as you are able, really.'

Allison wondered if Bennet attended the same psychology courses as Portia. Probably read the same books. Or – she hoped her sneer wasn't obvious – a cheat's summary of each. 'Yes, you're right, of course you are. Thank you for understanding, that's it exactly.' She was grovelling but it did the trick, the liaison officer's expression softening further.

'The coroner may issue an interim death certificate before the police investigation is completed,' Bennet said. 'I promise I'll keep on top of that and let you know as soon as that seems likely.'

'Thank you, that is kind of you.' Allison wasn't planning on depending on the liaison officer. Her solicitor, a man whose rather comical appearance belied his viciously sharp reputation, could be depended upon to expedite the certificate.

She was tired of dealing with liaison officer, and it was a relief to see Portia approaching. 'Here's my friend now. Thank you for your support this morning.'

Bennet turned automatically to see who approached, her eyes widening at the sight.

Allison wasn't surprised at her reaction. Portia was rarely seen without full make-up. Very pale foundation, high, arched, dark eyebrows, bright lipstick. Her black hair – Allison guessed it was a very expensive wig – was styled in stiff waves curling away from her face. That day, obviously relishing her role as chief mourner's supporter, she was dressed in a long, sleeveless, black velvet and lace dress, a shawl draped over her upper arms trailing almost to the floor. Allison had wondered what had been in the holdall she'd brought with her the night before; now she knew.

A classic film buff, Allison half expected Portia to channel her inner Gloria Swanson, stretch a slim arm towards her, and utter

Norma Desmond's immortal lines. *All right, Mr DeMille, I'm ready for my close-up now.*

'Darling!' Portia swooped in and enfolded Allison in her arms. Draping her with her shawl as she did so, she kissed the air each side of her head. 'Was it awful?'

'Hideous.' Allison pushed her gently away. 'My liaison officer, Sally Bennet.' She introduced the woman, who was still staring at Portia in something akin to disbelief. 'She's been very kind and supportive. Sally, this is my good friend, Portia Strong.'

'Ms Strong.' Bennet nodded, then looked to the door behind. 'I'd better be off. I'll be in touch, Mrs Fellowes.'

Allison linked her arm in Portia's. 'Let's get out of here.'

29

Allison didn't question the destination when she was urged into the taxi idling outside. She rested her head back and shut her eyes. Murmurs of conversation between Portia and the taxi driver drifted towards her without settling in her head. She didn't care where they were going, happy to let Portia take charge. As long as at the end of the journey a cold glass of wine was waiting. Several glasses. Temporary oblivion was bound to be lurking in the bottom of the first bottle.

'Here we are.'

Allison opened her eyes with little interest, half-expecting to see the façade of a restaurant. Probably one she knew, undoubtedly good, and since the choice had been Portia's, unquestionably expensive. What Allison hadn't anticipated was seeing her friend's elegant Kensington home.

Perhaps they were simply calling to pick up something... maybe for Portia to change into something slightly more suitable. Her hopes were dashed when Portia turned to her with a smile. 'I guessed you'd be too upset for a restaurant, so I've prepared lunch here.'

It was impossible to take offence. 'How thoughtful.' *Bugger, shit, fuck.* The last thing Allison wanted was to sit with Stuart and Portia's eyes fixed on her face for any length of time. Getting drunk in a restaurant where she could be poured into a taxi afterward was one thing; getting blotto in Portia's pristine, rather clinical dining room was another matter altogether. Anger made her movements jerky as she shoved open the taxi door and climbed out.

Portia had already reached the wrought-iron gate of her home. For a few seconds, Allison was tempted to slip back inside the taxi and tell him to drive away. She didn't, of course; until the funeral was over, till probate had cleared, she was stuck in London. Stuck and friendless sounded more pathetic.

'I've ordered food from that French bistro you like,' Portia explained as she searched through a large bunch of keys for the correct one. 'And there's a couple of bottles of your favourite Chablis chilling in the fridge.'

Maybe it wouldn't be too bad. Allison kicked off her stilettos inside the front door as she had done on the last visit when Portia had explained about the expensive cherrywood floors, and the damage heels could cause. Allison had shrugged off the offer of slippers then as she did now. 'No, I'm fine.'

Portia slipped on garish pink fluffy mules – a rather ridiculous contrast to her funereal dress – and flip-flopped noisily across the hallway to fling open the door to the large lounge that stretched across the front of the house. 'Sit, I'll get the wine. The food is due in about half an hour.'

Allison sank onto the sofa, relieved there was no sign of Stuart. His eyes were too sharp, too all-seeing for her liking. It had been a wearisome morning. She was sorry she'd been persuaded to have lunch with Portia and annoyed to have ended up in her house.

It had been months since she'd been there for dinner A frown creased her brow as she tried to remember if she'd refused invitations or if they'd simply dried up. She'd been so caught up in the initial excitement of her relationship with Peter, then their wedding, and the plans after that, she'd never noticed. Portia had met him, of course. At their wedding. Allison's frown deepened. Oddly, she and Peter had never been invited to Portia's home as a couple. Perhaps Portia and Stuart hadn't cared for him, which was strange; Peter might have been a bore but he'd been a charming one.

Allison rested her head on the back of the sofa and shut her eyes. The early afternoon sun was slanting rays through the tall bay windows. Their warmth was comforting, soporific. If she'd been at home, she'd have given in to it, let herself be lured to sleep, but she wouldn't do it here. Portia wouldn't wake her and would then try to persuade her to stay over as she had the previous visit.

Allison had dressed with more than usual care that morning. The only black dresses she possessed were totally unsuitable for the occasion, showing too much cleavage or leg, or both. A navy trouser suit paired with a navy shirt rather than the white she'd normally have chosen was suitably funereal, but it was heavy and the room excessively warm. She took off the jacket, flung it over the arm of the chair and pulled at the fabric of her shirt, flapping it, enjoying the cooling draught.

Portia was taking her time with that glass of wine. Allison would have preferred to have gone with her and sat in their kitchen, a much cooler room overlooking the lushly planted rear garden. But Portia had brought her to the lounge. Allison wasn't sure why. The sofa was comfortable enough, the ceiling high with attractive cornicing around the edges, the walls papered, not painted. Everything, the walls, furniture, rugs, were in shades of cream. Only the cherrywood floor had any warmth. There was also the same lack of personal details Allison had noted on her previous visit.

She shuffled restlessly. God, she needed that drink. She glanced towards the door, willing it to open. Perhaps she should go and ask if she could help. But Portia, for all her seeming casual laissez-faire, liked things done her way. If she'd wanted Allison to help, she'd have asked.

Checking her watch for the hundredth time, she wondered if time was standing still. It felt like she'd been waiting for hours; truth was, Portia had been gone a mere ten minutes.

It must simply be desperation for that drink.

She wanted that promised oblivion.

She'd pre-empt Portia's attempts to have her stay, though, and order a taxi. In fact – she checked her watch again – Portia had mentioned lunch arriving in half an hour. After a quick calculation, and allowing extra time for after-dinner drinks, she pulled out her mobile and ordered a taxi for five.

'Here you go.'

Allison dropped her mobile back into her bag as Portia came through, a glass in each hand.

It was clear what had taken her so long to pour the wine. Instead of the dramatic black costume she'd worn, she was a vision in pink, baby-pink wide-leg trousers with a loose silk shirt in a slightly darker tone. 'You don't mind me changing, I hope,' she said, sitting on the other end of the sofa, angling herself so she faced her friend.

'Of course not.' Allison wished she could do the same. There wasn't a breath of air in the room. She knew it was useless to ask if a window could be opened. Portia was paranoid about being burgled and every window was, she'd told Allison once when they were discussing the question of security, locked tight. She gulped a mouthful of the wine, feeling the chill trickle down her throat with far more pleasure than a mouthful of wine normally brought.

After another gulp, she felt a little cooler and smiled across at Portia. 'I needed that, thank you.'

Portia leaned closer and patted her arm. 'You're doing brilliantly. I don't know how you're keeping yourself together so well.'

Allison had spent several minutes in front of her bathroom mirror perfecting a slight quiver of her lower lip. It paid off now. Much better than trying to force tears. 'It's hard. I'm trying not to think of Peter, trying to get through one day at a time.' Another lip quiver, this time accompanied by a smile she knew Portia would see as *brave*. 'I keep expecting the reality of my loss to hit me, but I think, for the moment, shock is making me numb to it all.'

'You're being incredibly brave.' Portia reached for the wine bottle she'd placed on the table. 'Let me top up your glass. I know alcohol isn't the answer but there's no harm getting a little tipsy today of all days.'

Allison thought back to the last dinner she'd shared with Portia and her husband. Alcohol had flowed freely before, during and after. Neither husband nor wife had appeared drunk, at least not the falling-down variety, but their tongues had loosened, they'd become more touchy-feely, their conversation more risqué and, like most inebriated people, they'd become rather boring.

Not a heavy drinker, Allison was only ever mildly tipsy. That day, though, she was planning to get totally blotto.

The chime of the doorbell, a prosaic *ding-dong* that matched the house and not the flamboyant owner, brought both their attention towards the doorway to the hall.

'That'll be lunch.' Portia got to her feet, leaving the room in a flash of pink. She popped her head around the edge of the door seconds later. 'I'll pop the main in the oven, dish up the first course and be back to get you, okay?'

She'd left the wine, so Allison was more than happy. Happier, in fact. For a few minutes she didn't have to pretend to be the grieving widow whose life was over. She had to concentrate on the bright future before her. The lovely house that would soon be hers. She wouldn't remember Peter's smiling face, or think of his sad, crushed body.

She knocked back the end of the wine and reached for the bottle to pour herself a more generous glassful. She was sipping slowly, enjoying the buzz building in her head. No breakfast to slow it down, the alcohol was getting straight to work.

Portia had left the door open. In the distance she could hear a murmur of voices and sighed. Stuart was home. She put the glass down. Getting drunk and loose-lipped wasn't a risk she wanted to take.

When the door opened, she hurriedly settled her expression into a suitably mournful one.

'Allison, my dear girl.' Stuart strode across the floor and leaned down to plant a kiss on both cheeks, pulling back only slightly to stare into her eyes. 'I don't know what to say.'

He might not know but it didn't stop him trying. He sat slightly too close to her on the sofa and took her hand in his large, warm one. As he spoke on and on about how both he and Portia would be there for Allison for however long she needed them, her eyes stayed fixed on his long fingers and the thumb that swept over the back of her hand.

There was something mesmeric about the action, the rhythmic to and fro, the pressure – soft and gentle one way, hard and firm on the way back.

Maybe it was the wine, because suddenly she desperately wanted to leave.

30

Perhaps Allison would have left, made some vague excuse and run from the house to pick up a taxi somewhere on the street, but as she looked towards the door, wondering how fast she could move, it opened, and Portia entered, her face wreathed in a smile. 'Lunch is served.'

Stuart took his hand away and got to his feet. He reached the same hand out towards Allison. It was impossible to refuse his assistance and her hand was enveloped in his. She hid the quiver of distaste as, once more, his thumb did that sweep to and fro.

Did he somehow think it was comforting?

He drew her ahead of him, then thankfully released her. It took all her reserve of strength not to rub the back of her hand frantically against the material of her trousers. As they passed a cloakroom, she reached out and tapped the door. 'I'll just pop in here for a moment.'

Inside, she turned on the hot tap, squeezed a generous amount of liquid soap into the palm of her hand and rubbed it over the back of her hand, running the hot water over it, adding more soap.

Only after the second wash did she feel she'd succeeded in ridding herself of that odd, creepy sensation.

* * *

The food was good. Allison, who was hungry by that stage, would have liked to have cleared her plate. Instead, conscious of the role she was playing, she pecked at a little, pushed some around the plate before heaving a sigh as she placed her cutlery down. 'That's as much as I can manage, I'm afraid.'

They were seated at the end of the large dining room table, Allison at the head, Stuart to her left, closer than necessary and certainly closer than she liked. When he reached a hand to rest it on hers, it took all her control not to pull away.

'We're going to need to look after you.' He squeezed her hand. 'You're already so very slim. You'll fade away.'

His eyes seemed to be boring into her. Transfixing. Allison's mouth was suddenly dry. She wanted to pull her gaze away... to run away.

It was Portia's cough that broke his spell.

Spell. Allison shook away the odd notion, pulled her hand from Stuart's and picked up her cutlery again. 'You're right. Maybe I'll try a little more.' But this time, she didn't need to pretend her appetite had gone. It had vanished when she'd seen the look in Stuart's eyes. A knowing look.

What exactly did he know?

31

The only thing helping to keep Allison together was the knowledge of the taxi arriving at 5 p.m. It wasn't Stuart or Portia's fault. Or not Portia's anyway. She'd been a good friend and Allison knew she'd be horrified if she thought Stuart was... what? Allison flicked a glance in his direction. His expression as usual was bland, unexceptional. Compared to the colourful, eccentric Portia, he was dove-grey dull. But Allison hadn't imagined it... there had been something in the way he'd looked at her. As if he knew exactly what she'd done.

'Try to eat some more,' Portia urged.

Allison knew the food would have been good. It had come from her favourite bistro. Their food never tasted like dry sawdust that stuck to the inside of your mouth in a clagging, choking mess. Only a gulp of wine allowed her to swallow and not disgrace herself by putting her fingers down her throat to pull it out. 'I really can't eat any more, I'm sorry.' She pushed the plate away, turning her wrist to check the time as she did so. Only 4 p.m. Another hour – she wasn't sure she could manage it.

When she saw Portia stretch across with the wine bottle, she put her hand across the glass and shook her head. 'No, thanks, honestly, I really can't drink any more.' She managed to paste on a smile. 'I think I've already had too much.'

'A temporary crutch to help you get through these difficult times,' Stuart intoned as if he was the authority.

Allison waited for Portia to correct him, to tell him that alcohol wasn't the answer to anything. Even without her multitude of psychology courses, she'd have known the truth of that. Instead, she smiled at him as if he'd said something original and profound.

Portia was stupidly deferential when it came to her husband. It made Allison feel even more nauseous.

'No, really, I would prefer not,' she said, keeping her hand resting firmly across her glass. 'I'd love a coffee, though.'

'Coffee it shall be.' Portia got to her feet and with dexterity gathered all the plates and vanished in a flash of pink, leaving Allison uncomfortably aware of the eyes looking her way.

Refusing to turn to meet them, she glanced around for something to fix on. But in a room devoid of any ornaments or photographs of smiling family and friends, there was nothing.

With the silence increasingly uncomfortable and unable to keep staring into space, she turned to look at Stuart. 'You're keen minimalists, aren't you?'

'There is time for excess. Otherwise, I prefer my surroundings to be clean, so I'm not distracted by' – he flicked the fingers of one hand dismissively – 'non-essentials.'

I prefer. Anger simmered for her friend, and she was about to say something cutting when the door swung open, stopping her.

'Here we go.' Portia placed a laden tray gently on the table. 'You're in luck,' she said, lifting a plate and putting it in front of Allison. 'Fortnum & Mason Florentines.'

Yes, because expensive biscuits are a good trade-off against a dead husband. Allison lifted a hand to her forehead as she felt the beginning of a headache she knew would soon be crippling. 'My favourite, thank you.' She picked up one and took a small bite as Portia poured coffee.

'You'll stay over.' Stuart's statement seemed to forbid argument.

Allison nibbled the Florentine and thanked her foresight for booking a taxi. 'No, thank you, that's terribly kind, I'd prefer to go home.'

'Oh, do stay,' Portia said, topping up Allison's cup. 'You needn't worry about nightclothes and stuff. There's lots of Amy's belongings here still. I'd guess you're the same size. Even the same colouring—' She stopped, her cheeks flushing a matching shade to her clothes. 'I'm sorry, that's hardly relevant. All I'm saying is, you'd be perfectly at home here, perfectly comfortable.'

'It's very kind of you, really.' Allison forced down the remainder of the Florentine with a mouthful of coffee. 'But the taxi I ordered will be here soon. I need to get used to living in the house on my own.'

'Right, well, I'll go with you then.' Portia assumed a mulish, determined face.

'No.' The word came out stark and unadorned. It seemed it was necessary in the face of what was becoming unpleasant persistence. When she saw her friend's face fall, she felt a twinge of guilt. 'I'm sorry, that was rude.' She lifted a hand to her forehead again. The headache was worsening; soon, it would be unbearable. 'I'm tired, I have a headache, all I want to do is go home.' Her voice, now plaintive, seemed to get through to them.

'Oh, you poor love,' Portia said, getting to her feet and rushing around the table to gather Allison in a hug. 'Of course, you do whatever is best for you. We're just trying to help.'

'I know, and I am most grateful. You've been so kind.' Allison felt a twinge of guilt. Portia had been extremely kind, dashing around last night when she'd needed her, going with her that morning, going to the trouble of ordering her favourite food. *And don't forget the Fortnum & Mason Florentines.* 'Extremely kind.' She managed to include Stuart in her smile of gratitude.

It wasn't his fault she found him creepy.

32

The taxi arrived on the dot of five, allowing Allison to escape. In the hallway, she slipped her feet into her shoes. 'Thank you so much for everything,' she said, hugging Portia. It was sincerely meant. She'd been a good friend. When Allison pulled away to see Stuart waiting to say goodbye, she wondered if she could make a run for the front door, rush through it and jump into the waiting taxi before he could get closer.

But he was between her and the door. She didn't think she'd manage to rugby tackle him to the floor and step over his prostrate body. Or even better, grind the heels of her stilettos into the paunch oozing over his trouser belt.

She wondered if he'd read her mind when she saw a hint of a smile curve his lips. Or was he smiling in anticipation? She held her breath as he closed in on her.

'Poor, poor Allison. Don't forget, we're here if you need us.' He put his hands on her shoulders and pulled her into his arms. Too close. A musky scent, the combination of aftershave and deodorant perhaps, couldn't quite hide a nose-crinkling body odour. Too close and for too long.

Allison hoped she was imagining the heat she felt pressing against her belly. The tight band of his arms kept her pressed against him. Stretching her neck, she drew her face away. 'The taxi driver will be getting impatient.'

'Yes, yes,' he said, pressing his lips to hers. Briefly, but not briefly enough.

Allison would swear she felt the tip of his tongue pressing between them.

Finally released, she made her get-away with a final wave to both. Only inside the taxi did she relax, tense shoulders drooping. As the car pulled away, she looked back to the house and saw Portia and Stuart standing framed in the doorway, his arm around her shoulder. Both had a hand in the air. Not moving. Royal waves.

Allison raised hers in response, letting it flop onto her lap as they were lost to view.

She laid her head back onto the headrest and by the time the taxi had negotiated London traffic to her home, she'd managed to dismiss her imaginings. She didn't need a psychology degree, or even some of Portia's rather dubious courses, to know stress was responsible.

Allison caught her eyes in the rear-view mirror. Was it as simple as that? She was looking at Stuart and seeing a monster when she knew the monster was inside her, not very deep either. Only a few layers of civilised behaviour, manners and polish coated it. But they'd never cracked, not once over the years. Till recently. She was back in control now but perhaps there were after-effects.

Poor Stuart had got in the way. That was all. She'd imagined the rest.

When the taxi drew up outside her house... *her house*... satisfaction swept over her. It might take a little longer than she'd expected but soon she'd have enough money to give up her job and live the life she'd always wanted.

Inside, she switched on lights and walked from room to room, seeing each in a new light, making mental notes about what to do when the funds were released. She'd given up the idea of selling it. The house was in a good street, a good area. She'd planned to travel but wanted somewhere to come home to. In the future, she might rent it out. Lots of plans. Lots of options.

Upstairs, she stared at the king-size bed she'd shared with Peter. It was time to start a new chapter of her life. She stripped the bed linen and remade the bed with fresh, crisp sheets, slipping her two pillows into their slips, tossing Peter's through the doorway of the spare bedroom, where they landed to sag against the wall.

It was early but she was tired and despite the couple of painkillers she'd taken, the headache still simmered. A few minutes later, naked between the clean cotton, her future a rosy glow before her, she easily brought herself to a deep, satisfying orgasm. Before the pulsing pleasure had faded, she was asleep.

33

I spent weeks in hospital following the fire, staring through wide, unblinking eyes at those who questioned me, neither answering nor giving any indication that I'd heard. The doctors whispered to the uniformed police officers and the succession of other concerned individuals who came to peer down at me. Some wore expressions of sympathy, others of sheer horror. I didn't respond to either.

The word 'catatonic' was bandied back and forward. I knew what it meant and how to act the part. I didn't flinch when they inserted tubes into my arm and barely responded when they slid another down my nose.

I lay still, unresisting, when the nurses moved me back and forth with gentle efficiency to clean away the mess my body insisted on making. They alone treated me non-judgementally as the child I still was and rarely left without giving me a gentle pat and kindly word.

After a time, the others who came to stand and stare didn't bother to whisper and held long and often detailed conversations about what I'd done. It was difficult not to react when I learnt they'd found my scruffy schoolbag and had read my detailed notes.

From them, too, I first heard the word 'monster'.

It was this that dragged me out of the catatonia into a world of pain and sorrow.

34

When Allison woke, it was mid-morning. Rested and relaxed, she stretched arms and legs, feeling the vast emptiness surrounding her with pleasure.

Sunday. A day of rest.

Not for her. She had things to do. She needed to tell Peter's cousin and friends the bad news. It would have been so easy if there'd been a WhatsApp group of everyone who needed to be informed of his passing. She could have tapped out a suitable message. *Hi, everyone, sorry, Peter's dead.* Blunt and to the point. It would have been so much easier than making phone call after phone call, trying to maintain the same sorrowful tone in each.

Luckily, his relationship with his cousin was a distant one, and they hadn't spent much time with his friends. There was talk of dinner parties in some dim and distant future that Peter was never going to see.

After a mug of coffee, and with another in hand, she started the process, beginning with the cousin, who was suitably shocked. It took several minutes of spouting and listening to platitudes before she could hang up. One down, many to go. She worked her way through the contact list in the diary Peter had kept in his bedside locker drawer. Most of the names, she didn't recognise. If they answered, she told the shortest version of the story she could get away with, a variation on *He fell, he died, the police are investigating, the funeral won't be for a few months.*

Some of the names were work contacts who seemed puzzled she was contacting them. Some went so far as to say, *Who?*

There were also those who didn't answer. She wasn't spending more time trying to contact them. She sent a message:

Sorry to inform you my beloved husband, Peter Fellowes, was killed in a terrible accident on Friday. Funeral arrangements will be sent when available.

It took almost an hour to get through the list.

Her own contacts were simple. Her boss at work. She didn't bother phoning, sending her a version of the message she'd sent Peter's friends, adding:

I'm devastated and not sure when I'll be back.

It was a lie, of course, Allison knew exactly when she'd be going back. On the tenth of never. She had sufficient savings to last until Peter's largesse was delivered into her waiting hands. It was safer to lead a quiet life for the next few months, anyway. She didn't want to give anyone the wrong idea.

She'd wait a few days, then ring the office and explain she was simply too distraught to return, wasn't sure when that situation would change and rather than inconvenience the office, she felt it was preferable to hand in her notice. Allison practised the words in her head. They made her sound quite noble. She imagined her boss's expression and smiled. Harriet wasn't anyone's fool. She'd guess she wasn't hearing the full truth, but her hands would be tied in the face of the poor grieving widow.

It was mid-afternoon before she was satisfied she'd informed all, or certainly sufficient people. Tomorrow, she'd contact her solicitor and leave all the official things to him.

She brought up her favourite playlist on Spotify and increased the volume so the music blasted through the house. With a roll of black plastic refuse sacks in her hand, she went upstairs, ripped one off the roll and shook it open. Humming along to the music, she worked methodically and emptied Peter's clothes from the chest of drawers and the wardrobe until there were four bulging bags slouched on the spare bedroom floor. She knotted the top of each and stood back, satisfied with what she'd achieved. Poor Peter, soon there'd be little indication he'd lived there.

She'd left his bedside locker till the end. Books he'd never got around to reading, one he'd never finished. A two-year-old diary. An unopened packet of condoms, well out of date. Random keys. Pens with logos from meeting and hotels. A rather battered coaster. She picked up this last and looked at it. Recognition dawned with a twinge of guilt and a lash of sorrow. It was from the wine bar they'd gone to the first night. He'd kept it to remember. How much he'd loved her.

With a sigh, she tipped the contents of the drawer into a bag, sweeping the books in on top, checking into the corners, making sure every trace was gone. Leaving the bags of clothes in the spare room, she took this final one down and dropped it on the kitchen floor. Later she'd take it out and put it in the refuse bin in the side passageway.

It was late afternoon. She'd had nothing to eat, had eaten little the day before. There were numerous restaurants in the area willing to deliver. It took a few minutes to find the menus for a couple of them, less time to decide. Italian would hit the spot.

The order placed with a promise it would be delivered within half an hour, Allison opened the fridge and pulled out a bottle of Chardonnay. Unable to face the décor in the dining room, she took the bottle and a glass through to the living room and sat.

The first mouthful of wine slipped down nicely. She put the glass down and picked up the remote. There were a couple of movies she wanted to watch.

She was still trying to choose when she heard the doorbell, looking at her watch in surprise. Only fifteen minutes since she'd rung; the restaurant was being surprisingly efficient. Grabbing her purse, she went to answer. Her expectant smile faded quickly as she pulled the door open.

It wasn't a uniformed delivery person on her doorstep.

35

Allison felt her expression freeze in lines of disbelief. If she had to make a list of all the people she didn't want to see that evening, Jo would have been near the top. Unusually lost for words, she opened and shut her mouth like a gormless goldfish.

'I had to come when I heard the news.'

Disbelief was followed by confusion. What was she talking about? It couldn't have been about Peter... could it? Jo hadn't been one of the people she'd contacted earlier. Allison was almost sure. She lifted a hand to her face, pressing fingers to her eyes.

'I can't begin to know how you must feel.' Jo stepped close enough to reach out and rest a hand on Allison's arm.

She wanted to brush away her hand, look Jo straight in the eye and tell her to fuck off, that she neither wanted nor needed her concern. Strangely fake concern. Or was the woman simply incapable of creasing her stiff face into the correct position to imply sympathy?

'May I come in?'

Did she have a choice? 'Yes, of course, you'll have to forgive me; my head's all over the place, as I'm sure you'll understand.' She stood back and waved her unwanted visitor inside. Jo, she noticed, was good at taking liberties. She didn't wait to be directed, heading through the open door and taking a seat on the sofa. Allison's seat. Right beside her half-drunk glass of wine. Wasn't it a bit of a give-away she'd been sitting there?

Did Jo think it was odd Allison should be sitting there boozing only two days after her husband had been killed? She didn't really care, wasn't interested in knowing what Jo thought of her behaviour, but she was curious. 'How did you know?'

Jo smiled as if amused at the question, although it was hard to tell. She was, Allison decided, a great advert for the anti-plastic-surgery brigade.

'You should know, there are no secrets these days.'

No secrets. Allison felt her own expression becoming set and unmoving as she valiantly tried to fix the correct one in place. The grieving widow persona she would have worn if she'd known this bloody woman was going to be standing on her doorstep.

As if aware of her confusion, Jo reached into her pocket and pulled out her phone.

Allison looked at it, puzzled. Perhaps she had rung Jo, told her the bad news, desperate to get it all over with. Told her and forgotten? Perhaps. In the same way Allison had believed poor Stuart was a monster who'd come onto her when he was merely being kind.

Stress. She'd lost the ability to choose the correct response in social interactions. She needed to be very careful.

'My news feed.' Jo waggled the phone.

News feed? Allison looked blankly at her unwanted visitor for a few seconds before shaking her head and moving to the other sofa, sinking onto it with a sigh she hoped was taken as despair and not continued confusion. She rubbed a hand over her face. Only then did it hit her what Jo had meant. It was on the damn internet. Of course it would be. It wasn't every day someone fell under a Tube train and died.

'I should have rung you,' she said, taking her hand away. 'To be honest, I'm still trying to come to terms with it so I've not caught up on all I should be doing.' Maybe it was her imagination, but Jo's eyes appeared to linger a touch too long on the wine bottle, the half-empty glass.

'I've not eaten since I heard.' Allison waved a hand towards the wine. 'I've ordered a takeaway; I was hoping a glass of wine might give me an appetite.'

'It always does me although I prefer beer myself.'

It wasn't a subtle hint. 'There's beer in the fridge.' The only thing of Peter's she hadn't yet thrown out. 'Bishop's Finger. It was Peter's favourite. Would you like one?' *He won't be needing it any more.* Had she said that aloud? Allison looked at Jo in horror, relieved to see her expression hadn't changed to one of surprise. If it could.

'That would be very nice, thank you.'

Allison got to her feet. 'I'll be a sec.' She was longer. As she stepped into the hallway, the doorbell rang again. This time it was the delivery. In the kitchen, she put it on the counter with a grunt of annoyance at having her evening spoilt. Her irritation grew when she looked at the rubbish bag slouched by the back door. If Jo saw it, Allison wouldn't put it past her to ask what it was. It was better to pre-empt that question. She grabbed it, opened the door quietly and slipped outside to dump it in the rubbish bin.

Back in the kitchen, she opened the fridge for the beer. Rather than taking the first suitable glass, Peter's engraved tankard, a gift he told her he'd been given from a grateful client, she reached behind it for a plain pint glass. It took her a while to locate the bottle opener. When she returned to the living room, Jo was sitting back, relaxed, looking as if she was settled for the evening.

Biting back the sarcastic remark that was dying to jump out, the *Sit back and relax, why don't you* – she knew would be wasted on the thick-skinned woman – Allison put the beer and glass down on the coffee table. 'Here you go.' She handed Jo the opener before picking up her wine glass and sitting opposite.

'I never bother with a glass. Saves washing up.' Jo used the opener to flick off the lid, the accompanying *phsst* making her smile. 'One of my favourite sounds.'

Allison watched as the beer was necked greedily. She still had questions. Jo might very well have seen information about Peter's death on a news feed on the internet, they may even by now have named him, but what they wouldn't have done is given his address. Allison's address. And she knew, without a doubt, she'd never given it to this strange new friend. 'It was kind of you to come, but really you shouldn't have bothered. The shock is wearing off; now, I must get used to my new future.'

'It's no problem. That's what friends are for.'

'You're too kind.' The words – the lie – were uttered through gritted teeth. Allison sipped on her wine. She'd looked forward to having a few glasses with the dinner that was rapidly cooling in the kitchen, but it didn't look as if Jo was leaving anytime soon. 'I hope they didn't give our address in that piece you saw.'

Jo wiped a hand over her mouth. 'No, of course not.'

Short of asking her outright how she knew it, Allison was stuck. She wasn't usually slow at being blunt but there was something about Jo, something unsettling, that made her reluctant to ask any questions. It didn't really matter, did it? Did it?

'Was that your takeaway?'

Allison looked blankly at her. 'What?'

Jo pointed towards the door with the neck of the bottle. 'The doorbell. I heard you answer. You shouldn't let it go cold.' She took another pull from the bottle. 'I'll keep you company while you eat. Might help your appetite.'

Allison's fingers tightened around the bowl of her wine glass. Afraid she'd crush it, she put it down. 'I've ordered Italian. I was hoping it would appeal.' She raised a hand to her forehead. 'I've hardly slept since... you know... but I'm trying to stay strong, Peter would have wanted me to, so I need to try to eat. They always send far too much; would you like to have some?' In fact, her appetite had gone completely and the thought of eating with this bloody odd woman staring at her made her feel ill. If she thought the answer would be no, that her unwanted guest would take the hint and go, she was destined to be disappointed.

'That would be very nice, thank you.' Jo lifted her bottle. 'I always think beer goes well with Italian food.'

Was she expecting a pepperoni pizza, perhaps? This was gourmet food from an upmarket Italian restaurant. Allison felt her mouth twist in a sneer and covered her face with her hands until she regained control. 'Sorry.' She dragged her hands down her face. 'It keeps hitting me.'

'You'll be better after something to eat.' Jo got to her feet. With the beer in one hand, she picked up the wine bottle with the other. 'Shall we go through before it gets cold?'

Allison was caught off-guard by this move and, once again, was lost for words. Perhaps it was an accepted part of the bereavement process she'd not heard about, this insistence for people to take over her life. Her portrayal of a devastated widow was obviously spot on. She knew she was a good actress; after all, she'd been playing a part for most of her life, and her loyal, loving wife had been an Oscar-worthy performance, but portraying the recently bereaved was harder than she'd expected. Or perhaps merely more tiring.

'Gosh, this is a bit naff, isn't it?'

Jo's voice came from the hallway, dragging Allison back from her confused self-reflection. She stood, too quickly, a hand reaching for the wall when she was overcome with sudden weakness. Too little food, too much alcohol. The weakness passed as quickly as it had come and she followed Jo, who had switched on the light in the dining room and was walking around the table, staring at the frankly hideous paintings on the wall.

Allison stood in the doorway, a hand resting on the frame keeping her anchored. 'Peter inherited the house from his parents. The décor was their choice.'

'They died recently?' Jo put the bottles she held down on the table.

Allison wanted to remonstrate and tell her both bottles would leave ring marks on the wood. Peter had, frequently, and she'd resisted the temptation to argue the table was hideous and should be chopped up for firewood. Now, strangely, she wanted to save the damn ugly piece from ruin. Rather than remonstrating, she took coasters from a drawer and slipped them under each offender. 'No, they died several years ago.'

'And he never redecorated?' Jo looked at Allison in amazement. 'It's dreadfully dated, isn't it? Weren't you tempted to gut it when you moved in?'

'We had plans to knock the wall down between this room and the kitchen.' Allison pointed to the shared wall. 'We never got around to it. I suppose we were still in the honeymoon phase of our marriage.' The expression, one Peter had used so often, came unbidden. She wished tears would come, it would be a good effect, but she didn't cry. Never had, even when she'd had more reason years before.

'Sit, I'll get the food.' She placed her glass down on another coaster and left the room. The takeaway was sitting on the counter. She took the cartons out and placed the main course in the microwave. There was also a portion of tiramisu... she wasn't sharing it, and put it into the fridge. With two plates heating in the oven, she took cutlery through to the dining room and set them on the table. 'It's *spaghetti alle vongole* – I hope that's okay.'

She almost laughed when she saw Jo's blank reaction. Seriously, had she really expected pizza? 'I'm just giving it a blast to heat it; I'll be back in a second.' Allison was back sooner than her guest had expected, and she hid the smile to find Jo checking her mobile.

That she'd been doing an internet search was proven a moment later when she sniffed the food with assumed pleasure. 'I just adore clams.'

The restaurant was generous with their portions, but whereas it was more than sufficient for one, it was stretched for two.

'You've given me far too much,' Jo said, tucking a fork into the pasta.

Allison dropped her eyes to her plate. She'd given herself less than a quarter. It was unlikely she'd eat even that. 'If I manage this, I'll be happy enough.' She twirled spaghetti around the tines of her fork and dexterously transferred it, without sauce flying every which way, to her mouth. She expected Jo to make a mess or, sacrilegiously, cut the strings of pasta into more manageable lengths. Instead, to her surprise, Jo ate the pasta with as much skill as Allison did.

She must stop underestimating her strange new friend. She couldn't afford to make a mistake now; she'd too much to lose.

36

Jo swirled the spaghetti around her fork with a skill she'd acquired working in the kitchen of an Italian restaurant in her teens. It wasn't the only thing she'd learnt in the year she spent there. She'd learnt that in the dark, it didn't matter what you looked like. Through that long, endless year, at one stage or other, she'd serviced most of the staff in the windowless storeroom at the back of the restaurant.

Too many years had passed, and she hadn't recognised the word 'vongole', relieved to see they were nothing more exotic than clams. Those she could eat. She'd have eaten cuttlefish too, but with a lot less gusto.

Allison, she noticed, was eating little. She looked pathetically pale too. Almost as if she was really grieving. Maybe she was. People never ceased to surprise her. Jo's eyes flicked around the room. She was finding it hard to conflate this décor with the woman she'd been following for so long, whose appearance she'd tried at one time to emulate with little success. Nothing, she decided, could turn a pig's ear into a silk purse. Not the expensive plastic surgery or the wig. It was all the same in the dark.

The beer was gone. It was tempting to ask for another, but it was stronger than she was used to, and she couldn't afford to risk getting loose-lipped and letting her secrets tumble out before it was time.

Pushing her empty plate away, she leaned back and folded her arms. She'd heard the back door opening and shutting and wondered why Allison felt the need to go outside. Something she didn't want Jo to see, perhaps. She wondered what it could be.

'That was delicious,' she said. 'You haven't eaten much.'

Allison put her fork down. 'No, I'm afraid I just can't seem to stomach it.'

'Not surprising, really.' Jo would have liked to have asked what the police had said. It wasn't that she wanted the salacious details, more she wanted to watch Allison's face as she spoke. 'It must have been awful.' It was giving her an opening if she wanted to speak. Annoyingly, it didn't work. She saw Allison's expression harden. Any moment now she was going to ask Jo to leave. Putting her hands flat on the table, she pushed to her feet. 'You look done in. How about you sit and relax, and I make us some coffee?'

Allison held a hand up... to argue or stop Jo, she wasn't sure.

She caught the hand in hers and looked down into her startled eyes. 'I insist. It's what friends are for.' She swept from the room without another word, almost giggling to herself at her risky, and successful, strategy. Luckily, she didn't give in to amusement. Only a second later, she heard Allison's footsteps and turned to see her standing in the doorway.

'You'll never find anything. The cupboards are chock-a-block.'

Jo pointed to the kettle. 'I can do that at least.'

Allison opened the nearest cupboard door. Even from where Jo was standing with water streaming into the kettle, she could see the interior. Not so crammed she couldn't see the jar of instant coffee.

'D'you need sugar?'

'No, ta.' Jo flicked the switch on the kettle and leaned back against the counter, watching as Allison opened the next cupboard, removed two cups, and spooned coffee into each. Was there was a fancy coffee machine hidden behind one of the other doors? Jo would've liked a chance to snoop.

With nowhere to sit in the galley kitchen, she followed Allison from the room. Not into the far more comfortable living room where she might have relaxed, but back into the awful, depressing dining room. It wasn't a room conducive to conversation, but she wasn't one to give up easily. 'I suppose there'll be an investigation.'

'Yes.'

A stubbornness Jo didn't realise she possessed took hold and she persevered. 'You're going to need all the support you can get. This is the time for friends to rally around.' She knew she was on firm footing with this comment, had followed Allison for long enough to know there was nobody she was close to. There had been transitory connections in university, but none had lasted. She, like Jo, was a solitary soul. But Allison would need someone now, someone to hang on to while she draped herself in widow's weeds, and here was Jo, waiting to be her bestie. 'Is there anything I can help you with?'

'That's very kind of you,' Allison said with a slight inclination of her head.

Very bloody condescending. Jo kept a sympathetic expression in place by sheer force of will.

'But Portia, an old friend of mine, has already offered to help with a few things.'

Who the fuck was Portia? Jo had been lackadaisical about following Allison for several months, which was why she'd missed Peter's appearance on the scene. It seemed she'd missed Portia's too. But *old friend...* an exaggeration, surely. There was certainly no female friend on the scene, up to... Jo tried to think when she'd grown bored with her constant surveillance... maybe seven or eight months before. No longer. *Old friend, my ass.* 'Oh that's great. You need someone.'

The coffee was cold; she drank it back in two long gulps and got to her feet, startling the woman sitting opposite. 'It's time I headed,' Jo said. 'I'm staying in London for a few days, visiting friends, so I'll pop back. Now that I know where you live, I won't be a stranger.' She almost laughed as she saw a variety of expressions fight for supremacy on Allison's face, a look of horror quickly overlaid with an effort at grateful thanks.

'That's so kind, thank you,' she said, getting to her feet. 'But really, you don't need to.'

'Don't be silly.' Jo stepped closer and put her arms around Allison, drawing her into a hug. 'I'm going to stay in London for as long as you need me.'

As the body she was hugging became rigid, Jo smiled into Allison's hair.

37

Allison wanted to open her mouth and sink her teeth into Jo's neck. Right in, bite down, feel warm blood gush. She'd swallow the blood and keep her jaw clamped until the gush became a trickle, until the damn bloody woman slumped in her arms and slid to the floor.

Deep breath. Don't let the monster out. 'Thank you so much for coming; it was very kind of you.' The words almost choked her. What she wanted to say was, *Go away and don't come back.* What she wanted to ask was, *How did you get my address?*

She could block Jo on every social media account. Ignore her when she came to the house. She'd get the hint... wouldn't she? Allison wasn't normally the reticent type; she could have simply told Jo she didn't want to see her again, but she had the distinct feeling her words would fall on purposefully deaf ears.

'I'll call around tomorrow. I can't promise what time, though.'

'I'm going to be in and out. Perhaps ring first to make sure I'm here.'

Jo smiled. 'No, that's all right, if you're not here I'll wait or call back.'

Allison noticed that the smile curving Jo's lips didn't reach her eyes. Had it been the same when they'd met for lunch? Perhaps she'd been too distracted by her fall, by the plans she had for the remainder of the day to notice. She hadn't been sure she wanted to see Jo again after that first meeting... now she was absolutely certain. She didn't want to see this odd woman again. With a sudden clarity, she knew she'd somehow been lured into her net, the coincidences of commonality suddenly suspect.

Allison had been a fool. Was that why Jo had appeared on her doorstep? Did she think the new widow was going to be even more vulnerable to her scam?

No, she didn't want to see Jo again. If the woman didn't take the hint, Allison would get rid of her somehow.

38

The authorities did their best. After her discharge from hospital, she was sent to a remand centre for children that was segregated by age and sex for their protection. It had limited effect. The cruelty of children is legend. Especially when they sense a weaker prey.

A great emphasis was placed on confidentiality, but she wasn't there a week before she heard the whispers. Since children rarely bother to be sneaky, they weren't said behind her back but spat right into her face, and whispered only for protection from the wrath of supervisors.

At first, it was one or two of her fellow inmates. Soon, it had spread. And it was such a great word, lending itself to a wonderful two-syllable sing-song chorus.

Even now, she could hear them chanting.

Sometimes, she woke with it ringing in her ears.

Monster, monster, mon-ster.

Monster, monster, mon-ster.

Monster, monster, mon-ster.

39

Outside the house, Jo turned to wave a final farewell. Too late – the door was already shut.

Obviously, Allison couldn't wait to see the back of her. With bitterness burning a pain in her gut, Jo started the walk to the Underground station. She hadn't gone far, walking slowly, rehashing everything that had been said, and everything that had occurred, from the time she arrived to her departure. Her steps slowed, finally coming to a stop. Why had Allison found it necessary to go out the back door? Was she hiding something she hadn't wanted Jo to see? If there was something, whatever it was had to be nearby. With only a moment's hesitation, she retraced her steps to the garden gate.

The front gate had rattled ominously when she'd come through it moments before. Despite her best efforts, opening it as slowly as possible and only sufficiently wide to squeeze through, it rattled again. She stood still, waiting to see if a curtain twitched. When there was no sign of Allison coming to investigate, Jo stepped carefully across the patch of grass that served as a front garden and slipped around the side of the house.

A high wall separated the side passageway from the one next door. Enough light from the street light filtered through to show her she was out of luck. A sturdy-looking gate stopped her from going further. She swore softly and pressed the handle down, more from irritation than from any belief it would work, her eyes widening in surprise when it opened quietly.

She slipped through, shut it behind her and felt in her pocket for her mobile. Turning on the torch, she kept the beam low and moved it along the ground in front. There was nothing to see ahead apart from three wheelie bins sitting side by side.

Was that all it was? No big mystery. Allison had simply been putting out the rubbish. Jo felt a twinge of disappointment. Unwilling to accept that was all, she walked to the end of the passage and peered around the corner of the house. It was dark, no light filtering through from the kitchen or dining room. She risked a quick sweep of the beam across the garden, but it was lost before it reached the end of what appeared to be a massive space.

Nothing suspicious.

She picked up the lid of the first wheelie bin and shone the torch inside, closing it quickly when the stink of rotting garden waste hit her. More tentatively, she lifted the lid of the next, expecting a worse stink. It wasn't pleasant, but the smell was less offensive, the rubbish contained in refuse bags. Jo's curiosity wasn't strong enough to send her rummaging in each.

She shone the torch over the bags. Why had Allison felt it necessary to bring out rubbish just then? None of the bags were bulging.

The first one certainly wasn't.

Holding her mobile in her mouth, Jo found the top of the plastic bag and quickly untied it. It wasn't tightly fastened and was the work of seconds to have it undone. Opening it as wide as she could, she retrieved her phone and aimed the beam of the torch over the tangled contents. There were a couple of books that looked okay. Who threw out books? More stuff lurked underneath. She itched to look through it all. But not there. Tying the bag again, she lifted it out. It wasn't heavy.

She carried it casually, conspicuously, it being the easiest way to avert suspicion. At home, she made space in the middle of her living room floor, spread sheets of newspaper out and emptied the contents of the bag onto it.

The books, three of them, were relatively recent releases. Crime thrillers, not her favourite genre but beggars, like herself, couldn't afford to be choosy. Putting them on the sofa, she sifted through the rest. A diary! She picked it up, eyes gleaming with excitement that quickly died when she discovered it was two years old. The only interesting thing written in it was the name on the details page: Peter Fellowes.

Jo sat back on her haunches. This was Peter's stuff. An unopened box of condoms gave her a clue where it had come from. She'd have bet money, if she had any, that it was the contents of his bedside locker. There was nothing of any interest among the jumble of items. Pieces of what looked like a coaster grabbed her attention. Hoping there was something scribbled on it, she gathered the pieces and reassembled them. But there was nothing written on it. It was simply a coaster from an upmarket wine bar. Why had Peter kept it? And if he had, why had he torn it into pieces? Or had it been Allison who'd found it and, for reasons of her own, ripped it up?

A minor mystery Jo might never solve. The contents of the bag, however, did solve the question of why Allison was desperate to get rid of it. She wouldn't have liked anyone to have seen how soon she was clearing her beloved late husband's belongings from the house. It didn't fit with the grieving widow mantle she'd laid about her shoulders.

Tossing the torn coaster back on top of the remainder of rubbish – the old receipts, keys, pens, timetables for buses that probably no longer ran – she folded the edges of the newspaper over the lot and shoved the untidy parcel back into the black bag.

Poor Allison. Really, she needed to be much more careful.

Somebody could get the wrong idea.

40

Jo opened the door of her apartment. It was late and the corridor outside was dark. She flicked the switch, blinking when the space filled with light. The black bag hung from one hand; she swung it gently, then harder and let it go, the bag sailing along the corridor to land with a flat *flump* against the wall further along. She waited till the light, on a timer, switched out before softly shutting her door.

One of her neighbours would open the bag, find Peter's name and go through the current list of occupants to find a connection. Of course, they wouldn't find any and since her neighbours were far more law-abiding than she, they'd be forced to get rid of the rubbish themselves. It saved Jo the walk down to the refuse shed behind the apartment block.

Restless, she tossed the cushions off the sofa bed and unfolded it. She wasn't tired and lay with her hands behind her head, thinking.

Her plan to befriend Allison had hit a problem. It was becoming clear she didn't much like Jo. She wasn't sure why – she'd gone to so much trouble to ensure they had things in common. All lies, of course; it was too soon to share what they really did have in common. It wasn't necessary that they be friends, not really, but it suddenly seemed an important step.

Allison didn't want her as a friend and with this woman – this Portia – she didn't need her either. The only solution was to get rid of Portia, but first Jo needed to find her. Without a surname, it was going to be hard, but not impossible. She would simply hang around outside Allison's house until an unknown woman turned up and follow her. It wasn't as if Jo had anything better to do.

Luckily, there was no hurry. With her husband's death under investigation, Allison would be forced to stay put for a while. Jo's plan for her was vague, revenge a concept rather than a predetermined pathway.

Throwing back the bedcovers, she got to her feet and crossed the room to the bathroom door. She didn't bother switching the light on. There were no curtains on the windows of her tiny bedsit. There had been, of course, the place advertised as being *fully furnished*. But the curtains, with their black-out lining, made the tiny space not just smaller but claustrophobic. They were rolled up and shoved to the back of one of the kitchen cupboards.

It meant the bedsit was never dark; light streamed in from neon signs, street lamps, oozed from the other apartments that crowded around hers. With the bathroom door open wide, there was sufficient illumination for Jo to see her reflection in the small, toothpaste-spotted mirror hanging over the wash handbasin. A soft-focus version of her. Perhaps the woman she would have been if it hadn't been for Allison.

Reaching up, Jo pushed her fingers into her hair and pulled gently, the wig sliding over the scarred skin of her scalp with a soft whisper. She dropped the poor creature into the basin and rubbed her hands over her head. Sometimes, especially when the temperature rose into the high twenties and London became hot and sticky, her scalp became unbearably itchy. Sometimes, in desperation, she'd go into toilets of department stores, take the wig off and scratch until her skin was torn. Jagged scratches that would bleed and itch as they healed. A cycle of dismal discomfort.

If she could wear her hair shorter... her fingers went up to trace the scars at the curve of her jaw. They used to be on her cheek. Plastic surgery had successfully moved them to a less prominent position, leaving Jo with what she'd seen described by sneering critics as a wind-tunnel effect. If she wore shorter hair, the scars would be visible. She wasn't ready for that.

Maybe someday. Maybe after she'd exacted her revenge on Allison.

Reaching out, she pulled the cord to switch on the light over the basin. A bright halogen light, it was unforgiving.

Perhaps this would be her revenge.

Perhaps it would be enough to stand in front of Allison. Take off the wig. Show her the consequences of what she'd done all those years before.

41

Allison didn't bother to wait till Jo left the garden before shutting the door with forced restraint. She'd wanted to slam it, to have the aggressive sound chase Jo up the street, to make it absolutely clear Allison didn't want her to return. She wanted to bang her head against the door for being so stupid as to have become embroiled with someone she'd met on Facebook.

How many lies had Jo told her... had anything she'd said been true?

Allison pushed away from the door. It was tempting to have more wine, but she'd hardly eaten, and her thoughts were scrambled enough without adding alcohol to the mix.

She remembered her suspicions about Stuart the previous evening. Perhaps this was something the same. Stress making her suspicious of everyone. Truth was, she'd known from the first meeting that she and Jo weren't going to be friends, that the meeting had been a bad idea. But it seemed as if Jo felt differently. Perhaps that was all it was. Not a scam at all. She wanted a friend and had latched on to Allison because of their similarities.

Maybe. Allison tried to convince herself she was right, but she couldn't shake the feeling there was something suspicious about the relationship with Jo. She sat at the dining room table with her coffee and laptop. It didn't take long; she wasn't in too many Facebook groups. She went into each, used the search option and viewed every post and every comment she'd made since she'd joined. It took a couple of hours, her expression settling into grim lines as she realised how much personal information she'd given out in dribs and drabs over the years. It would have been easy for someone determined to have discovered Allison was originally from Oxford, that she was an accountant and what books she enjoyed.

She went back over the comments Jo posted, the messages she'd sent, from the first *I hope you don't mind me contacting you but...* to the comments where she'd casually dropped a reference to being from Oxford, to her husband being a solicitor... lots of laughing emojis about the number of coincidences. All done over months, carefully, coolly, reeling the usually suspicious Allison in little by little.

Jo had gone to a lot of trouble... and spent a lot of time. It was clear she wanted something, but what?

And why now?

The relaxing evening Allison had planned was spoilt. Restlessly, she rinsed the plates they'd used and slipped them into the dishwasher. Then, because she suddenly felt hungry, she took out the tiramisu, leaned against the counter and used a teaspoon to eat it from the container. The luscious sweetness had a calming effect. When every morsel was scraped out, she tossed container and spoon into the sink.

Determined to keep her hard-earned calmness intact, she decided a glass of wine and a book would be the perfect finish to the evening. A good book... only then did she remember the book Peter had been reading was one she'd been looking forward to reading herself. It was satisfying to be able to blame Jo for her panicked rush to get rid of the bag of rubbish. Allison was almost amused at the effect stress was having on her usual calm approach to life. The life she'd planned for herself.

She switched on the outside lights and went to retrieve the rubbish bag. The bin was almost full; the bag she'd dropped into it a short time before should have been sitting on top. It wasn't.

Panic lashed her and she fumbled with the other bags, opening one after the other, staring at the detritus of their daily life, ignoring the whiff that oozed from a couple, retying them and dropping them to the ground until she was surrounded by a sea of baggy blackness, tilting the wheelie bin in order to reach the last item, knowing as she struggled to untie it, she wasn't going to see what she wanted.

The lid of the bin fell shut with a snap. Loud in the silence of the side passage, it startled her and made her stumble backwards and trip on the discarded rubbish. Her fall was cushioned but as luck would have it that night, the bag she landed on, bursting open under her weight, was the whiffiest. She lay stunned, surrounded by the stink, as realisation hit her with a harder blow. The bag was gone and only one person could have taken it.

Jo.

42

As she got older, the chanting stopped, but the name-calling never did and by the time she left institutional care, it had been beaten so far into her mind that she could never get rid of it. It was what she was.

And if she ever forgot, the chanting came... in the middle of the night... sometimes when she was somewhere pretty and peaceful... it never went away... she could hear the high-pitched sing-song words as clearly as if those delightful children were standing right beside her.

Monster, monster, mon-ster.

Monster, monster, mon-ster.

Monster, monster, mon-ster.

43

Allison lay awake most of the night worrying about the woman she'd stupidly let into her life. Dawn had barely tinted the day when she flung the duvet back and reached for her robe. She hesitated. There was something vulnerable about a naked body dressed in a thin robe and although Jo was hardly going to arrive on her doorstep at cockcrow, Allison wasn't taking any chances.

In black jeans and a long-sleeved maroon T-shirt, she felt suitably clad and ready to face whatever the day threw at her.

She sat with a mug of coffee and went over the items she'd thrown into the rubbish bag Jo had taken. There had been nothing suspicious in it. She might have wondered at Allison's haste in divesting herself of her late husband's personal belongings, but she could easily explain it away if the woman dared to ask. 'Grief affects people in different ways.' No, too impersonal. She tried again. 'My grief' – better, owning it – 'was almost overwhelming. The only way I could cope with such catastrophic loss was to divest myself of the physical trappings of Peter's life.' That sounded deep, profound even. If she could say it with enough pathos, it would fool anyone.

Okay, so Jo could find nothing in what Allison had discarded. Good, but it didn't answer the simple question, why was she looking? And what the fuck was she looking for?

Allison pushed her fingers through her hair. Lifting it from her neck, she held it on top of her head with her clasped hands. At nine, she'd ring the solicitor. She debated whether it would be in her interest to hire someone new. Benjamin Brown had been looking after the Fellowes' legal matters for many years. She'd met him only the once when, on Peter's insistence, she'd drawn up her own will to leave all she owned to her darling husband. It had been easy; she hadn't owned anything, had no savings worth talking about and a pension plan unfit for purpose.

On the dot of nine, she dialled the number she'd saved in her phone. It was answered immediately by a voice that was probably assumed to soothe the more irate and demanding of callers. It immediately got under Allison's skin, making her voice sharper, her tone more insistent.

'It's Allison Fellowes; I'd like to speak to Mr Brown.' She took a breath before forcing a sound she hoped came across as a pathetic sob and not gastric reflux. 'It's urgent. My husband...' A long pause for dramatic effect. 'He was killed on Friday in a tragic accident.'

The indrawn breath down the line sounded suitably shocked, as did the response. 'Oh, oh, goodness, I don't know what to say. I'm so sorry. I've met Mr Fellowes several times over the years. Always such a pleasant man. Goodness, I'm lost for words.'

People who purported to be lost for words and then kept spouting drivel were a pet hate of Allison's. But she stuck to her grieving widow role and swallowed her irritation. 'It's been a horrendous shock and I'm feeling a little lost.' Grieving widow, pathetic weak female. Two lying roles, neither of which reflected the real Allison. She'd struggle to maintain them long term, so the sooner probate was settled, the better. 'I really need to speak to Mr Brown; I know he'll advise me what to do.'

'Gosh, yes, of course. He'll be shocked. Stunned.' Another indrawn breath. 'He knew Mr Fellowes' parents too, of course. This will come as a blow. End of an era, I suppose.'

Allison mouthed, *Get on with it, you silly cow.* 'Yes, indeed it is. Is Mr Brown available?' A heavy hint that fell flat as another sigh shushed down the line.

'No, I'm so sorry, he's out of the office until mid-morning. Meeting a client. He sometimes rings before he heads back so if he does, I'll get him to ring you straight away. Straight away.' She repeated the words as if it was a major consolation.

Allison, who wanted to slam the phone down in annoyance, settled for, 'Fine, thank you. As soon as he can, please.'

She sat, tapping the phone against the palm of her hand, willing the phone to ring. She'd downed yet another coffee before it did, and she tapped to answer without looking at the screen. 'Benjamin, thanks for getting back to me so quickly. I'm so distraught. I—'

'Allison, it's me, Hazel.'

The interruption, coming as it did when Allison had launched her carefully phrased spiel of devastation and sorrow, threw her completely. When she tried to adjust and address the caller, she drew a complete blank. Who the hell was Hazel?

'Hazel Manners.'

As if that made it clearer. Allison's free hand thumped the side of her head as if that would loosen the information she needed. 'I'm sorry...'

'Hazel, from work.' The voice sounded offended. 'I rang to offer my condolences on your loss, see if there was anything I could do for you.'

Her! Bloody marvellous, just what she needed. 'How kind,

sorry, as you can imagine I'm all over the place, and not sleeping either. All I can think about is poor Peter.'

'So awful for you. Such a terrible shock. When I heard the news, I went straight to management and offered to take on your workload until you were feeling up to coming back, so don't worry about here. Take all the time you need.'

'So kind.' The conniving bitch! No doubt she'd move into Allison's office for convenience, making herself completely at home. From having no intention of returning to work, ever, Allison did a complete about-face. 'Work can be a kind of solace, though, can't it? I'm planning on being back next week so, although your offer is extremely kind and considerate, I wouldn't think of putting you out. But thank you, it means so much to know how kind and supportive my colleagues are.'

'Next week!'

Allison smiled to hear part shock, part irritation in those two words. She dropped her voice to a lower, more sorrowful register before speaking. 'It'll be a relief to bury myself in my work, to take my mind off my loss.'

'Yes, yes, I see. Well, I'm here if you need me, and willing to accept any work you're finding too difficult to get through, okay?'

'So kind.' Allison couldn't trust herself to say more. She hadn't wanted to go back to the job, but she was damned if she was letting that bloody woman gain from her loss. Anyway, it would be better to return if probate was going to be delayed for as long as the liaison officer had implied. She'd know better after speaking to the solicitor.

She'd go back to work for a few weeks, maybe even a couple of months. Plenty of time to deal with Hazel, her feigned concern and obvious attempt to leapfrog into Allison's job.

Work might not take her mind off her loss but dealing with that scheming cow would.

44

It was another hour before Allison's mobile rang again. This time, she'd learnt her lesson and checked carefully before answering, relieved to see the solicitor's name flash up on the screen.

'Benjamin, thank you for returning my call.'

'Mrs Fellowes... Allison, I was shocked to hear the dreadful news. My apologies for not being available immediately, I was stuck in a meeting that went on far longer than I'd anticipated. Please accept my profoundest commiserations on your loss. I've known Peter for several years; I considered him as much a friend as a client.'

'I'm struggling to process it all. The suddenness of it. We were celebrating three months together. It's simply not fair to lose him.' A gulp, indrawn breath, obvious attempt to regain control. 'Sorry, it's so hard...'

'Of course, I can't begin to comprehend your loss, Allison, but rest assured, I'll be here for you. Whatever you need.'

It was what she'd expected to hear, what she'd be paying a hefty price to achieve. 'I'd better fill you in on the details. I'm not sure I can do so over the phone; would it be possible for you to call round?'

'Of course. I'll get my secretary to cancel my early-afternoon appointments and call straight around now if that suits you.'

Now? She looked down at her black jeans and maroon T-shirt. 'That's so kind, thank you. How soon will you get here? I'll have coffee waiting.'

'Please, don't go to any trouble. I'll be about twenty minutes.'

Plenty of time to get prepared. 'So kind. Twenty minutes, then.' She hung up, finished her coffee, then dashed upstairs to swap her casual clothes for something more formal. Black wide-legged trousers, a black pussy-bow shirt she'd bought and never worn. With her hair pulled back into a low ponytail and no make-up, she looked suitably funereal.

She shut the curtains on all the windows, covered the mirror in the living room with a dark scarf, and stopped the hall table clock. Over the top, without a doubt, but these were details the rather pedantic, conservative Benjamin would notice, and consider appropriate.

When the doorbell chimed, almost thirty minutes later, Allison took a deep breath and released it slowly. With her shoulders slumped and the corners of her mouth turned down, she fixed her thoughts on the genuinely sad picture of Peter's crushed body rather than the sunny future his death was going to allow her. As ready as she could be, she turned the handle and pulled open the door.

Benjamin Brown – by name and description – was a small, round man with thinning hair, a sallow complexion and bad teeth. His habit of tilting his head to one side at the end of every state-ment or question made him creepily sparrow-like.

'My dear,' he said, stepping into the hall, both hands extended. Taking hers, he held her at arm's length for so long that Allison wondered if she'd failed dismally in her portrayal of a grieving widow. 'My dear, you look wretched.'

Since this was exactly the look she was aiming for, she gave a mental air-punch before making her lower lip quiver like a curious rabbit. 'It's so awfully, awfully hard.' The solicitor, thankfully, wasn't the hugging type; instead, he squeezed the hands with enough vigour to have Allison wince. 'Come into the living room,' she said, indicating the room behind with a jerk of her head. 'I'll make some coffee, or would you prefer tea?'

With a final press of her hands, he released her. 'Tea would be lovely, thank you.'

She saw him glance around the room, the imperceptible nod of satisfaction he gave to see the curtains drawn, the mirror covered.

It was, however, far too gloomy to sit in. 'Rather than switching on the light, I'll open the curtains.' She threw him a sad smile. 'Just while you're here, of course.' She crossed to the window, pulled the heavy drapes and straightened the net curtains. 'Please, have a seat and I'll get that tea.'

A teabag bunged into a mug wasn't going to be sufficient. While the kettle boiled, she rummaged in a cupboard for the rarely used teapot and teacups and set them on a tray. It took longer to find a jug, the Tetra Pak looking completely out of place... with the minutes ticking by, and a sheen of perspiration on her face, she gave up on the search for a sugar bowl.

Carrying the tray in her two hands, she opened the door to the living room with a tap of her hip. 'Sorry for taking so long,' she said, lowering the tray to the coffee table. 'I hope you don't take sugar; we're completely out.' She threw the solicitor a smile, allowing it to waver and die as she sank onto the sofa.

'You're being so brave.'

He didn't know the half of it, she thought, busying herself with the palaver of pouring tea, adding milk when he nodded. It had been brave to make the decision she'd made, to do what she'd done. Some may have a different word, probably several of them: manipulative, self-obsessed, monstrous. That last was most appropriate.

The clink of china on china as she and the solicitor drank their tea was a hypnotic, relaxing sound. Everything was going to be okay. She almost smiled, hiding it quickly as the solicitor looked up from his cup. She reached for the pot and lifted it. 'Another cup?'

'No, thank you, that was an elegant sufficiency.'

She topped her own, barely touched cup with a dribble.

Brown put his cup and saucer down. He sat back, crossed one knee over the other and rested his clasped hands on the prominent curve of his belly. 'To spare you the distress of having to give me the details of this appalling tragedy, I took the liberty of contacting the police and am fully conversant with the specifics of the matter.'

Allison was a little annoyed – she'd been looking forward to reciting her monologue of woe, but she was also relieved. Benjamin may look sparrow-like and speak like an escapee from a Victorian melodrama, but she wasn't stupid enough to be fooled. By reputation, he was all hawk, little sparrow.

'That's such a relief, thank you. It's hard to talk about it although it's never out of my head. Those last few minutes. Wondering if he knew what was happening, if it was quick, if there was pain.' She shut her eyes for a second. When she opened them, she found Benjamin's eyes fixed on her and forced herself not to react, to meet his gaze without flinching and allow her lower lip to tremble... just a little; she didn't want to drift into a pantomime caricature.

She reached for her tea and took a sip. It was cold and strong. When the solicitor went, she was going to reward herself with a drink. 'The police have said it might take months before their investigation is complete,' she said, replacing the cup and saucer on the table. 'The funeral is such a milestone in the grieving process, and to have that delayed is going to be so difficult.'

She held her breath, waiting for him to grab hold of the wriggling worm she'd dangled right in front of his sparrow face, reluctant to come straight out with: *Is there anything you can do to speed up the process?*

Brown tapped stubby thumbs together, each movement measured and slow. Allison felt irritation begin to bubble and dropped her eyes to her hands.

'The police, understandably, will have to investigate this terrible tragedy,' the solicitor said, 'but I'm sure I can speak to the coroner and have a death certificate expedited to allow you to proceed with the funeral.'

Exactly what she'd hoped he'd say. 'That would be so terribly kind of you.' Bloody hell, he had her speaking like him now. 'It'll be good to get that first step done. Luckily, my finances are good, so I'm not rushing to have Peter's estate settled. Although it will be nice to have that done too.' Take the hint, Benjamin.

'Will you stay in this area? Or perhaps you'll want to make a clean break and decide to move out of London.'

Allison frowned. It felt like she'd skipped a page in a book. Suddenly she didn't know where she was in the story. 'I don't understand. Of course I'm going to stay here.' She dragged a smile into place. 'Peter loved this house; I owe it to him to stay.'

It was the solicitor's turn to frown. 'Stay? Oh, I'm sorry, but that's impossible!'

45

Allison cast her widow's weeds aside, her expression hardening, her voice sharp when she spoke. 'What do you mean, *impossible*?' She saw confusion flit across the solicitor's face before it was set into rigid, professional lines.

'I assumed you were aware, that Peter had told you.' He looked disappointed, as if he'd been let down. 'I'm surprised he didn't. He should have done.'

Allison felt as if her world had suddenly tilted, throwing her off balance. She barely recognised her voice when she finally managed to speak. 'What should he have told me?'

Perhaps it was easier for the solicitor to adopt a formal manner when delivering bad news. He straightened in the seat, clasped his hands together again and spoke slowly, as if aware of the repercussions of what he was about to say. 'You can't stay here, my dear, because this house was left to Peter for his lifetime only. Now, I'm afraid, it will need to be sold and the proceeds given to charity. The RSPCA to be exact.'

It was a joke. It had to be. Perhaps this odd, bird-like man was trying to lighten the mood by making a joke in very poor taste. She waited for the punchline... and waited... watching the solicitor's expression soften in sympathy. *In pity.*

'I think you'd better explain.'

Brown tilted his head and nodded. 'You know Peter had issues with substance abuse when he was younger—'

Allison's gasp of disbelief must have been louder than she'd thought, stopping the solicitor's flow.

He took a handkerchief from his jacket pocket and dabbed his upper lip in evident discomfiture. 'You didn't know?'

'It seems I know very little about anything.'

'You did marry very soon after meeting, of course.' He folded the handkerchief and replaced it in his pocket. 'It was while he was in university. His parents maintained he'd fallen in with the wrong crowd.' He shrugged, the movement sending a ripple over his ill-fitting suit. 'I'd met him a couple of times by then; it struck me he wasn't the strongest of characters. Easily led, you know. When he dropped out—'

'Dropped out?' Allison held a hand up. 'He never qualified?'

'No, I'm afraid not. His parents did help, though; they paid for him to go to a private clinic to get clean and it seemed to work. As far as I'm aware he hasn't indulged in anything more dangerous than tobacco since.'

Allison tried to get her feet back on solid ground. 'Did he go back to college, then? And qualify?'

The solicitor looked puzzled. 'No, he didn't. I'm sorry, you seem to be under some misapprehension. Peter refused to return to college. I think his parents were quite relieved, actually, preferring to lay the blame for his addiction at the feet of an institute of learning rather than holding their over-indulged son to account. As a result, Peter never qualified as anything.'

'He's not a solicitor.' A statement, not a question. Of course he wasn't. She remembered the business card he'd handed her, how she'd been foolishly impressed. Or had she seen what she'd wanted to see? A handsome, successful man, obviously interested in her, ripe for the plucking. Except she'd been the one plucked.

Brown raised an eyebrow. 'A solicitor? Is that what he told you?'

Her silence told him enough.

'I'm sorry. No, he's not a solicitor. He did work in a law office, though.'

As if that should be a solace for her. As if Peter's lie could simply be seen as a different shade of truth.

'Some kind of administrative position, I believe,' Brown added.

'Right.' It was all she could manage as she tried to make sense of this unbelievable truth.

He looked as if he was uncertain whether to continue or not. 'Perhaps we should leave it at that.'

'No. I need to hear it all.' Just how bad was it going to be?

'Okay.' He drew out the word, then stopped as if searching for the easiest way to continue. 'Peter's parents wanted to protect him. When they drew up their will, they wanted to provide stability for him but also wanted to ensure he couldn't access large amounts of money and slide back into bad habits. That's why they wrote their will as they did. Peter was able to live here for the remainder of his life, but he couldn't sell the house nor, of course, was he able to leave it to you.'

No house. Her future plans shot to hell. 'He told me he'd rewritten his will when we married.'

Brown nodded. 'Yes, he did, but I'm afraid his estate amounts to little. A savings account with some several hundred pounds and a current account that I'm afraid is likely to be in debit. When he came in about the new will, I encouraged him to think about life insurance, but I doubt if he took out a policy.'

Several hundred pounds. Allison heard the creaks as the life she'd planned, the future she'd imagined, shifted on the unexpectedly unstable foundation... shifted, cracked and fell in shards, slicing into her, leaving gaping bleeding wounds before landing with an ear-splitting crash around her feet.

Brown took out his handkerchief again and blotted his top lip and forehead as if the stress of his disclosures were causing him to melt. 'Perhaps, under the circumstances, it would be best not to expedite the death certificate. Until it's released, I'm not obliged to settle his estate. It would give you a few months to make decisions about your future.'

She'd have to rent an apartment. Smaller than her last one. In a cheaper area. Her future had been so determined, she'd allowed herself to indulge in expensive clothes, bags, shoes. Using her savings. She still had some – not enough, though. She was back to where she'd started... further back.

Peter had fooled her completely.

Silence weighed heavily in the room. The solicitor had obviously said all he needed to say and Allison, unable to think of one word that wasn't scatological or blasphemous, sat silently even when the solicitor got to his feet.

'I'll be in touch as soon as I've heard anything from the police.' He shuffled uncertainly as she continued to sit, staring blankly into space. 'Don't get up. I'll show myself out.'

She didn't move for a long time after she heard the quiet clunk of the front door shutting behind him and then only to smooth a trembling hand over her forehead as if to soothe the thoughts that were hammering against her skull.

What a mess.

All her brilliant plans reduced to rubble.

She thought she'd been so clever. Seeing what she wanted to see, she'd never realised it was all smoke and shadows. *Peter.* She almost admired him. Sadly, if she'd known the truth, she'd never have married him... if she hadn't, he wouldn't have been on the platform at that time... wouldn't have died.

She thought his death had finally given her the life she'd craved... how ironic that it had, in fact, pushed it further out of reach.

She'd thought she'd covered every eventuality, and she had, apart from one. That Peter was a bigger liar than she was.

46

Luckily, Jo wasn't easily bored, because little happened on the street where Allison lived. Neighbours slid into cars and drove away, giving her only a glimpse of designer jeans, large leather bags, expensively highlighted hair. All the trappings of middle-class England. Jo didn't envy what they had, but she did their casual belief it was all theirs by right. Only a childhood steeped in love could imbue such self-belief. It wasn't something you could buy, and this was the hardest to accept.

The weather was warm, sunny, not a cloud in the sky. It was a good day for stalking. Union Square park, she was delighted to discover, wasn't locked and kept solely for the pleasure of the residents of the surrounding streets. She was in luck, too; one side of the small park was heavily planted with view-obscuring shrubs but not the side facing Allison's house. The densely planted shrubs were a backdrop for a line of benches. Original Victorian, she guessed, eyeing the cast-iron arms and legs. Overhanging branches provided shade from the sun, the downside of their protection being the green algae that covered most of the wood. Jo wasn't precious and sat on the end of the bench, the seat with the clearest view of Allison's front door. Taking a pair of powerful binoculars from her pocket, she settled for a long wait.

The arrival of a man on Allison's doorstep had Jo straighten and press the binoculars tighter to her eyes. A veritable Tweedledum... or perhaps Tweedledee. She watched as he straightened his jacket, fixed his tie and ran a hand over the sparse hair that barely covered his head. Only then did he reach for the bell. Seconds later, the door was opened. Jo zoomed in as much as she could on the figure appearing in the gap.

Allison's black garb emphasised her pallor. No make-up, her hair scraped back from her face, a severe style that highlighted her high cheekbones. And her perfect, unblemished skin. In that moment, Jo hated her more than she'd ever done before.

Tweedledum was admitted, the door was shut, and Jo was where she aways was... on the outside. The weight of sorrow was an old friend; it settled in her chest, as it always did. Only anger rid her of it, and that came surging in now, bringing her to her feet in an abrupt, jerky motion. Had there been anyone nearby, they'd have given the wide-eyed, panting woman a wide berth, might even have seen the manic expression on her face and rung the authorities. But apart from a stooped, elderly woman walking an equally old dog, the park was empty.

The burst of anger never lasted. Time had taught Jo it was a wasted emotion and a minute later it had faded.

The binoculars were useless, and she hadn't developed superpowers to allow her to see through walls. Leaving the park, she crossed the street and walked slowly past the house. There was movement in the front room. Allison had taken the man, whoever he was, into the living room, not the dreary dining room. Perhaps Tweedledum was an undertaker, and she was acting in anticipation of the death certificate to organise a funeral for her late departed. If so, she was being very optimistic. Jo had done an internet search and knew the police could take months to complete the investigation.

She walked on, turned around and retraced her steps. Curiosity, always her biggest fault, drove her to open the garden gate and, with a glance around to make sure the coast was clear, she sidled up to the edge of the living-room window. The net curtains, a relic she assumed of the same parents who'd left their mark on the dining room, blurred her view, but the heavy drapes to either side provided her with a shield to peer around.

Through the glass, she could hear the faint to and fro of conversation. When it stopped, she risked a glance around the edge of her shield. Of the two sofas in the room, only one was occupied. Pressing her nose to the glass, she was close enough to see Tweedledum's bad comb-over. Peering past him, she could see the coffee table was empty. It made her reconsider the man's occupation. An undertaker would have brought brochures, wouldn't he? Photographs of coffins for Allison's delectation.

The small, round man was unlikely to be a lover. Too short to be a police officer. Just then, Tweedle lifted his wrist, shucking the sleeve back to expose his watch. And cufflinks. A solicitor, perhaps. Yes, that made sense. Allison would want to know exactly where she stood.

Jo took a step backward and looked up at the house. This part of London. Two million, easily. Probably more despite the ghastly kitchen and dining room. Not bad for a few months of marriage.

With no sign of Allison returning, Jo slipped across to the other side of the window, which allowed her to see the living-room doorway. Allison wouldn't be expecting anyone to be peering in; Jo could safely watch, maybe get a clue to what was being said.

She was mildly irritated, and a little amused, to see Allison was out to impress the man with a fancy teapot and cups and saucers. Different to the mugs she'd offered Jo. Something else she'd make her pay for.

A few minutes later, she saw Allison's expression change. Even through the soft-focus layer of netting, it was obvious she'd heard something shocking. Jo risked pressing closer. Whatever Tweedledum was saying had been unexpected, and it wasn't good news.

It was frustrating to be standing there out of the loop. Jo pulled back when Allison put down her cup and saucer and stared straight ahead. Oddly, it looked as if she was in shock. Jo sneered. Perhaps she'd just learnt the extent of her wealth. Maybe the house was worth much more than she'd expected. Three million, perhaps. And perhaps millions more in the bank and yet more in insurance policies. Gazillions of pounds. It would be enough to shock Jo.

She ducked down, crossed to the other side of the window and made her escape. Retaking her seat in the park, she kept her binoculars fixed in place to watch for Tweedledum's exit. It came only minutes later, the man striding down the street in short, jerky steps.

Dropping the binoculars into her pocket, Jo sat staring at the house, considering her next step. Her plan had been to find the Portia woman and get rid of her but perhaps that was an unnecessary step.

Much better to keep it simple. Better, too, to proceed with speed. If she was right, if Allison had come into such colossal wealth, perhaps she wouldn't have to linger in London until the investigation was over. She'd leave London, might even vanish from sight and Jo would have to start all over again.

She was weary from her search, from the years of planning for revenge, from everything she'd been through. Now that Allison had succeeded beyond her dreams, it was time for Jo to finally make her move.

Slowly, though. Too many years of pain had built up. She wasn't planning to let Allison off lightly.

47

Allison hadn't moved following Benjamin Brown's earth-shattering visit. Everything, even the simple act of getting to her feet, seemed a waste of time. She was floundering in a deep pool of despondency when the doorbell rang, making her surface with a gasp and gulp. Was it the solicitor, back to tell her he'd made a mistake? That what he'd said had all been one big fucking joke?

She remembered the pity in the funny little man's face. *Pity.* For her. No, it wouldn't be him.

When the doorbell rang again, more insistently, as if the caller was putting their whole weight behind their finger, she knew who it was. That bloody woman, Jo. No way was Allison going to answer the door. And she would have remained steadfast if Jo had possessed any sense of decorum. But she didn't, and seconds later Allison looked up, startled, when something banged the window. Jo. Nose pressed against the glass, knuckles poised to strike again. There was no bloody getting away from her.

Allison raised a hand in greeting to prevent another clatter against the window and shuffled to the edge of her seat. Despair sat heavily on her shoulders, pushing her down as she tried to stand. She groaned at the effort, conscious of the woman staring through the net curtains. Sweat gathered in her armpits, at her hairline. She wished for Brown's pristine handkerchief, settling for the sleeve of her blouse, wiping it across her forehead, sweat leaving unsightly darker streaks on the black fabric.

By the time she reached the front door, she could smell the acrid stink of body odour. It smelt of fear. She stopped with a hand on the doorknob, suddenly afraid to open the door. *Maybe she's an axe murderer.* Peter's voice was so clear in her head, she jerked around, searching for him. She remembered she'd laughed, had insisted Jo was no danger to her. But now... well, it appeared Peter knew more about dodgy types than she'd given him credit for. Jo possibly – probably – wasn't an axe murderer, but she was certainly a dubious character.

The doorbell sounded again. A short burst this time. A little reminder from the woman standing expectantly on her doorstep. It seemed Allison was left with little choice. She'd open the door, tell Jo she wasn't up to visitors and send her on her way.

A good plan. She hoped it worked out better than her plan for her wealthy, comfortable future.

As it happened, the only part that worked out was opening the door.

'I thought you weren't going to let me in!'

'I'm sorry. It's been a tiring morning and I'm really not up to visitors. You'll understand, I'm sure.' That should have been it. Jo should have agreed her understanding of Allison's position and fucked off. Instead, she found herself being grabbed in a hug and propelled backwards into the house. Before she could regain control, the front door was shut and she was sitting on the sofa in the living room, Jo standing over her like some bloody avenging angel.

'You need someone to take care of you.' Jo nodded to the tray. 'Looks like you've had a visitor already this morning.'

'My solicitor visited to see if I was okay.' Allison had been, before his arrival, before he'd turned her expectations into a mirage. 'It was more tiring than I'd expected so I'm sorry, I think I'd better head back to bed.'

'I bet you've had nothing to eat.' Jo bent to pick up the tray. 'You sit there, rest; I'll make us fresh tea and find something for us to eat.'

Allison, still stunned from the earlier revelation, tried to stand firm. 'I'd prefer—' But it was too late; with a smile that was possibly supposed to convey understanding and sympathy but merely looked creepy, Jo was gone.

Maybe she was right. Perhaps after something to eat, Allison would feel... something, anything... because she felt numb and unable to process the reality of her situation. The stark, unbearable reality that all her carefully made plans had come to nothing.

'Here we go!' Jo bustled through the door several minutes later, carrying a laden tray. She placed it gently on the coffee table. 'I raided your cupboards so there's tinned salmon sandwiches, and chocolate biscuits. Enough to keep us going till we can think about something more substantial for dinner.'

Dinner? Allison gave a half-hearted laugh. 'If I can manage a sandwich, I'll be doing well. Dinner is out of the question.'

Instead of answering, Jo handed her a side plate and held out the sandwiches.

They were, Allison was amazed to see, cut into triangles, the crusts removed. She took one, then another when she was urged, the voice refusing to accept no for an answer.

'You need someone to bully you for a while,' Jo said in justification, sitting back with a smile of satisfaction. 'Eat those, drink some tea, then maybe have a couple more – they're only small.'

Only small, but Allison nearly choked trying to swallow the first. She felt like she'd fallen down a well. There was light at a distance, but a rigid circle restrained her, making it difficult to breathe. Panic shot through her. She gagged on the bolus of chewed bread and tinned fish and, with a hand over her mouth, rushed from the room.

Desperate, she made it as far as the kitchen sink before retching, sending the chewed food and tea gushing into the sink. She reached out for the roll of kitchen towel and tore a few sheets from it, dampening them and wiping her face. A few deep breaths and she felt calmer.

A voice drifted from the living room. 'Are you okay?'

'Yes, I'll be there in a sec.' Allison grabbed a glass and filled it with cold water, leaning against the sink and sipping it slowly. She needed to get rid of Jo. After a final wipe of her face, she pressed her foot to the pedal of the bin to dispose of the damp tissue and gasped. Inside, in pieces, were her beautiful teacups and the lovely teapot.

'Oh, sorry, I was going to tell you.'

The voice, coming from immediately behind Allison, startled her; she stepped backwards, the lid of the bin dropping with a bang. 'You shouldn't creep up on people!'

'Sorry.' Jo shrugged apologetically. 'I came to check if you were okay.'

Allison jabbed a finger at the bin. 'What happened?' She'd priced that teapot on eBay, had seen similar selling for upward of eight hundred pounds. What had seemed a drop in the ocean at the time now looked completely different. 'It's a Sadler teapot.'

'I've no idea if that means it's good or it's tat,' Jo said. 'I'm afraid I was a little clumsy and they slipped from the tray.'

Slipped? Two cups, two saucers and a teapot all went crashing to the ground without making a sound? 'I didn't hear anything.'

'No?' Jo reached out and put a hand on Allison's arm. 'You look so pale; come and sit down.'

She shook the hand off, swayed with the effort and, with one hand sliding along the wall, went back to the living room. The plate of sandwiches was empty. In the few minutes she'd been retching into the sink, Jo had devoured them. Not the biscuits. Not yet. She watched, frustrated, as Jo sat, picked up her mug of tea and ate them, dunking each into the tea before popping it whole into her mouth and munching.

'I want you to leave.' How many ways did Allison need to say it? 'Now, please. I'm tired, I can't have this.' Whatever *this* was... it felt like an invasion, a takeover, as if Jo was in control of her strings, making her dance to a tune Allison had never heard before. 'Please, just go.' She resented the need to beseech, and the first twinge of anger made its way to the surface. 'Get out, Jo. I don't want you here.' There, she couldn't make herself any clearer than that. She moved to the doorway and stood waiting for Jo to get to her feet and leave. She would, wouldn't she?

Jo picked up the last biscuit and waved it towards the other sofa. 'You may as well sit down, Allison; I'm not going anywhere.' She smiled as she continued her dunk and munch, finally slurping the end of the tea and putting the mug back on the tray. 'Seriously, sit before you fall down. We have a lot to talk about.'

Allison didn't move, seething at Jo's obstinacy. They had nothing to talk about, she and this increasingly strange woman. 'Another day. Now, I'm tired. You seem to forget I'm recently bereaved.'

Jo lounged back, folding her arms across her chest. 'Recently bereaved. The devastated, grieving widow, eh?' Her laugh was cruel, her eyes sharp as they swept Allison from head to toe. 'Sit down. You don't look too hot; you're going to look a lot worse when I tell you what I know.'

48

Allison, unwilling to give in, stood a moment longer, holding Jo's gaze. Her amused gaze. It was this that made Allison growl in frustrated annoyance, take two strides across the room and flop heavily onto the sofa to face her tormentor. 'Right, listen up, say whatever it is you want to say and get out of my face. I've had a pretty shit morning and you're making it a million times worse.' Her voice was rising with each word, screechy at the end, like fingernails dragged down a blackboard.

Jo crossed one leg over the other. It wasn't a good move. Some women managed the action with elegance, but it was a hard manoeuvre when your thighs are squeezed into non-stretch denim possibly a size too small. As a result, one leg was balanced precariously on the other knee. It was obviously uncomfortable as, rather than holding the pose, Jo dropped her foot to the floor.

Watching her, Allison relaxed. There was no reason to be so wary of this silly woman. It was everything else that had been thrown at her. Jo was being dramatic for effect. Allison would listen to her, send her on her way.

'I enjoyed meeting you for lunch on Friday. And it was kind of you to walk me to the Underground afterward, but you didn't really need to; I know London fairly well.'

'Right.' Allison frowned. She'd a vague memory of Jo saying she wasn't sure of the way. Wasn't that why she'd gone with her? It certainly wasn't to prolong their time together; by then she'd already had enough. 'I'm sorry, could you get to the point?'

'The point... always in such a rush, Al. You don't mind me calling you Al, do you? Allison is such a mouthful. And if you don't mind me saying, you look more like an *Al* kind of woman.'

Allison wondered what an *Al* kind of woman looked like, what made her different to an *Allison* kind of woman. She had no intention of asking; Jo could call her whatever she liked if it made her leave sooner. 'I'll answer to whatever makes life easier.'

Jo smiled. 'So reasonable.'

'I try to be.'

'I suppose it'll be a while before your late husband's estate will be settled. There's bound to be a police investigation, isn't there?'

None of your damn business. 'My solicitor is dealing with all that for me.' Allison hoped her tone was sufficiently curt to make Jo drop this line of questioning. What an impossible, ignorant woman.

And persistent. 'You're going to be a wealthy lady, aren't you?'

Allison would have liked to have told her the truth. To tell this objectionable woman that she was worse off than she had been before she'd met Peter. That she could have done with selling the teapot that had, for some reason, been trashed. The few hundred quid she'd have got for it would have helped with a deposit for an apartment. She'd have liked to have been honest, but she wasn't. 'Peter has left me more than comfortable, thank you. It isn't the kind of thing I feel easy talking about, however.'

If she hoped that would bring the conversation to a halt, she knew by the smile on Jo's face that she'd failed, that it would take more than polite words to get through her cast-iron hide.

'And you get to keep this lovely house.' Jo looked slowly around the living room and nodded. 'Despite the hideous décor in the dining room, and the too-small-for-purpose kitchen, it must be worth what...' She sat forward expectantly.

Did she really expect Allison to discuss the value of the house? She knew it, of course, she'd spent enough time poring over estate agents' sites to have a fair idea it was worth between two point five and three million. And that was in its current condition. All that money going to the RSPCA. It curdled her gut to think about it.

'I'd say it's worth about three mil,' Jo said, oblivious to the tension that tightened Allison's expression. 'That's a hefty reward for three months' marriage.'

'I would, of course, prefer to have my husband.'

Jo laughed. A forced, too-loud noise, lacking any humour. 'Really? It's a shame he fell under that train, then, isn't it?'

49

Jo laughed aloud to see Allison's jaw drop and her eyes widen so much she thought they might pop out of her head. It made Jo laugh louder, tears of merriment running down her cheek. 'Your face, oh my goodness, that's the best laugh I've had in a while.'

'What a wicked, insensitive thing to say!'

'You were in such a hurry to leave me that day, you never bothered to look back to see if I went into the station. I didn't, of course; I followed you.'

Jo saw the fear in her eyes, the doubt. 'That's a very neat raincoat you keep folded in your handbag, isn't it? I was surprised to see you take it out and slip it on as you walked, more so to see you pull the hood up as you entered the station. Nobody paid any attention, of course; this is London – laissez-faire rules the day. You were walking fast, but not too fast, nothing to draw attention to yourself. I'd no idea what you were planning till we reached the platform, then I remembered you saying you'd made your poor husband promise to leave his office at a certain time. It wasn't rocket science to realise you'd planned to arrive at the same time.

'I'm guessing you knew he liked to stand in a certain place on the platform. Frequent travellers often do, I notice. The platform was unusually crowded. You must have been delighted. It made your job ever so much easier.'

It was interesting to watch the play of emotions on Allison's face, a determination to deny morphing into acceptance before changing again, this time settling on an acknowledgement she'd been outmanoeuvred.

'You were good, honestly, I was impressed. If I hadn't been watching you so carefully, I'd never have noticed you pushing through the crowd to get to his side.' She shook her head. 'I'm guessing the police don't know you were there that day, do they?'

Allison got to her feet. 'If that's what you came to tell me, you've done it, now fuck off. I don't want to see you ever again. If I do, I'll tell the police you've been harassing me.'

She was good; Jo could almost believe she had it all wrong. Except she had proof. She reached into her jacket pocket for her mobile. 'I knew you were up to something, Al, so I was ready with my phone, prepared to snap whatever I saw.' She tapped her screen and peered at it before turning it to face Allison. 'I'm guessing the police would be interested in seeing this. Proof you were in the same station where your husband' – she crooked an index finger in the air – '*accidentally* fell in front of a train.'

When Allison stayed silent, Jo used two fingers to enlarge the image on the screen and held it out to her again. 'I was quite pleased with the clarity of my picture. Even with your hood up, it's quite obviously you.' This time, she was pleased to see fear shimmy across Allison's face. 'Absolutely no doubt at all, is there?' She put her mobile on the seat beside her, folded her arms and watched as the other woman sank back onto the sofa as if all the fight had melted away.

'Since you haven't, I assume, brought this to the police's attention, I take it that you want something.'

'I knew we'd get on.' Jo smirked. 'It seems to me your freedom is worth a considerable amount. After all, what good would the millions do you if you were locked away for the foreseeable.'

'How much?'

A woman for whom the material things counted for so much, of course Allison would assume it was all about money. It wasn't. Jo had no interest in what her money could buy... although a lighter wig would be nice. Nice but not essential. There was a time when she'd wished for money to pay for more and more plastic surgery. Only the passage of time had taught her that the pain wasn't worth it, that no matter how good the surgeon, the scars went too deep. No, she'd little interest in the money, but she knew Allison did.

'Two million.'

Allison stared, then laughed in disbelief. 'Dream on!'

Jo waved a hand around the room. 'You'll get three million for this, no problem. I'm not greedy; I'll leave you with a million and whatever else your dearly departed has left you and my word to destroy the evidence.'

'Your word! How on earth could I ever trust you? Are you even who you say you are? Peter told me I should be careful, that you could be an axe murderer...'

Jo laughed. Really, this was proving to be more fun than she'd expected. 'Peter – the man you murdered for his money – that Peter?' She was glad Allison had the sense to say nothing. 'I tell you what's going to happen now,' Jo said. 'I'm going to move in until the estate is settled, and the house is sold. Then, I'll take my share and leave you in peace. You'll never see me again.'

50

Allison could have told her tormentor the truth, that the house was never going to be hers, there was never going to be a million, never mind three. She could have told her all this, but she needed time to process everything. The video footage Jo had was clear, placing Allison somewhere she shouldn't have been. She couldn't take the risk; prison wasn't where she'd planned to spend her future.

'It could take months before Peter's estate is settled and I'm able to sell.'

'That's okay.' Jo snuggled down on the cushion behind her. 'I think I'll be quite comfortable living here.'

'What about what's-his-name... your husband? Your job?'

'Lie and lie.'

Allison struggled to keep a reign on her temper. She needed to keep calm, find a crack in this woman's carapace. She'd already lost so much this morning... all her dreams of a glorious future... but she was free to try again; this woman was trying to take that freedom away. She wasn't sure what she could do but she had to do something. Jo was sitting back, looking perfectly at home. Allison was missing something. If it had all been a scam from the beginning, if Jo had lured her into this relationship, to what end?

She'd gained her knowledge of Allison from reading her Facebook posts, trawling her Instagram. All the recent shots of designer bags, expensive meals, weekend spa breaks. Had she given the impression she'd come into money? Had she made herself vulnerable to be scammed?

Feeling foolish, she pressed her lips together, gathering what strength she could muster. 'Why have you done this?' When Jo's eyebrow rose, she shook her head angrily. 'I don't mean this...' She indicated the mobile phone with a jerk of her head. 'I mean contacting me, trying to be friends.' She yelped in shock when Jo grabbed her mobile and jumped to her feet.

'That's a story for another day. I need a house key. I'll go and pick up my stuff. No point in wasting money renting an apartment at London's crazy prices when you have all this space wasting.'

An apartment in London. Not a house in Swindon. More lies – Allison shouldn't be surprised. It was unlikely anything she'd been told was true. She wasn't sure why she bothered to ask, 'Is your name really Jo?'

Jo looked at her as if she was going to say something profound and Allison held her breath.

But the moment passed, and Jo grinned down at her. 'It is now.' She juggled the mobile. 'A key, please. I won't be long, it's not far.'

Until Allison could get her thoughts together, she seemed to be out of options. 'Right,' she said, getting to her feet. Jo didn't step back, and they ended up almost nose to nose. This close, Allison could see the unnatural stretch of skin across Jo's cheeks. This close, she could see that the upward tilt at the corner of her mouth wasn't down to an inherent cheerfulness but merely a side-effect of the facelift. Only then did Allison understand why she felt so unsettled by her... it was the conflicting contrast between the almost-smile and the hard, derisive, condemning eyes. She shivered under their gaze. 'A key, right, I'll go and get one.'

She brushed by, taking a deep breath in the hallway. Maybe she should cut her losses. Pack her bags and disappear before Jo got back. Disappear. It was a tempting thought. If she had more money, she might have done but what she had wouldn't get her far. She hadn't checked her credit card recently, not since her last spending spree.

No, she needed to stay where she was. Find a solution to all her problems. Financial... and Jo. She'd think of something. She always did.

'Here you go.' She handed Jo the key. It was attached to a totally inappropriate fuzzy pink ball. 'It was to make it easy to find.'

'Good idea.' Jo took the ball off and threw it onto the sofa. 'I'll just check it's the right key, if you don't mind. I wouldn't want to get locked out and have to ring the doorbell again.'

Allison stood by as the key was tried. It had crossed her mind to give the wrong key, one of the many unknown ones that lay in the back of the kitchen drawer. She was glad she'd resisted. She needed to get this bloody woman to trust her... even a little.

Jo slipped the key into the pocket of her jeans. 'And the alarm code? I wouldn't want to be disturbing the neighbours by accidentally setting it off, would I?'

'Of course.' Allison reeled off the code.

'1990?' Jo stared at her, a strange expression on her face. 'Nineteen ninety. Right. Okay, I'll be back in a couple of hours. You should get some rest. You look like shit, if you don't mind me saying.'

'I suppose if we're going to be housemates, I'll need to get used to your rather blunt way of speaking.' Blunt, aka bloody ignorant and rude. Allison could have replied that she'd look better after a good night's sleep, whereas Jo was always going to look as she did… scary. One day, she'd tell the woman exactly what she thought of her. For now, she'd play the game her way.

51

Hog-tied. Wasn't that the expression that suited? It was several minutes after the door shut behind Jo before Allison felt able to return to the living room and collapse onto the sofa.

She needed a break; she deserved one. Not one catastrophe after the other. She was still trying to take in Peter's colossal deception. Had he thought she'd never find out? There had been no indication he wasn't what he'd purported to be. How could she have guessed he was as devious as she?

She remembered all those phone calls from important clients... how considerate she'd thought him switching his phone to vibrate rather than ring... how easy it was for him to fool her. And all those late-night meetings. Once or twice, she'd caught the whiff of alcohol on his breath, accepting without any hesitation his explanation he'd gone for a drink with a client to clinch a deal.

How gullible he must have thought her. She had no suspicions of him; he had none of her. What a pair they were. It would have been nice to think that, as the survivor, she was the winner, but it looked like Peter would get that honour posthumously.

She didn't know how long she sat there, trying not to think, to give her head a rest from the painfully bouncing ideas. Too long. The doorbell chimed noisily, jerking her head around to stare at the open doorway, expecting Jo to be framed in it any moment. Surprisingly polite but unnecessary of her to ring the doorbell. Or was it done with the intention of waking a sleeping housemate up?

Allison sneered. Looked like it was going to be fun and games.

When the doorbell sounded again, she jumped to her feet, irritation driving her in jerky movements to the door. Wrenching it open, angry words balancing on her tongue ready to jump and slice, she had to swallow quickly when she saw not Jo, but her friend Portia. 'Hi.' It was all she could manage.

'Darling, you look wretched.' Portia stepped inside. She was wearing an oversized fine jersey jacket over a dress of the same fabric. Both black, the overall effect was bat-like. She draped an arm around Allison's shoulder. Smaller than Allison by a few inches, Portia had to stretch upward on her narrow, pointed-toed stiletto shoes. 'Poor, poor dear. I'm here now.'

After two traumatic visits, it was good to know she was in safe hands. Allison relaxed for the first time that day. 'It's been a tiring morning.' She almost laughed at the understatement.

Portia drew back. 'Come inside, I'll make us a cuppa and you can tell me all about it. Then I'm taking you out for lunch. No argument,' she added, stopping Allison's objection with a finger placed lightly across her lips. 'Now you sit there, and I'll put the kettle on.'

Tea was the last thing Allison wanted but it gave her time to get back into her role as grieving widow.

'Here you go, darling.' Portia put the tray down. 'I was throwing the teabag into the bin, couldn't miss the smashed crockery.' She sat opposite and picked up one of the mugs of tea. 'Shame about the teapot.'

'It fell.' Allison brought the mug up, sipped, holding it in front of her face.

'Shame – worth a lot, that particular style. Possibly nearly two grand.'

Two grand! She could kill Jo. In fact, she might have to. 'It belonged to Peter's mother. I wouldn't have put you down as a fan of Victorian china.' What a mundane conversation. It would have made her smile on any other day.

'Oh, I have eclectic taste. Anything pretty appeals.'

Portia tilted her head, the movement reminding Allison of the sparrow-like solicitor who'd stuck a pin in her dreams only a few hours before. Her expression must have told a tale because she saw tears appear in Portia's eyes. Any moment they'd fall. Allison envied her the ability.

'I wish I could take your pain away,' Portia said.

'Thank you. I'll be fine. It's just been a difficult morning.' Perhaps she was looking for sympathy, and for once she thought, *Why not?* She deserved it. As she had that wonderful future she'd planned.

'Do you want to talk about it?'

'Our...' She smiled sadly. 'I'll have to get used to saying "my", won't I?' She lied; she'd never bothered adapting to saying *our*. 'My solicitor called around first thing. It was kind of him, but I thought it was way too soon to be thinking of Peter's estate, you know, it makes it all so final.'

'Of course, I can understand completely.' A tear trickled down Portia's heavily made-up face. 'So distressing for you.'

Even someone as hard-hearted as Allison couldn't fail to be affected by the sympathy in Portia's voice. It was a relief after Jo. 'Yes, and then a friend called around. Well, I say friend, but she isn't really, just a woman I've met a few times. She meant well but I found her visit intrusive. Some people feed off others' grief and, unfortunately, she is one of those. When she finally left, I felt as if every positive thought had been sucked out of me.' It wasn't even close to the truth, but it felt good to be dismissing Jo in this fashion.

'Sounds like someone you could do without in your life. I hope you won't be seeing her again.'

Seeing her, living with her, until she could figure out a way to get rid of her. 'No, I won't.' She hadn't mentioned Jo by name. If Portia happened to meet her, and that might happen, Allison would introduce her as an old friend. Portia would be none the wiser.

Portia pushed back the sleeve of her jacket to expose a thin, ropy-veined wrist and a slim gold watch. 'I have a taxi booked; it'll be here in five minutes.' Dropping her arm, she looked at Allison. 'A good lunch will make you feel better. I even went to the trouble of cooking myself, something I wouldn't do for just anyone, you know.'

Allison, aware of her friend's dislike of cooking, was touched. Impossible now to say she'd prefer to go to a restaurant, that she was still slightly wary of Stuart's over-familiarity. 'That's so kind of you. I hate putting you to so much trouble.'

Portia crossed and sat beside her. 'I know you say you don't care about being alone in the world, and you've often said you've no need for friends, so I was quite pleased you allowed me into your life—'

'You were rather insistent,' Allison interrupted her with a smile to show she meant no harm.

'And I'm here for you now, for however long it takes to get you back on your feet.'

Allison felt fragile, weak, truly the grieving widow she was trying to be. It was quite a nice part to play. Perhaps she should have more friends like Portia. 'You're so kind.'

'Nonsense, it's what friends are for.' She gave Allison's arm a squeeze and got to her feet. 'Run upstairs and slap a bit of make-up on. I don't want the taxi driver to think I'm transporting a corpse.'

With a laugh, Allison did as she was told. She would have liked to have changed from her widow's weeds. Black wasn't her colour, her skin too naturally pale. Opening her make-up drawer, she applied enough to put some colour on her face, finishing with a pale red lipstick. She took the band from her ponytail, shook her hair out and ran a brush through it. Much better. She was even looking forward to getting out of the house.

Staring at her reflection, she admitted she was also glad not to be there when Jo arrived back. What would the woman think – that Allison had scarpered? Perhaps she should have told her the truth about Peter's estate. It might have made her think twice about returning. Too late now.

Peter's estate. The bastard! Shock had worn off. Now she felt anger towards the man who'd deliberately misled her. *I've made an appointment to see my solicitor to change my will, leaving everything to you.* There had been no guile in his eyes when he'd spoken about it. God, he'd been good. She could almost admire him... almost.

She heard Portia shout up the stairs. 'Allison, taxi's here.'

'Coming.' She grabbed a jacket from her wardrobe. Fuchsia pink. Not funereal. *Fuck it.* She slipped it on and ran lightly down the stairs. 'I'm sure I've a dark jacket somewhere...' She joined her friend in the open doorway. 'But for the life of me I can't find it.'

'It's just us, remember. Stuart would be happy if you came naked.'

Allison, in the process of setting the house alarm, looked around in surprise. Surely, she'd misheard. 'What did you say?'

'Just that we're glad you're coming, whatever you wear.' Portia tucked a hand in her elbow as they walked to the waiting taxi.

But it wasn't what she'd said. Was it?

Was it?

52

Jo packed everything she owned into two cheap suitcases that had seen better days, the edges scuffed, the handles worn. Standing at the door, she looked around before shutting the door and posting the keys through the letter box. She was in arrears, but she doubted the landlord would chase her for the money she owed. He'd give it a cursory clean and rent it out as soon as he discovered she'd flitted.

Although she didn't have much in the way of possessions, the cases were old and heavy and dragged uncomfortably. She was reluctant to splurge the little money she had for a taxi but when one passed, its vacant light calling to her, she hailed it before she changed her mind. When she got to Union Square, she'd ask Allison to pay for it. She'd money to spare after all.

Money. It had never been Jo's driving force. Perhaps she was being stupid, though. With two million, the world would be at her feet. People who looked down on her, people like Allison, who saw her stretched skin and jumped to the wrong conclusions... they'd look at her differently when she was dressed in designer clothes and roped in diamonds. Wouldn't they? Never having mixed with those types of people, she'd no idea. But with millions, if it didn't work out that way, she could leave, start over elsewhere. With kinder people.

The taxi chugged through congested streets, rocking her gently, calming her thoughts. It was easily done. She didn't allow life to stress her too much. A lesson hard-learnt. Pain, she could have told anyone who'd listen, was a tough, unforgiving teacher.

The journey seemed endless, but finally the taxi pulled up outside her new, far more salubrious home. 'I'll have to get money from my friend,' she said. 'I'll be a sec.'

The driver shrugged. 'Clock's ticking.'

Jo pulled the key from her back pocket and slipped it into the lock. When it turned smoothly and the door opened, she smiled in relief. She'd half expected Allison to play some trick. Get the locks changed, maybe even put a safety chain up. But although one hung from the door, she hadn't bothered. Accepting the future so clearly laid out for her. Jo was surprised, and wary. A woman who could so coldly dispatch her husband was capable of anything.

To her surprise, she heard the beep of the house alarm. Allison hadn't waited in to welcome her new house guest. Swallowing the dart of irritation, Jo hurried to key in the code. The most annoying part of Allison's absence, of course, was having to pay for the taxi herself. With a sigh of frustration, Jo pulled out her purse. She had enough for the fare, nothing for a tip.

Maybe the battered suitcases the driver had set on the footpath had told him enough about her circumstances. He took the fare without comment, gave a nod of thanks and took off.

She stood with her luggage, and she looked up at the lovely house. She'd be happy living here. But then she was easily pleased. She lugged her cases inside. Leaving them in the hallway, she decided to make the most of her new landlady's absence and have a nosey upstairs. In the main bedroom, she discovered she'd been right about the contents of the rubbish bag she'd taken from Allison's bin. One bedside table was empty, the other filled with the tat every woman accumulates. She took out a packet of medication – the contraceptive pill. Jo wasn't surprised. Allison didn't strike her as the maternal type.

To the back of the house, she found a large spare bedroom overlooking a rather beautiful and lushly planted garden. This would do nicely for her.

It took her less than thirty minutes to unpack her bags. The old wardrobe was cavernous, the chest of drawers equally so. Her meagre selection of clothes were lost inside. Perhaps, with two million, she could buy clothes and keep them rather than having to bring them back. Money had never been a driving force... this is what she kept telling herself all the years she'd looked for Allison, the years stalking her... but maybe it was simply because she'd never had it.

Two million pounds. That could maybe change her thinking.

Restless, she returned to the main bedroom and rummaged through the drawers, finding little of interest, amused rather than surprised by the vibrator she found in the bottom drawer of the dresser. Downstairs, she did the same, opening cupboards, peering inside. Nothing interesting. In fact, for all their money and fancy designer clothes, Allison and Peter were rather dull.

They had good taste in wine, though. Jo took a bottle of Pinot Noir from the rack and opened it. With a large glass in her hand, she stood looking out at the back garden. Where was Allison? Gone shopping for food to celebrate Jo's arrival? Highly unlikely.

Food, though, was a good point. She opened the fridge. They liked their cheese, too. Unfortunately, Jo didn't. She'd more success in the freezer and took out a frozen chicken curry and a smaller carton of rice.

The microwave was a complicated contraption that took her a

minute to figure out, shoving both containers inside and pressing buttons randomly until it whirred into life.

It was nice to have the place to herself, to play pretend it was her home. She was humming happily as she searched for a plate and cutlery. She wasn't going to sit in that miserable dining room with her solitary meal. When she had the meal dished up, she found a tray and took it into the living room, returning for her glass of wine, hesitating only seconds before taking the bottle too. It had been a long time since she'd had wine, longer still since she'd had wine as good as this.

She quickly discovered she'd overheated the food. It was volcanic. Leaving it to cool, she switched on the TV and channel-hopped to find something to watch. An old black-and-white movie with a very young Cary Grant in the lead role fitted her mood.

When it was over, her dinner finished and the wine bottle nearly empty, Allison still hadn't returned. Jo checked her mobile on the off-chance there was a message from her, unsurprised to find none. She sent one of her own, weighing heavily on sarcasm.

Hi, remember me?

She sat back with the last of the wine, her head pleasantly buzzing. *Allison can't have gone far.* Until Peter's estate was settled, she wouldn't have access to his money and although she no doubt had a good salary, it wouldn't be enough to keep her in the style she so enjoyed.

Jo knew she'd no friends, apart from that woman, Portia. Was that where Allison had gone? To pour out her woes. Tell her friend some nasty woman was trying to steal her inheritance. She couldn't, could she, because she'd have to confess to why, and she wasn't going to do that.

Allison would come home eventually. She had to. Perhaps

when she did, Jo would tell her the real reason she'd been following her for so long.

She pulled off the wig, threw it across the room and let her fingers trace the lines of scars that decorated her skull. Yes, it was time.

53

Allison tried to convince herself she'd imagined what Portia had said or she'd simply misheard. Her friend couldn't possibly have said *Stuart would be happy if you came naked*, could she? It was inappropriate, seriously creepy, and wrong.

When the taxi pulled up outside Portia's house, Allison wanted to stay in the taxi and say she'd changed her mind, that she wasn't up to lunch, to ask, even beg, the driver to take her home. Portia had seemed such a comfort after Jo's visit; now, Allison wasn't too sure.

Portia climbed out and turned to look in at her. 'Come on, darling, I've a nice bottle of your favourite Prosecco chilling in the fridge.'

Perhaps it was the mantle of grieving widow she'd taken on with such enthusiasm making Allison feel weak, biddable, because she swallowed the lump of intuition that was stuck in her throat and climbed from the car, almost crying out as the taxi took off, feeling instantly abandoned.

Portia put an arm around her shoulders and led her on, chattering about something, the words going over Allison's head. It was stress, the understandable result of a seriously fucked-up day. Nothing more than that. She was being foolish to worry. These were good people. Allison had simply misheard.

Inside, Portia took the bright pink jacket and hung it on the ornate coat stand that stood in the corner of the large entrance hallway. 'Now, let's get you comfy, and I'll get that Prosecco.'

Her concern and her low, murmured words were calming, soothing. Allison allowed herself to be guided into the lounge and pressed into the corner of the sofa, feeling cosseted when a cushion was placed behind her head. She'd no idea what she was going to do about Jo. Right at that moment, basking in her friend's support, she didn't care.

'Here you go.' Portia swept in, a glass in each hand. She handed one to Allison and took the seat beside her. 'Here's to happier days.'

The power of positive thinking, probably taken straight from one of her psychology books; it was as good a toast as any. 'Happier days.' She clinked her glass gently.

'A few glasses of Prosecco and you'll feel more the thing,' Portia insisted. 'I probably should have brought the bottle through but never mind; it's good exercise for me, getting up and down.'

Allison took a sip. It might have been a good idea to have asked the taxi driver to come back in a couple of hours to take her home. She should have done, would have done normally. It was definitely a good idea to book one now, before she drank any more. Looking around for her handbag, she frowned and shook her head. Portia must have taken it with her coat.

'Are you okay? You look concerned.'

Portia was being so kind, so generous and sympathetic, Allison was being stupid. 'No... well, not as such, I was simply thinking I should order a taxi for later.'

'I can do that when I go for a refill. You sit back, relax, and stop worrying.'

Allison smiled at the motherly tone. The Prosecco was delicious; it was gone in a few sips and Portia got to her feet. 'Give me that, I'll get you another, then we'll have lunch.'

It would have been simpler, Allison wanted to say, to bring the bottle through but she wasn't going to argue with her hostess.

'Here you go, round two.' Portia handed the glass over.

'Thank you.' Allison took a sip. 'You're not having any?'

'I will, I'm keeping an eye on lunch. Stuart is there but, bless him, he's a little lackadaisical when it comes to timing things.' She sank onto the sofa beside Allison. 'You drink up, though. It'll help you relax.'

'I'm feeling better already. I think I needed to get out of the house for a while. Thank you, you're a life saver.' Allison was feeling more relaxed, the earlier worries floating away. The disappointment over Peter's estate... ha! Estate – she had to stop calling it that. Jo's infamy, the silly twist she'd put on Portia's harmless words, all these things felt less worrisome. She was a survivor; it was simply a matter of starting again. The future she wanted – it was there for the taking. The power of positive thinking. Perhaps Portia was right. Next time...

* * *

She'd fallen asleep. How embarrassing. What must Portia think of her? Allison would explain she hadn't slept well recently so it was understandable. She was still so tired her eyelids felt heavy, sticky. And she ached. No, that wasn't quite the right word; she didn't ache – she hurt. In places she shouldn't be hurting. Fear kept her eyes shut but her hand moved, slowly, seeking knowledge through her fingertips. What she discovered terrified her.

She was naked.

54

Jo expected Allison to return during the night. Several times, she woke, shaking off disorientation and swinging her feet from the bed to walk across the landing, only to stare into the empty room and swear loudly.

Morning arrived too early, sparrows erupting in a series of noisy squeaks in the shrubbery outside. She grabbed her phone, groaning to see it was only five. *Bloody birds.* Too early to be awake, she was too sleepy to attempt to solve the mystery of Allison's whereabouts. Wherever it was, it didn't look as if she'd be home that morning. No point in wasting her bed.

A minute later, Jo was curled up in a significantly more comfortable bed. There were still birds twittering outside but the sound was more muted. Only the odd car passed, the sound a low grumble. For someone used to the constant growl of traffic outside, the sound of others living too closely in badly insulated apartments, the peace here was heavenly. A short while later, she fell into a deep sleep.

It was almost nine before she woke again, stretching and yawning. Allison could stay away for as long as she liked if it meant Jo could sleep in her room.

She liked the en suite too, especially the range of shower gels more expensive than she'd ever used. After a long shower, doused in layers of Chanel Coco Mademoiselle, she wrapped a soft bath sheet around herself and headed downstairs for breakfast.

There was coffee, but no cereal and she'd used the last of the bread the previous day. Did Allison live on bloody cheese and wine? Jo would have her coffee, get dressed and do some shopping. Bread and milk. There was plenty of food in the freezer for dinner, plenty of wine in the rack. When Allison returned, Jo would ask her for her credit card and stock up the cupboards. Perhaps she should have explained that she expected bed and board till the estate was settled.

She took her coffee into the living room and sat on the sofa, feeling strangely content. This was the life she should have been living, perhaps the life she would have lived if not for Allison.

It wasn't too late.

She put the mug down, sat back and gazed out the window. This could be hers... and for the first time, she acknowledged she wanted it. When Allison returned, she'd ask her if the solicitor had given her any idea of a time frame for dealing with the estate. Only then could the house be sold, and Jo be able to get her share. Two million pounds.

She'd need to tread carefully till then. Allison was capable of anything but Jo, probably more than anyone, already knew that. Knowledge in this case was safety; she wouldn't let her guard down. She certainly wouldn't stand on the edge of a train station platform.

There was no rush. It was pleasant to sit in comfort and not worry about anything. Or anyone... But where the hell was Allison? Jo knew her to be a loner. No school or university friends. She rarely joined colleagues for drinks after work. It had amused Jo to see how alike they were.

She had never expected Allison to marry, thought she, like Jo, was destined for the single life. She should have guessed there was an ulterior motive for her rush to the altar. A three-million-pound motive.

Jo was almost relieved to have been proved right. She and Allison *were* alike.

No family to flee to, no friends, apart from one... she had to have gone to stay with Portia. Such a shame Jo hadn't managed to find out where she lived. She'd have to do some fishing when Allison came back and see what she could find out. Knowledge was safety; it was also power.

Back upstairs, she looked in Allison's wardrobe. What a pity she was slimmer and taller than Jo. She pulled out a silk shirt. It was loose-fitting; it might be okay. Dropping the towel to the floor, she slipped it on. It did fit... if she didn't need to fasten the buttons. She pulled it off roughly, rolled it into a ball and threw it into the bottom of the wardrobe. The slam of the wardrobe door echoed around the room. Before it faded, her flash of anger had too.

Her own clothes would have to suffice. For the moment.

Dressed, she pulled out her purse and checked her funds. The taxi fare had knocked her a bit. She'd enough for milk and bread, maybe butter. Nothing fancy, and she'd have killed for a biscuit.

Back in Allison's bedroom, she went through the pockets of her coats and jackets, finding two pounds in small change. It all helped. Doing a quick check on her phone, she found a Co-op store a short walk away. It was a good place for an economical shop.

Better value than she expected. She arrived back less than twenty minutes later with everything she needed, including biscuits and a four-pack of cheap beer. Wine was all well and good, but beer was her drink of choice.

The day was warm enough to take her toast and coffee into the back garden. The wooden garden furniture was obviously expensive but had stupidly been positioned under the branches of a large tree and was streaked with bird droppings. Rather than using it, she sat on the back doorstep. It wasn't particularly comfortable, but she was used to roughing it. As she worked through two slices of toast, her fingers slippery with melted butter, she thought about Allison.

Jo was surprised she'd been left alone. How did Allison know she wouldn't wreck the place or steal the silver?

That thought brought her to her feet. Was there anything worth hocking? She'd sold stuff on eBay before; it was surprisingly easy and lucrative. Allison's designer bags and shoes would fetch a few quid; it was something to keep in mind. She hadn't found much else of worth.

The rubbish bags she'd spied in the spare bedroom were, she supposed, Peter's clothes. Like the contents of his bedside table, Allison hadn't wasted any time in getting rid of them. Good suits might bring a few quid. Worth thinking about too.

She couldn't drum up any enthusiasm, though. Where the hell was Allison?

Three days later, having heard nothing from her, Jo was worried. She watched the news, bought a newspaper, combed every page for any reference to Allison's death or to the discovery of an unnamed dead woman. Nothing.

Was it possible she was going to stay away until after probate was settled? Sell the house in a quick cash sale, contents included? Was this her response to Jo's demand?

The bitch!

Jo frowned. She could go to the police with the video she had. They'd have ways to find her, trace her phone or something. They'd find her, arrest her and charge her with her husband's murder. Wouldn't they? Or would she be able to explain away her presence in the station that day? A downside of being short, Jo had been unable to see over the shoulders of crowds to capture Allison pushing her husband onto the track.

Jo gave a harsh laugh. Even if she did have footage of the actual moment, she wouldn't go to the police. She hadn't wasted all these years only to see Allison locked safely behind bars out of Jo's reach.

But Allison didn't know that...

So where the fuck was she?

55

Allison's eyes snapped open. Why was she lying naked in a strange bedroom with a sore body and a woolly head? The last thing she remembered was drinking Prosecco in Portia's clinically elegant living room. Had she drunk too much and passed out? She squeezed her eyes shut again, blocking out the light, trying to find answers in the dark. There weren't any.

Struggling to get her thoughts in order, she distinctly remembered enjoying the first Prosecco and Portia taking her empty glass away and returning with it full. Hadn't Allison been puzzled that she hadn't brought the bottle through? Yes! And she remembered feeling more relaxed as she sipped the second drink... sipped – she hadn't knocked it back. Two glasses. On an empty stomach, she might have been tipsy; she wouldn't have been drunk.

Difficult as it was to accept, never mind understand, it seemed clear her drink had been spiked.

Portia had drugged her.

Facing the truth was, in Allison's experience, the best way to deal with it, the fastest way to find solutions to a problem. She looked around the room. Apart from the bed she lay on, it was empty of furniture. A skylight overhead let in light. Daylight... how long had she been here? There were two doors. One the exit, the other perhaps to a bathroom.

She hoped so; her need was suddenly urgent.

Pushing back the sheet, she got to her feet, swallowing the lump in her throat to see the bruising to her ribs, her hip, the multiple finger-sized bruises on her arms that indicated, even in her drugged state, she'd tried to resist whatever had occurred. Good. She hoped she'd made it bloody difficult for them to get her wherever the hell she was.

Them. Portia and Stuart? Someone else? Whoever had done this to her, she'd make them pay. Somehow. She clung to that thought as she crossed unsteadily to the door. The first was, as she'd expected, locked; the other, to her relief, opened into a small en suite with a standard toilet, shower and wash handbasin. There was a tiny towel and a roll of toilet paper. Nothing else. Nothing Allison could use as a weapon against them. Keeping them safe from her anger. *Keeping her.*

She used the toilet, wincing as even the mundane act of sitting hurt, gasping when she got to her feet again at the sudden sharp pain in her side. Moving a hand gently over the area, she guessed she'd broken a rib or two. It wasn't going to make her panic. She'd broken one when she'd fallen against a doorknob years before and had spent hours waiting to be seen in the A&E department of her local hospital only to be told in the end that they didn't do anything for broken ribs.

Bruises and broken bones wouldn't make her panic... being locked in a room would. Being naked made her vulnerable. Not knowing what the fuck was going on made her very afraid.

She felt weak, but desperately wanted a shower to wash away the feeling of strange hands touching her bare skin. In the shower cubicle, she slid down the tiled wall to the floor and let the warm water cascade around her. There was some tiny consolation that as far as she could determine, she'd not been sexually abused. She ached in a lot of places but not *there*.

Not yet anyway.

Stuart. That bastard with his over-familiarity, his creepy touchy-feely behaviour. That kiss – it had been his tongue she'd felt, she was sure of it now. And that remark Portia had made about him liking to have seen her naked... why hadn't she trusted her instincts, the ones that were screaming something wasn't right? Allison wanted to weep for being such a fool.

But Portia...? Allison had trusted her. She groaned, holding her head up to the water, letting the spray fill her mouth, spitting and choking. What a fool she'd been... what a pathetic, needy, sad fool... there had been no friendship; Portia had targeted her from the beginning. All the sympathetic questions about Allison's lack of family and friends that she'd seen as friendly curiosity now took on a more sinister cast. Her isolation had made her the perfect victim. No wonder Portia had been taken aback at the sudden appearance of Peter. It must have upset her plans but it didn't take her long to resume after his death.

It had been Allison's desperation to get away from Jo that had made her play right into Portia and Stuart's hands. Struggling to her feet, she switched off the water and used the too-small towel to dry herself, rubbing the damp rag over her hair.

There was nothing to wear in the bedroom. Pulling the top sheet off the bed, she wrapped it around her damp body. Although she knew it was useless, she tried the door handle again, rattling it harder as anger took over from despair. She rested an ear against the door, straining to hear something... anything... hearing nothing but the uncomfortably loud thump of her heart and the pathetic hitch of her breath.

56

Allison assumed someone would eventually come. She wasn't sure how long she'd been unconscious. A day perhaps, maybe two. When hours after she woke passed without contact, she banged on the door and yelled until she was hoarse. All she achieved was to make herself more scared.

More scared. It was good to acknowledge it.

There was water. She drank mouthfuls from the tap, slurping it from her cupped hands, drying her hands and face on the small damp towel. There wasn't a mirror anywhere – too dangerous, never mind the seven years' bad luck; shards of smashed mirror would make a good weapon. It didn't matter. Allison didn't need to see her reflection to know her skin would be ghostly pale, her eyes wide with fear and... she pressed tentative fingers to her face... there would be a swathe of colour across her cheek.

She hoped Stuart and Portia had matching bruises, hoped she'd managed to get one or two punches in. Stupid people, they didn't know what she was made of. The fight she'd already won.

Banging and yelling had resulted in nothing apart from sore hands and a strained throat. She needed to be more meticulous.

Wrapping the sheet tighter, she examined the edges of the door, looking for any weakness. Another waste of time.

As was banging on the walls.

And moving the bed, grunting to turn it on its side, looking for something, anything she could use. She even failed to find something useful under the carpet. Hoping for floorboards she could prise up with her fingers, she found sheets of plywood nailed to whatever lay underneath, breaking two nails in an attempt to loosen the edge.

She sat back against the wall, sucking on the bubble of blood that welled at the base of her broken nail. If she could cry, this would be the time to do it. Instead, she got to her feet and restored order to her prison. The mattress had fallen from the upended bed. Her lip curled to see the stains on the reverse. With a grunt, she flipped it over and back onto the base and threw the sheet over it. She sat with her back against the wall and considered her options.

Whatever way she looked at it, it didn't appear she had any. It seemed wiser to consider theirs. Stuart and Portia. What were their plans? If she was right, if this had been a set-up from her first meeting with Portia, they'd gone to a hell of a lot of trouble. They'd drugged her to get her here. Were they planning to drug her again for whatever was planned next? She shivered when she thought of Stuart's fat, sweaty hands on her. His mouth. His... 'Argh!' The thought of any part of him touching her made her nauseous. Had they hoped she'd be compliant when she realised she'd no choice?

Compliant!

Over her dead body.

Or maybe over theirs.

57

Allison only noticed the passage of time by looking at the skylight overhead. There were no lights in either the bedroom or en suite and once night came, she was left in darkness. The lack of lights or light switch puzzled her. The slanted angle of the room indicated her prison was an attic conversion. The doors and bathroom fixtures looked relatively new... so why weren't there light fixtures?

For safety? So that she couldn't take them apart and do herself damage?

The thought took root and horrified her... had this room been prepared solely for the purpose it was currently being used for?

Perhaps she wasn't the first woman Stuart and Portia had kept here.

If she wasn't, what had happened to the others? Kept prisoner here until what? They managed to find a way to end their lives or – a horrendous thought – they starved to death. This was accompanied by a growl as if her stomach was complaining about the future she'd considered.

The room was warm. She slept sometimes, exhausted by the various scenarios spinning around her head, by the hunger, by the sheer unknowingness of her situation. Sleep at least passed the long, wearisome hours. She tried to keep track of the days but when she finally heard a sound at the door, she wasn't sure if she'd been there three or four days.

For a few seconds, she thought it was a dream, or the recurring nightmares that had her waking in a sweat, the one where Stuart came through and advanced on her with an engorged phallus and a lewd light in his eye.

She shuffled up, her back against the wall, staring as the sound came again and slowly, very slowly, the door opened. Expecting a monster to appear, it was an anti-climax to see Portia standing there with a sad expression on her face, a large double-bladed knife held almost listlessly in one hand.

Allison was about to jump up and charge her, knock her down, climb over her scrawny body, stamping on it for good measure, maybe give a few kicks and punches while she was at it. Maybe spit in her damn face. She'd have done it, wouldn't have hesitated to run out in the street naked as the day she was born if she managed to get away. She would have done it if Portia's expression hadn't suddenly hardened as she raised the knife with clear intent.

'Did you think I'd walk in unarmed? Don't underestimate me, my dear.'

Allison had tensed for the flight. She slumped back as Portia approached.

'Very wise. I wouldn't hesitate to use it. Not to kill you, you understand, I've gone through far too much trouble for that, but I'd certainly cause you considerable pain.'

Allison frowned. The words were hard, deliberately cruel but the tone was wrong. An actor reciting a part without any real feeling. 'Why are you doing this? I thought we were friends.'

The knife wavered as Portia's hand trembled. 'We were friends.' She shook her head and tightened her grip. 'You couldn't possibly understand so there's no point in wasting my breath. Suffice to say, we were searching for someone, and you fit the bill. I told you how much we missed Amy, didn't I?'

'Your daughter who went to the States? I don't understand.' How many days since she'd eaten? The weakness was making it hard to concentrate, making it difficult to understand.

'I knew you'd be perfect from the first day we met; you're so unbelievably gullible.'

Was she? Portia and Stuart, Jo, even Peter. Gullible, sad, desperate, bloody pathetic. 'There's no daughter.'

A slight nod of agreement before Portia waved the tip of the knife around the room as if casting a spell. 'There's no daughter. There was, however, a young woman called Amy. She was the previous occupant of this suite.'

What happened to her? The words were on the tip of Allison's tongue, but she didn't ask, didn't want to give Portia the satisfaction of telling her because it was obvious from the hard glint in her eye that her predecessor was dead.

Portia used the knife to point to Allison's face. 'That bruise looks painful.'

Allison put a hand to her cheek. 'You beat me up.'

'No, we're not guilty on that count. You struggled, far more than we'd anticipated, and fell down a few stairs. Luckily you didn't do any major damage—'

A surge of anger made Allison tense. 'You don't count broken ribs?'

'Broken ribs?'

'At least one, possibly two.'

'They'll heal. In a week or two.'

It was probably a hangover from the drugs, the lack of food, or the continuous simmering pain from her injuries, but Allison was confused by Portia's expression; she looked almost pleased. 'I don't understand what's going on.'

'You don't need to understand; you just need to behave.' Portia waved the knife up and down Allison's body. 'Now, since my clothes wouldn't fit, and unless you want to remain wrapped in a sheet forever, I'm going to go and fetch you some clothes. The ones you were wearing when you arrived became a little torn during your journey.'

'Torn?' Allison knew she was lying.

'I suppose "cut off" is more appropriate. Stuart wanted to have a look at his prize.'

She thought of lying there, helpless and naked, while that little toad of a man leered over her, maybe touched her with his long, bony fingers. She'd make them pay. If it was the last thing she did.

Portia was swinging the knife, looking a little bored. 'I have your house key but I'm sure you're sensible enough to have an alarm, so I need the code. And don't try to trick me. Stuart doesn't like it when I'm upset.'

Allison would make them pay, but she'd have to wait for the opportunity. That knife looked sharp. 'Seems my hands are tied. It's 1990.'

Portia frowned. 'That's not your date of birth.'

'That's right.' It was Allison's turn to smile. A forced uplift of the corners of her mouth. There was no need to tell Portia why the number was important to her, why it was lodged in her brain more completely than the year of her birth.

'Okay, I'll go and get you some clothes. When I return, if you behave, I'll let you have something to eat.'

And without another word, she backed out of the room. The sound of the key being turned in the lock was loud in the silence of Allison's prison.

She'd told Portia the truth about the alarm code. What she

hadn't told her, because she hadn't been asked, was that Jo was living there.

Allison went to the en suite and slurped water into her dry mouth.

If Jo heard someone in the house, she'd assume it was Allison returning at last. She'd be surprised to see a stranger. So would Portia. Maybe they'd come to blows, kill one another off. That would be the ideal outcome for Allison.

She remembered what Portia had said about Stuart not liking it if she was upset. How would he feel if she was dead? Would he take it out on Allison? But this time, he'd be on his own, and she wouldn't be drugged.

This time she'd be ready for him.

58

Running out of money, Jo thought about selling Allison's designer bags and shoes. They'd fetch a fair amount. Deciding to give her another day to return, Jo emptied the plastic bags she'd found in the spare bedroom. There were some decent suits. She hung them on the back of the wardrobe door and photographed them to put on eBay. They were good brands... not designer, unfortunately, but good enough to sell. She wanted a fast sale, put a reasonable price, gave the option of buying immediately at this price rather than getting into a bidding war, wasn't surprised to get a reply within a few hours.

That evening she was fifty pounds better off. Money for beer, for food to stock the emptying cupboards. Enough to get a take-away that night.

The following morning, she headed back to the Co-op and spent almost half the money. With the handles of two bags biting into the palms of her hands, she headed home. *Home...* it was nice to pretend, to imagine it was hers, that she had the right to live there, to stay, but it was unsettling to never know when Allison was going to return, a smug expression on her pretty face. Jo turned the corner of Union Square, head down, heavy, obsessive thoughts weighing her down more than the bags hanging from her hands. It was only when she lifted her eyes to check for traffic prior to crossing the road that she glanced towards the house. One glance, it brought her to an abrupt halt. Allison was on the doorstep!

Two passing cars prevented her from rushing across to accost the prodigal house owner and in those few valuable seconds, with her eyes fixed on the figure, she realised she was wrong. The woman on the doorstep was too short to be the tall, willowy Allison. And her profile... the nose was too large, chin too receding.

Whoever she was, if she was looking for Allison, her visit was in vain.

Jo waited for the woman to leave. When she turned, she'd get a better look at her face. File it in her head in case she saw her again.

But the woman didn't leave. Instead, she pushed open the door.

A burglar! Jo had lived in London for long enough to know not to take chances. She'd put on the alarm before she'd left and waited now for it to wail. When it didn't, she swore loudly, startling a cyclist passing by, who wobbled precariously, shook a fist at her and cycled on.

Jo hadn't considered what type of alarm system had been installed. Perhaps it was a silent one that alerted a security company, or the police. If so, it wouldn't be long before the air was filled with their wail as they dashed to the rescue. Jo bent to pick up her bags. If the police were going to descend on the house, it wouldn't do to stand there looking conspicuous.

She retreated into the safety of the park, took up a position behind a shrub with a good view over the house and waited for the outcome.

Ten minutes. Shuffling from foot to foot, the shopping bags slumped by her feet already attracting attention from an army of ants. She kicked them away and put one bag on top of the other. If she had to wait much longer, the frozen meals she'd bought would be spoilt

No alarm howling. No police racing to the rescue. Jo had been wrong... the alarm hadn't gone off; whoever had entered the house had a key and knew the alarm code. Not Allison but perhaps someone acting for her.

Portia?

Possibly.

When the front door opened several minutes later, she saw the holdall the woman held and nodded, satisfied. Her second scenario had been correct. Someone sent by Allison to fetch some belongings.

Jo hesitated only seconds before picking up her two bags. Tying a knot in the top of each, she shoved them under the leafy boughs of a nearby bush and took off after the unknown woman.

59

It was easy for Jo to follow the woman with the holdall. She didn't appear to be in any hurry. Jo stayed a few feet behind, sufficient distance to allow time to turn away should the woman glance around. Portia. It was as good a name to call her as any until Jo was proved wrong.

Luck stayed with her. The holdall didn't appear to be heavy, so they continued on foot. Jo would have quite liked to have jumped into a taxi and utter the immortal words *follow that cab*, but she'd a strange idea a London taxi driver would look askance at such a crazy demand, plus she didn't want to waste her money on what could be a protracted chase through the city.

After a short walk, Portia stopped at a café. Unwilling to risk being seen or paying what would be an extortionate amount of money for a coffee that was sure to be half froth, Jo stood on the other side of the street, trying to look inconspicuous.

She wasn't kept waiting long and soon they were off again.

Only to the nearest Underground station. It wasn't too busy and easy to keep Portia in view. Keeping a few people between them, she stood fairly close to her on the platform, needing to get into the same carriage.

Jo looked at the few commuters who stood near to the edge, impatient to catch sight of their train and thought of Peter. Had he known? Maybe felt the push, had time to look around to see his nemesis as she walked away. It had been one of the questions she'd wanted to ask Allison. Would she have lied or told the truth? Jo liked to think she knew her well enough to be able to tell the difference.

It wasn't difficult to follow Portia, but it was tiring to be constantly on alert and Jo was relieved when her journey came to an end outside a very elegant house in Kensington.

She was on the other side of the street, slowing to watch as Portia climbed the steps to the front door. Jo held her breath, hoping it wasn't a visit, that this was where the woman lived, where, if she was right, Allison was hiding away.

She felt like punching the air in triumph when Portia reached into her handbag, fumbled inside for a few seconds then pulled out what looked like a ridiculously large bunch of keys.

Home, then. Not a visit.

Jo waited until the front door shut before turning for the journey home.

Her two bags of shopping were still under the bush where she'd left them. She brushed off the investigating ants and woodlice and took them home. The two frozen meals were defrosted. It didn't matter; neither was overlarge – she'd cook both and pig out while she considered her next step.

She could simply knock on the door and ask to speak to

Allison but if that failed, she'd have given her advantage away. No, a better plan was to stake out the house and wait for Allison to come out. Allison had completely underestimated her... a very bad idea.

60

Allison spent her time imagining several different scenarios for what might happen when Portia entered her house in Union Square and for what she'd do when Stuart came to her door. Violence played a large part in her imagining. She wasn't a stranger to it, of course; it had played a formative part in her childhood. It was, she'd long come to accept, a necessary evil.

These people had no idea what she was capable of. Portia had called her gullible. She'd certainly been so when she accepted the older woman at face value, but who would have expected her to be a procurer for the awful Stuart?

Whatever happened in Union Square, her situation couldn't be any worse.

* * *

When she heard the key in the lock, she was ready. Getting to her feet, she tensed, ready to fight. Stuart wouldn't know what hit him.

It wasn't him. Portia, a bundle of garments under one arm, the knife clasped in the other, stood in the doorway. 'Here you go,' she said, dropping the bundle on the floor. 'Get dressed; I'll be back in a few minutes with some food.'

The door was shut again before Allison could speak. It looked as if it had all gone to plan for Portia. Where the hell was Jo? Had she given up when Allison hadn't returned, and left? Maybe she'd been bluffing and had never planned on returning.

So much for her grand hopes. With a sigh, she bent to pick up the clothes Portia had chosen for her. Clothes... Allison combed through the wisps of material for something substantial. It was quickly clear Portia had opened only one drawer of her dresser, the one holding underwear. All she'd brought were camisoles and French knickers, garments Allison had bought for Peter's delectation in the early days of their relationship, spending a ridiculous amount of money on underwear that wasn't designed to be either warm or practical.

She hooked her fingers into the lacy fabric of one after the other and rent it apart. No way was she wrapping herself up like a bloody Christmas gift for Stuart to unwrap.

It was half an hour before the door opened again. If Portia noticed Allison wasn't wearing the underwear she'd brought, or recognised the torn scraps that had been tossed about the room, she said nothing. The knife was attached to one hand like an appendage; in the other, she balanced a cardboard tray. 'You must be hungry. There's a couple of glasses of Prosecco too.' She placed the tray on the bed, her eyes never leaving Allison's face. 'Enjoy.'

The cardboard tray held an assortment of food. All on disposable plates. The cutlery, too, was plastic and flimsy. Allison picked up the first plate. Pasta in a sauce. Her mouth filled with saliva and her stomach growled. Taking a fork, she scooped up some and shoved it into her mouth, almost groaning with pleasure. It was delicious. Sitting on the edge of the bed, she finished it, scraping the last of the sauce with the edge of the fork.

It would have been nice to have washed it all down with the Prosecco. Two plastic cups of it. She took a sip. It tasted okay. But then so had the couple she'd had that fateful day and look where that had landed her. Taking both glasses into the en suite, she poured the drinks down the sink, rinsed them out several times before filling both with water. Better than using her hand, anyway. She gulped down a glass, refilled it and took both back to the bedroom.

There were cheese and crackers and a slice of chocolate cake too. She nibbled on one of the pieces of Cheddar, munched on a few crackers, drank one of the glasses of water, then picked up the cake. It was very good, chocolatey without being over-sweet.

It had all been good. She certainly felt better for having eaten it. Stronger. Less stressed. Almost relaxed. She put the tray on the floor and sat back on the bed, eating the last piece of cheese with tiny bites. By the time it was finished, she understood the mistake she'd made. It hadn't been the Prosecco this time. She guessed it had probably been the pasta dish, the garlic strong enough to cover any after taste of whatever drug they'd used this time.

It didn't matter. It was all too late.

61

The morning after following Portia, Jo returned to the Kensington house. It wasn't easy to look inconspicuous on the quiet street. It wasn't en route to anywhere, there were no shops on it, no logical reason for anyone to be hanging around.

She walked up one side of the road, down the other. She hadn't really thought it through, but it was impossible to do this all day. It was on her third perambulation that she noticed something that brought a smile to her face. Across from Portia's house, and one house down, a car sat in the driveway. Nothing exceptional about that. And most people wouldn't have noticed the layer of dust on the car, the small weeds growing in the cobble-locked driveway immediately behind the wheels. The car hadn't been moved in a while.

Maybe the owners of the house didn't use the car much... or maybe they were on holiday.

Sometimes, it was worth taking a risk. If someone came out, she'd scarper and regroup. With a glance towards the house, Jo slipped inside the gate. It wasn't perfect. There was nowhere to sit. In the shelter of the wall, it was damp, chilly and filled with insects scurrying out of her way. But it would do for a while.

Hopefully, any moment, the door would open, and Allison would come down the steps. Jo would wait for a minute, then follow her and pounce.

It was a good plan, but it didn't work that day. The door didn't open at all. She waited till early evening, till she was stiff and cold to the bone from standing in the damp garden.

The good news was that it looked as if she'd been correct about the house behind her. As soon as the day began to wane, a pop of light appeared in one of the downstairs windows, followed only a minute later by a second in an upstairs window. Lights on timers. Such a giveaway. Jo shook her head at such stupidity. Honestly, some people deserved to get burgled.

With a final glance at the house across the street, she headed for home. Tomorrow, she'd return. And the day after. Three days was giving her plan a good try. After that, well, she'd reconsider.

* * *

It looked like she was going to have to go for a third day when by the end of the second day the front door remained resolutely shut. Did the two women never go out? They lived in London. Didn't they go to the theatre, out for dinner, shopping, do anything?

Frustrated, she slipped out from behind the pillar to make her way home. She'd gone a few steps when she saw the door she'd been watching open. She almost fell over her feet in her haste to return to her hiding place, slamming her knee painfully against the stone, swallowing the yelp of pain as she concentrated on the figures leaving the house.

Not Allison. Portia and a man. Arm in arm. Their faces wreathed in big, toothy smiles. Both dressed up, she in a flowing, multi-coloured dress, he in a dark suit. They looked well together. Their laughter floated on the air to where she stood, and she felt a moment's envy for how obviously happy they were.

A night out for two. Leaving one behind. Jo smiled. If she dashed across now, rang the doorbell, or banged on the knocker, Allison would assume her friend had forgotten something and would hurry to open it.

What a surprise she'd get when Jo pushed her way in.

She almost bounced across the road, so sure was she of her success. There was both a doorbell and knocker. She pressed the bell once and waited. She didn't think Portia would be the impatient type.

Jo was, though, and when the single ring resulted in silence, she rang again. Twice this time. Then she lifted the knocker and rapped it twice. Soon she was pounding the knocker, hammering on the bell, unable to believe her bloody brilliant plan was failing.

62

This time when Allison woke, she knew exactly where she was. She was lying on her side, curled up in the foetal position. She didn't know why she'd resorted to returning to the womb in her distress. Her mother had rarely offered her comfort or support after birth; Allison doubted she had before.

The after-effects of whatever drug her food had been laced with made her thoughts woolly, her head woozy. She stretched slowly. One aching limb after the other. Even after so many days, her bruises still caused her discomfort. There didn't seem to be a part of her that didn't hurt. A sudden spasm sent her rushing to the toilet, where she heaved and shot a gush of undigested food into the bowl.

A wave of weakness kept her there, gripping the edges of the toilet, her face staring into the mess. The stink from it, from her despair, from her bruised body, loosened a hand and sent it trembling for the handle to flush away at least one of her problems.

It was several minutes before she was able to get to her feet and stagger back to the bed. The sheets, both bottom and top, were twisted as if she'd struggled with nightmares during her drugged sojourn. She lay down and wrapped the top sheet around her again.

Whether it was the remnant of the drugs floating around her body or the depth of her despair pushing her mind into survival mode, she drifted into an uneasy sleep filled with rabid monsters. She ran from them but fast as she ran, they caught her. When she finally managed to lock herself into a room, she heard the savage knocking from the other side. She wasn't safe. They'd get through. This was her life. Forever. There was no point in resisting. She unlocked the door and opened it. To her surprise, the monster wasn't there. Even more oddly, the knocking continued.

More violently. More persistent.

Perhaps there were other monsters out there she couldn't see.

63

Jo kept hammering on the door as if persistence would achieve results. With a final slam of the knocker, she stepped back and glared at the house as if it alone was to blame for her failure.

The curtains on the ground-level windows were open but, from where she stood, there was nothing to see. With a glance around to see if the coast was clear, she went down a wrought-iron spiral staircase to the lower garden level of the house. Here, the one window was barred on the outside and shuttered on the inside. Bloody useless.

Returning to the front door, she knocked again. Less enthusiastically, already giving up. Even the letter box was against her. Pushing it open, hoping to view the hallway, maybe even to see a cowering Allison, she was unable to see anything. She pushed her fingers through a brush. A draught excluder. Spy defeater. She took her hand away.

Giving up wasn't something Jo did easily. Not until she'd tried every option. If Allison wasn't going to open the damn door, perhaps there was another way to get her attention. Break in. Was it possible?

She wouldn't know without trying. Old houses, such as this one, frequently had weak points. No harm in searching for one. The bars on the garden-room window ruled that out. It was time to see what options the back of the house offered.

The house was separated from its neighbour by a wide drive with plenty of room for the Volvo parked on it. She slipped by the car to the gate dividing the front from the rear. The luck she'd had at the side entrance to Allison's house didn't hold here. It was locked. Jo took out her frustration on it and kicked it viciously. The gate looked solid, but it was old, the wood weakened by age and the elements. She smiled to see what one kick had done. Without wasting time, she put her shoulder to the door and shoved. It looked easier on the TV. On a second try, she heard a definite creak, louder on the next. She kept at it till, finally, it gave with an ominously loud crack. She held her breath, wondering if someone would come to investigate.

When they didn't, giddy with her success, she slipped through the gate and pressed the wood back into place. It wouldn't fool anyone who came to investigate, but she guessed from the road, the damage would be unnoticeable.

The light was fading, and the long back garden stretched away into darkness. As Jo edged around the house, a security light flashed on, bringing her to an abrupt stop. It went off again after a minute but not until she'd had a good look at the rear elevation of the house. She punched the air in excitement. There was an open window. On the first floor, true, but it showed a laxity in security that augured well for her success.

When she moved, the security light switched on again. Maybe Allison would come to investigate? No such luck. Jo checked the back door. It was locked. A uPVC door. Solid as hell. Further along there were bifold doors into what looked like a dining room. With little optimism that the owners of the house would be stupid enough to leave them unlocked, she pushed and almost toppled inside when the door slid back with a *shush*. *Unfuckingbelievable!*

She slapped a hand over her mouth when giggles threatened to erupt. No point in getting cocky now and ruining everything. The room she was in – a huge space that seemed to incorporate cooking and relaxing – was plunged into darkness when the sensor light outside switched off.

Standing still, Jo listened intently, expecting to hear the faint sound of a TV or music drifting from further inside the house. But strain as she might, she couldn't hear a thing. In her small bedsit, she could hear when a toilet flushed in the property on either side. She'd like this quiet. Mentally, she added to the list in her head of the things she would get with her two million. Peace and quiet could be bought.

She switched on the torch of her mobile and crossed to a doorway. It opened quietly into another room. Light drifted in from the street outside to show her a large, well-furnished living room. Thick carpet underfoot deadened her footsteps as she walked around looking for something personal, surprised to find no photographs, no *stuff*.

Neat freaks.

Another doorway to one side opened into a hallway. She went through, shutting it quietly behind her. The front door she'd hammered on several minutes before seemed to taunt her. She went to it, twisted the catch and pulled it open. Pushing the snib down on the catch, she closed it over. If she had to make a quick getaway, she'd be safe now.

Safer. She turned and looked up the stairway. The house was eerily quiet. Too quiet; it didn't feel right. An understatement... it felt very wrong. Focusing on why she was there kept her from cutting her losses and fleeing this creepy house. Allison had to be here somewhere. Perhaps she was asleep. Worn out from playing her exhausting role as grieving widow. The sneer carried Jo up the stairs, one step at a time, stopping now and then to listen.

On the first-floor landing, she opened door after door but only one of the four bedrooms showed signs of being used, damp towels in the en suite, a blouse thrown on a chair. The main bathroom, a room as big as her entire bedsit, held none of the paraphernalia that said someone used it.

Returning to the stairway, Jo stared upward, her mouth suddenly dry. The house looked to be a two-storey over garden-level building from the front. This narrower stairway, she guessed, was a later addition. An attic conversion.

At the top, she stopped on a small landing and looked at the only door. There was a key in the lock. The feeling something was wrong had grown stronger. Reaching for the handle, the cold metal grounding her in a suddenly unstable world, she pressed it down and pulled, then pushed. Nothing happened; it was locked. She turned the key and tried again.

This time the door opened.

64

Allison was struggling to shake away the dreams of monsters chasing her. The knocking had stopped a few minutes before and she'd drifted, not to sleep, but to that fuzzy in-between space.

The sound of the key being turned in the lock penetrated her thoughts and sent fear jolting through her. Fear of Portia, of Stuart, or what they had planned for her future. This was her life. Forever. How had Amy escaped? Allison would find a way. Death was preferable.

'Allison?'

The word was whispered in disbelief.

She opened her eyes then, turned onto her back, wincing as pain shot through her. She looked towards the door, expecting Portia, doing a double-take to see someone else standing there. 'Jo?'

'Yes.' Jo approached the bed, her eyes round, lips pressed together as if afraid of what would come tumbling out.

Allison levered herself up on her elbow. 'Bet you wondered where I'd gone?'

'I did a bit of speculating. I didn't come close.'

It made Allison laugh, which made her wince, then groan.

'Shit, what have they done to you?'

Allison was allowing relief to soak in. She'd been rescued. By Jo of all people. 'They drugged me, starved me, covered me in bruises and broke some ribs. But they never got what they wanted, and if you help me out of here, they won't.'

'Can you walk?' Jo ran a hand over her face. 'Fuck, can you even stand?'

Allison wasn't sure she could do either but if she had to slither across the floor like a snake, she was getting out of there.

Jo was shifting her weight from foot to foot. 'I should ring for an ambulance. Shit, I should ring the police. Those two, they should be arrested.'

Allison struggled to sit, letting the dizziness settle before shuffling around to put her feet to the floor. 'No ambulance, no police.' She pushed the sheet to one side. 'Could you find me something to wear?'

'Yes, I can do that.' Jo turned for the door, then looked back, a worried expression on her face. 'Don't move; I'll be back in a sec.'

'Right.' Allison waited till her rescuer had gone before getting shakily to her feet, steadying herself with a hand on the wall. She straightened, stretching upright, wincing at the pain. When she took her hand from the wall, she swayed and collapsed to the bed behind. She was safe now. Wasn't she? The doubt in her head pushed her to her feet again. This time, when she took her hand from the wall, she swayed only a little.

'You okay?' Jo was back, hovering in the doorway. 'I mean obviously you're not okay, I just mean...' Her voice faded away.

Allison wiped a hand over her mouth. 'I need a shower.'

Jo turned to look nervously down the stairway. 'We don't know how long they're going to be gone. Best not to tempt fate. When you're home, you can have a long shower, change into your own clothes. Okay?' She stepped into the room and dropped an array of clothes on the bed. 'I wasn't sure what would fit so I just grabbed a selection.'

Allison picked up a fine navy jumper. She pulled it on. It was soft and wide, caressing her bruised body. Rummaging through the rest, she found a wrap skirt. She tried to drape it around her waist, handing it over to Jo without a word when she'd failed for the second time.

'There you go,' Jo said, tying the belt in a bow at her side. She pushed a pair of mules towards Allison with her foot. 'Best I could do. Portia has small feet.'

They were probably a size too small, and Allison's heels jutted out over the end. 'They'll do.'

Jo handed her the bag she'd been holding. 'I found this on the dressing table. It's yours.'

Allison opened it and looked inside. Everything as she'd left it. Her phone, though, was flat. 'Can you ring for a taxi?'

'Sure, if you can pay for it. I'm all out of dosh.'

'That's fine, just get a taxi so we can get out of here.'

Allison left her to make the call and started her slow descent, a hand on the banister to steady her as she went, feeling the painful grate of her broken ribs, each aching bruise. She heard Jo's voice ordering the taxi. Soon Allison would be out of this hell... the thought made it easier to move faster.

Jo slipped by her, stopping a few steps further on to turn and look back. 'You look like death; do you want to hold on to me?'

'No, that's okay, I can cling to the banister.' It was slow going. When Allison reached the first-floor landing, a wave of nausea hit her, followed by a dizzy spell that almost brought her down. 'I just need a minute,' she said when she felt Jo hovering nearby. In fact, it was several minutes before she could take another step. At the top of the second staircase, she looked downward. The steps swayed alarmingly. She wasn't going to make it.

'Put an arm around my shoulder.' Jo stood beside her. 'One hand on the banister, one around me. Together we'll make it.'

Together. It wasn't a word Allison used. She lifted an arm and draped it around the shoulder of the shorter, stockier woman, her free hand gripping the banister. It made it easier, but the going was slow, the steps continuing to dip and dive under Allison's feet. She heard Jo grunt as she leaned more heavily on her.

They were only halfway down when the front door opened.

Allison looked down and made an instant decision. She'd rather throw herself down the rest of the stairs and hope for a quick death than return to the prison upstairs.

65

When Jo saw the door open, she was tempted to shuck off the arm that lay heavily on her shoulder and run like hell. She wasn't going to end up battered and bruised like Allison, who'd let out a whimper of absolute terror when the door opened. Why hadn't Jo grabbed a knife from the kitchen? *Idiot.*

It was only seconds before a figure appeared. One neither woman recognised.

The man held a hand up. 'Sorry. I was going to ring the bell but the door was open.'

'It's the bloody taxi driver,' Jo said in relief. The arm over her shoulder had tensed. She felt it relax at her words, the body she was propping up slumping and swaying dangerously. 'Come on,' she said, 'hold it together a bit longer. We're almost there.' She looked down to the driver. 'Can you bring the car to the door?'

He stood looking up at them, a frown dividing his forehead. 'She's not going to be sick in my cab, is she?'

'No, she isn't. She's recovering from a stroke, that's all. Don't be so discriminatory.'

He held both palms out in surrender. 'Fine, sorry. I'll pull up close as I can to the door.'

'Hear that, Al, we're almost there.'

Almost... it was a struggle to get Allison to lift her feet over the threshold of the front door, a further struggle to get her down the few steps to the waiting car. Luckily, the taxi driver had taken the criticism to heart and held the door open. By dint of turning Allison around and pushing down on her head, she got her into the car.

Only when the taxi was back on the road and on its way did Allison turn to her. 'Thank you. I owe you.'

Jo leaned closer, dropped her voice to a whisper. 'Two million will pay me nicely.'

'It's certainly worth it.' Allison sighed and shut her eyes.

'You sure you shouldn't go to the police? They don't need to know about the other thing.'

'The other thing?' Allison smiled briefly. 'No, no police.'

The words were firm... and loud. Jo saw the driver's eyes flick to the rear-view mirror. She waited till he shrugged and looked away before leaning close to Allison again. 'You can't let them get away with it.'

'Don't be stupid! Of course I'm not. I'm going to make them pay.'

'I know you're capable—'

Allison grabbed her hand and squeezed it. 'You have no idea what I'm capable of, Jo, no idea at all.'

Jo pulled her hand away. She knew exactly what Allison was capable of, had had first-hand experience of it. But it wasn't the time to tell her. Not while the woman was in such a sorry, pathetic state. When she was back in full health, when Peter's estate had been settled and Jo had the money in her bank account, only then would she make her revelation. And make Allison pay.

66

The taxi double-parked outside Allison's house. With help from Jo, she struggled from the car, pain in every step as she tottered weakly to her front door. She stood with a hand on the railing dividing her small front garden from the neighbour's as Jo slipped her key into the lock, opened the door and hurried through to switch off the alarm and turn on a hallway light.

Allison didn't think she'd seen a more beautiful sight, relief helping her move more easily. 'I'm going to have a shower, then I'll be back down. We can talk.'

'Okay. I'll find us something to eat.'

'Good.' Allison didn't think she'd ever want to eat again. She swayed, grabbing hold of the newel post.

'You sure you'll manage?'

She looked up the stairway. Had it always been so high, so steep? She was sure it hadn't always moved, like a bloody roller coaster. 'No, I don't think so.'

Jo slipped a hand around her waist. 'Come on, let me help you.'

Allison wanted to push her away but the pressure of the hand on her back increased, pushing her forward. One step after the other. For the moment, she needed the help. But even though Jo had saved her, Allison wasn't going to forget she was a liar, a blackmailer, a scam artist. There were also too many unanswered questions. She'd never discovered how Jo had found out her address. Now there was an added mystery – how had she found out where she was being kept prisoner? In the en suite, she co-operated as Jo helped her out of the borrowed clothes and urged her into the shower cubicle. She stood unmoving as the water was turned on, and took the opened bottle of shower gel that was handed to her.

'Stay as long as you want,' Jo said, shaking water from her hand. 'I'll find something easy for you to put on when you're finished and leave it on the bed. If you need me, shout, but I'll pop back in a while anyway to make sure you're okay.'

Allison gripped the bottle too hard, gel shooting out of the top. It was empty before she was finished, foam filling the base of the cubicle, her skin red from the loofah she used to scrub away the sensation of Stuart's fingers running over her skin. That she couldn't remember him touching her bizarrely made it worse.

Finally, she switched off the shower. The sudden silence was almost overpowering. The cubicle felt safe, protected. Outside, anything could be happening. Stuart and Portia might have returned, come looking for their prisoner. Two of them would easily overpower the smaller Jo. Fear of what might be happening kept Allison where she was, her skin rapidly cooling. She knew she was being silly, but she was unable to stop the fearful thoughts cascading, nor could she stop herself squeaking in fear when the door was opened suddenly.

If Jo had heard, she gave no sign as she handed Allison a large bath sheet and put another smaller towel on the floor. 'Come on, dry yourself or you'll catch cold.'

Chivvied along, Allison stepped out. The bathroom mirror was steamed over. She was glad. She'd no desire to see her face. It was enough to look down at her body and see the multiple bruises.

With Jo's help, Allison was soon dry and dressed in warm brushed-cotton pyjamas she hadn't known she possessed.

'They're mine,' Jo explained. 'I couldn't find anything suitable in your drawers.'

'They're comfortable, thank you.' Allison was surprised at the thoughtfulness. Did this strange woman pity her?

She didn't want her pity, or her help. Didn't want to feel grateful for the arm she leaned on as she slowly descended the stairway. She allowed herself to be settled on the sofa, raised an eyebrow when a rug was placed over her knees but said nothing. How ironic it was – she'd fled from Jo and sought refuge with Portia and Stuart and now it was Jo providing the refuge. Allison would have laughed if she could have found one thing amusing about this whole damn scenario.

She looked up to see Jo hovering.

'I'll bring your dinner in on a tray. Would you like a glass of wine to go with it?'

'As long as it's not Prosecco.' Allison saw the puzzled frown and shook her head. 'I'll explain later. Yes, a glass of wine would be nice, thank you.' She rested her head back. She was feeling a little better. The drugs were working themselves out of her system. Tomorrow she'd be good as new. *Keep telling yourself that!*

Jo pushed open the door a few minutes later. 'It's only a Co-op lasagne, I'm afraid.' She put a tray on the table. 'I'll get the wine.'

An unopened bottle, Allison was glad to see. It'd be a long time before she'd drink something without being perfectly sure where it came from. 'Only a small glass, please.'

Jo poured half a glass and handed it over. 'Eat up, I'll go and get mine.'

Soon, they were sitting opposite each other in what might have been companionable silence if the room wasn't filled with an air of expectation.

67

Allison ate a few mouthfuls before she put her fork down and pushed the tray onto the sofa beside her. The glass of wine sat untouched on the coffee table. She reached for it, took a sip then put it down. Maybe, after all, alcohol wasn't a good idea. She felt Jo's eyes on her, examining her in an almost predatory fashion. Allison owed her; it wasn't a sensation she enjoyed.

'I haven't thanked you for coming to my rescue. You probably saved my life.'

'I thought you were hiding out there. From me.' Jo shrugged and scraped the last of the lasagne from her plate with a noisy screech of metal on china before tossing the fork down and lifting her glass. 'I thought you were trying to do me out of my share.'

It seemed the better option to feign forgetfulness. 'Your share?'

Jo emptied her glass in two noisy gulps and slammed it down on the table. 'I know you've been through a lot but please, don't treat me like a fool. My share of your beloved, much-lamented late husband's estate. The two million we settled on for my keeping quiet about your presence in the station when your husband accidentally fell in front of a train.'

Allison nodded slowly. 'I owe you a lot for saving me—'

Jo interrupted her. 'How did they do it?'

'You want the details, do you?' Allison couldn't blame her. She'd have wanted to know how an intelligent woman had been so easily conned. 'Portia, it seems, set me up. The friendship, etc., was all an act to get my trust. I think my marriage to Peter threw her for a while; I saw less of her while we were married. That morning after you'd left, she called around and invited me to lunch. Getting out of the house seemed like a good plan so I went.' She shook her head. 'Bad idea. She gave me drugged Prosecco. When I woke, it was in that room. On that bed.' The memory stopped her words for several minutes.

'They look such a normal couple.'

'I'm not the first.' Allison told Jo about Amy. 'I'm guessing there were women before her too.'

'You think they killed Amy?'

'No, I think she might have killed herself. I'd have done so if I'd had the chance rather than stay locked up in that room.'

'Did they... you know...'

'No, I was spared that horror.' She remembered Stuart's lascivious eyes and shivered. 'It was only a matter of time, though.' She reached a hand to feel her damaged ribs. 'Maybe they were afraid to do anything until all my bruises had healed.' She saw a question in Jo's eyes. Perhaps she was being too careful of Allison's sensibilities to ask whatever it was. 'What's puzzling you?'

'When the drugs wore off, couldn't you have fought back?'

'Portia wasn't stupid. When she opened the door, she held a very large, sharp knife and threatened to hurt me.' Allison sighed. 'I probably would eventually have fought regardless but they drugged me again. This time, it was in the food.' She hadn't given much thought to what would have happened next. She'd have been reluctant to either eat or drink anything she was given, so how had they hoped to keep her subdued? 'I don't know what the next step in their plan was, how they were going to force me to be compliant, and thanks to you, I'm never going to find out.'

'You said you were going to make them pay.'

'Yes. And I will.' Allison reached for the glass, took another sip of the wine. She was feeling stronger. It was going to take her a long time to recover both physically and mentally; getting revenge on Portia and Stuart would certainly help. *Make them pay.* An idea came to her, and she looked across at Jo. 'You could help me.'

'That depends on what you're planning. I'm going to be hanging around for a few months so I might as well make myself useful.' She looked suddenly worried. 'I don't do violence, though, in case that's what you were thinking.'

'No, nothing violent.' At least not initially. Not till they'd paid for their crimes. 'When Portia and Stuart get home and find I've escaped, they'll be surprised when the police don't arrive, sirens wailing, lights flashing. Then they'll sit back and wonder what I want.'

'Money? They do seem obscenely wealthy.'

'Yes, so my plan is to relieve them of some of that, to help me buy this.' She waved her free hand around the room, then laughed at Jo's puzzled expression. 'Oh, yes, I never did get around to telling you the truth about Peter's estate, did I? Getting held prisoner does tend to make one forget. Let me make it clear. Your share of my dearly departed husband's estate would keep you in beer for a few days, no more than that.'

'You're lying!'

'Nope. It seems dear Peter forgot to tell me a few things. Like he didn't own this house, he wasn't a solicitor, and the few hundred quid he had in the bank possibly won't be enough to clear his credit card debt. There might be a pound or two over. As long as you stick to cheap beer, you should get a few cans out of it.'

Jo's response was unexpected. She sat back and laughed till tears ran down her cheeks.

'Glad you're taking the news so well.' Allison was surprised and more than a little suspicious.

Jo reached for the wine bottle and poured a generous amount into her glass. 'I'd never planned to ask for money, you know, it wasn't my motivator.'

Allison huffed a grunt of disbelief. 'You seemed pretty motivated to me.'

'Only because it's what floats *your* boat.' Jo jerked a thumb towards the ceiling. 'I've seen the designer bags, the expensive clothes, the Chanel body lotion. You've come a long way.'

You've come a long way. What the fuck was that supposed to mean? It struck Allison that she'd never discovered why Jo had hooked up with her on Facebook, why she'd lied to her. If she wasn't motivated by money, what had she wanted? She should have asked; it was the perfect opportunity, but she didn't, unsure whether she could handle any more revelations. She was still trying to understand how she, who considered herself so clever, had been fooled by Peter, Portia and Jo. Such a galling thought. 'You don't want money. In that case, I've no wish to be ungrateful, but you've no need to hang around.'

Jo held her glass up. 'I could get used to drinking decent wine rather than cheap beer.' She waved the glass around the room, the wine sloshing around the inside without spilling. 'It didn't take me long to get used to living in luxury either. You didn't see the bedsit I lived in; it wasn't much bigger than this room. I'm not sure I'll ever hanker for designer bags, but somewhere nice to live, maybe some travelling, good food. I could get used to all that.'

A better life. Hadn't that been what Allison had wanted, why she'd gone to such extreme measures? Maybe she and this odd woman weren't so different after all. She took another sip of her wine. 'I want revenge; you deserve a reward. We could get both from Portia and Stuart. By now, they'll know the police aren't going to arrive. They'll expect my next move.'

'Blackmail?'

'A nasty word. I'd prefer to call it payback.' She was surprised to find her wine glass almost empty. Annoyed with her weakness, she was already beginning to feel a little woozy. 'Of course, they might do a runner and flee the country. It's what I'd do. If so...' If they did, she'd get nothing... no money, worse, no revenge.

'No, they won't do that.' Jo reached into a pocket of her jacket. 'When I was looking for appropriate clothes, I found these.' She waved two passports, the gold crest on each shining in the light from a nearby lamp. 'I have to admit, I was thinking of their resale value, but it also means the diabolical duo are stuck in the UK.'

Allison looked at her and smiled. The diabolical duo. It seemed appropriate for both sides of the game that was yet to play out.

But none of the other parties, not Stuart, Portia or Jo, knew just how diabolical Allison could be.

68

Despite my every attempt, it proved impossible to escape what I'd done all those years before.

The path I'd chosen had become a deep trench. Trapped, unable to climb out, I peered over the edge to see all the lives I could have lived... should have lived.

Would have lived if I hadn't done something shockingly evil when I was barely old enough to know right from wrong.

If I could have changed what I'd done... if I could have chosen a different path... of course I'd have done it.

But it isn't possible to unlight a fire or to unkill someone.

I was stuck in the trench – me and the monster – desperate for the life of our dreams. And when, finally, I managed to scramble out, I didn't go alone.

The monster tagged along.

I kept it hidden, but I knew it was there. Waiting. Haunting me. Never ever letting me forget what I was.

69

Allison barely slept. It wasn't a fear of sleeping that caused the problem; it was the terror of opening her eyes to find she was still in that attic room. Worse, her imagination filled in the colours of the next chapter, and they were all shades of red and black, Stuart's lecherous face appearing in every frame. It was a nightmare, but the rape felt real, and she woke feeling soiled, grubby, scrambling from the bed to have a shower and wash the final wisps of the imaginary assault away.

It was still dark when she made her way down the stairs, switching on the lights as she went to dispel the darkness. Nothing lurked in it, she was being silly, but she felt easier in the light.

A mug of coffee cupped in her hands, she stood and looked around the kitchen. First thing she was going to do was to knock that damn wall down, gut the kitchen and dining room. Make a big, bright, light room with windows looking over the garden. A nice garden with plenty of flowers. Colour. All year round.

Then her life would be the one she'd been seeking most of her life.

She stood drinking her coffee, looking out the kitchen window till a hint of colour appeared over the roof ridges opposite and night gave way to day. Only when she heard footsteps on the stairs did she turn.

Jo, clad in pyjamas unseasonably patterned with Christmas trees, yawned and stretched as she stood in the doorway. 'Did you sleep at all?'

'Not much.' Allison indicated the kettle. 'It's not long boiled.'

Jo flicked the switch to boil the water again, then turned to open the fridge. She peered around the edge of the door and asked, 'Want some toast?'

Allison watched her unwanted visitor, this woman who had saved her, treating the place as if it belonged to her. She'd made herself completely at home in the few days Allison had been held captive. Held captive, drugged and abused.

'Allison?'

She jumped, startled. Jo was staring at her, a strange expression on her face. On the counter beside her, butter was melting on the two pieces of toast, steam spiralling from her mug of coffee.

Jo pointed at her with a greasy knife. 'You were out of it. For a minute or two.'

Allison stared at the knife. She wanted to grab it, use it to do some damage, but wasn't sure who it was she wanted to hurt most. Jo... or herself for all the stupid decisions that had helped get her where she was. 'It was a bad night.' A bad week. *Bad*. What a crazy understatement. Turning away from Jo's intent gaze, she made another coffee. 'Let's sit inside and talk about what we're going to do with the delightful twosome.' She went into the dining room.

Following her, Jo stood in the doorway, a mug in one hand, plate in the other. 'I hate sitting in this room. It has bad vibes.'

Allison ignored her. Daylight had done nothing to alleviate the dull dreariness of the space. She put her mug down and moved to the curtains. When, despite her best attempts, she couldn't uncover more of the window, she grabbed hold of first one, then the other, and wrenched the curtains from the rail. It didn't make a huge impact – the room was still incredibly gloomy – but it released some of the tension that had been building in her head.

Jo had taken a seat at the table. 'It's an improvement,' she said as she munched on a slice of toast.

Allison turned. It really was a hideous room and now, with a fine layer of dust coating the table and dresser, it had taken on a rather macabre air. Or maybe it was simply that everything had changed.

She took the chair opposite Jo and picked up her mug. 'You're putting crumbs everywhere.'

'Like a few crumbs are going to ruin the ambiance of the place.'

'They're not going to improve it.'

Jo sniffed. 'Fine, have it your way.' She brushed the crumbs onto the plate. 'So what's the plan?'

Allison drained her mug and put it down. 'Make them pay for what they did to me.'

'Money?' Jo put the last of the toast in her mouth and chewed thoughtfully. 'I've a feeling a financial transaction isn't going to be sufficient revenge for you, am I right?'

What made Jo think she understood Allison? She didn't have a clue.

'It'll be a start.'

70

Allison straightened, the movement making her wince. 'I'll ring Portia now; she and Stuart have had enough time to consider what I'm planning.'

'You really think they're going to hand over money, just like that?' Jo sounded sceptical.

'You don't know them. Portia and Stuart always look immaculate and their house... you saw it; didn't you think it was a bit clinical? Everything of the best, of course, but nothing personal, no tat, no piles of stuff anywhere. Scarily tidy.'

Jo nodded. 'Yes, I thought it was like a show house, beautiful but not a home.'

'They like things perfect.' Allison gripped her mug tighter. 'Do you know why I think I wasn't raped?'

'I assume that wasn't their plan.'

'On no, you're wrong, I think it was.' She reached up with one hand to run her fingers over the bruise on her cheek. It was still tender. 'It's fading a bit now, but it would have been a lovely shade of purple within an hour of happening. I must have fought like hell. Portia said I struggled so much I fell down some steps, which is probably when I broke at least one rib too. I think the lecherous Stuart is fussy about the women he assaults. I think he likes them perfect... like his damn house. I think this' – she touched her cheek again, patting it gently – 'is what saved me.'

Jo frowned and raised a hand. 'I don't want to rain on your parade, but it seems you don't have a great case to blackmail them. Your bruises were caused by you falling down the stairs, not because they assaulted you. You weren't sexually assaulted. All they're guilty of is locking you in a room for a few days.' Her hand was still in the air; she reached across and grasped Allison's hand. 'I'm not dismissing what you went through, how frightened you must have been, but I'm not sure you have enough for what you're planning.'

'You think it would be better if I had been raped, do you?'

'That's not what I'm saying!'

It was Allison's turn to raise a hand, brushing off Jo's as she did so. 'You're wrong. I have enough... enough to turn their neat, perfect, orderly world on its head.' She picked up her mobile, now fully charged, and rang Portia's number. She half expected a message to say the number was no longer in use or for it to ring out, so when it was answered, almost immediately, she was stunned into silence by the bizarrely normal tone of Portia's voice as she said, 'Hello.'

She'd have known it was Allison on the phone. Would have known why she was ringing. Was it Portia's plan to bluff it out? 'I think you know why I'm ringing.'

'No, actually, I've absolutely no idea.' She sounded bored.

Allison regretted choosing to phone rather than appear on her doorstep with Jo in tow for safety. She'd have liked to have seen Portia's face, to see if she was as unconcerned as her voice seemed to indicate. 'You think drugging me and holding me prisoner is something I'm simply going to let pass without doing something?'

'You're imagining things, Allison. You came over to ours for lunch, drank way too much, and when I tried to help you to bed to sleep it off, you became quite violent. If I'm being honest, I was quite scared. You were so out of control, you fell down several steps. We did think about calling an ambulance but between us, Stuart and I managed to get you to bed. Honestly, we'd have been poor friends to have allowed you to go home until you were recovered. You were still rambling and out of it, so we had to lock the room for your safety.'

Had Portia and Stuart sat up all night planning what to say, what to do? Worryingly, it was almost believable. It looked as if their game plan was plausible deniability. Perhaps they believed if Allison was going to do anything, she'd have had the police on their doorstep by now. They were rich. Obviously, with their money came an arrogant belief in their ability to wriggle out of every situation.

It firmed Allison's resolve. 'Before I tell you what I want, you should know that a letter has been delivered to my solicitor with instructions it was to be opened should anything happened to me.' She shrugged when she saw Jo raise an eyebrow.

'You think you're so damn clever.' There was a vicious bite to Portia's words now, the façade of calm cracking. 'You've no proof of anything.'

Allison forced her laugh to sound amused. 'But then you don't know what I have, do you?' She wanted to believe Portia was gripping the phone in fear, wanted to believe that for once, for once in her damn life, Allison finally had the upper hand.

'You should have changed the mattress, Portia. Really, that was sloppy of you. Or maybe you didn't think I'd look underneath. Wouldn't see the stains, the blonde hairs that weren't mine. The man who rescued me took swabs and samples.' Allison almost smiled at the look of amazement on Jo's face and gave her a thumbs up. There was no comment from Portia. It was doubtful if she was giving Stuart a thumbs up. Hopefully she was looking at him in shock. 'My friend' – Allison was amazed how easily all the lies tumbled out – 'is convinced the DNA will be linked to Amy and to other women who have been reported missing.'

Still no comment. She pictured Portia, one hand gripped in Stuart's. They were probably holding the phone between their two heads, both listening, both quaking in fear in the face of her threats, waiting to hear how bad it was going to be.

It was time for the punchline. 'Here's what I want. Six million pounds, transferred into my bank account by one o'clock today. And please don't insult my intelligence by saying you can't get your hands on that sort of money because I know people like you and Stuart can do whatever they want. Six million. Once the payment has been confirmed, all the evidence against you will be destroyed and your passports will be returned.'

She smiled across the table at Jo. 'You have realised they're missing, I suppose?'

Allison held the phone out for Jo to hear when their answer, both voices in tandem, was a stream of colourful expletives.

When the tirade finished, she said quietly, 'You have till one o'clock. I'm sending you my bank details by messenger. If the money isn't there, I'll go to the police, give them the passports, show them the photographs I took of the room, show them my bruises. They'll have to wait for the DNA report, I assume, but I would imagine they'll proceed to arrest you based on my complaint. Me, a poor, grieving, vulnerable widow. Then I'll have my solicitor sue you for distress. I might not get six million, but I'll get quite a bit. And you'll be in prison. It's up to you, Portia.'

Allison hung up without waiting for answer.

'What happens if she calls your bluff?' Jo said. 'You have nothing.'

Allison was tapping her bank details into a message for Portia; she finished before she looked up to answer Jo's question. 'I wasn't lying about the mattress. I bet she's there now, turning it over, inspecting it, regretting she hadn't tossed it and bought a new one. She'll never risk calling my bluff. What she will do, I'll bet, is try to negotiate. So, how much are we willing to accept?'

71

Neither Jo nor Allison was surprised when the phone rang less than twenty minutes later. There was no preamble, Portia jumping straight in. 'We've had a look at our cash flow and here's the deal. One million. Take it or leave it.'

'One million? You're having a laugh. Okay, I'll leave it.' Allison hung up. She kept the phone in her hand, looking at it for a few seconds when it rang again almost immediately. Finally, she answered. 'Stop taking the piss, Portia.'

'Fine, fine, okay. Two million. It's all we have. The rest of our money is tied up in property.'

Allison could have stood firm, insisted Portia and Stuart get the money somehow. They probably could have taken out loans, sold or mortgaged their properties, but all that would have taken time. Two million, like a bird in the hand, was the better option. It was, too, the minimum she and Jo had said they'd accept.

'Two million is far less than I'd wanted but...'

'You'll take it?'

Allison allowed a loud sigh to drift down the line. 'Yes. As long as it's in my account by one. You have my bank details?'

'Yes. How do we know we can trust you?'

'As soon as the money has cleared, you'll have your passports returned and I promise the evidence we have will be destroyed. You'll have to trust me on that.'

'It doesn't look as if we have much choice.'

Portia sounded defeated. Allison remembered the friend she thought she'd had and felt a twinge of regret it had all been a fantasy. She'd have felt sad for that woman, for the friend who'd seemed so supportive. For this woman, who'd have facilitated her husband's depraved appetite, she had nothing but disgust. 'Just have the money in my account, Portia. One o'clock. No later.'

'Bitch!' It was Portia's final word.

'Nice,' Allison said. She put the phone down and sat back with a satisfied smile. 'Two million. One each. Not as good as the three you'd hoped for, but better than the nothing you currently have.'

'I won't start spending till it's in my bank account.' Jo sat back and folded her arms, a strange expression on her face. 'If the money comes, what are you planning to do?'

'As I promised, give them back their passports and destroy the evidence.'

'Evidence you don't have.'

'Makes that job even easier, then, doesn't it?' Allison got slowly to her feet. 'Looks like we're going to be sitting twiddling our thumbs till one; you want more coffee?' She waited till Jo nodded a yes before going into the kitchen to make coffee. A pot this time; it was going to be a long morning.

'What are you going to do?' Jo asked again when she returned with the coffee, two clean mugs and a jug of milk.

'Drink coffee and wait.'

Jo's face wasn't mobile enough to show irritation. A raised eyebrow seemed to be the most she could do to show emotion.

Allison relented. She had to keep reminding herself that Jo had saved her. She wished she wasn't beholden to her. A million would clear that. 'I don't know exactly.' She shrugged. 'I'd like to stop them from doing the same to any other woman.'

Jo reached for her coffee. 'I'm not helping you with anything violent, Allison; I told you, it's not my thing.'

'Nor mine, relax.'

Jo sputtered on the mouthful of coffee, sending an arc of fine spray across the table. 'Nor yours? Give me a break; you forget I saw you push your husband under a train!'

Allison had lifted her mug to her lips. At this, it fell from her hands, clattering onto the table and sending a wave of coffee washing over the wood.

'That's a hell of a lot worse than a few crumbs,' Jo said, moving out of the way of the coffee dripping from the edge of the table. 'You don't care so much now, of course; even with a million, you won't be able to afford to buy this house.'

Allison went into the kitchen. She returned with a towel and spread it across the mess of liquid, swiping it carelessly and dropping the towel onto the floor. The mug she'd dropped lay on its side, intact. She picked it up and refilled it before sitting and looking at Jo with a frown. 'What are you talking about?'

Jo waved a hand around the room. 'This. A million won't get you this house.'

'Of course not, I'm not stupid. That wasn't what I was asking you. What did you mean when you said you saw me pushing Peter under the train?'

Jo shrugged. 'Sounds self-explanatory to me.'

Allison got to her feet and walked to the window. She stared into the garden, wishing the sun was shining, that she could sit outside and let it warm her face. But it was raining. A heavy downpour, rain slanting to hit the window and send drops chasing one another down the pane. Almost hypnotic.

She waited till she was calm, till she could find the words before she turned. 'You have it wrong, Jo. I didn't kill Peter.'

72

Jo laughed uncertainly. It was a bit late for Allison to be pleading innocence, wasn't it? 'I saw you, remember. That's why you're willing to pay me a million quid.'

'No.' Allison shook her head. Returning to the table, she took her seat. 'You didn't see me do any such thing.'

Jo had spent so many years stalking this woman, she'd thought there were no surprises, nothing she didn't know. It seemed she was wrong. She thought back to that day on the platform. She had seen Allison near Peter, then she'd heard a scream, the ensuing kerfuffle hiding everything from sight for a few seconds. The next thing she remembered seeing, as clearly as she was seeing her now, was Allison hurrying away, her face pale. Jo had put one and one together and come up with a believable two. 'You were on the platform.'

'Yes.'

'You'd told Peter to make sure he left the office on time, knew when he'd be taking a train.'

'Yes.'

Jo struggled to keep her temper. 'But you didn't push him, is that what you're telling me? Seriously, you think I believe that, that the police would?'

'No.'

Jo wanted to scream at the woman sitting across the table from her, forearms resting on the coffee-damp table, the sleeves of her robe soaking up the residue left behind by the swipe of the towel. How could she sit there looking so calm and dare to insist she hadn't killed her husband? 'No? What the fuck is that supposed to mean?'

She had to wait for an answer. Allison got to her feet again and left the room. She could hear her opening and shutting cupboards in the kitchen. Food? In the middle of this. Shit, what kind of woman was she?

But when Allison returned, it was with a bottle of whisky and two glasses. She put both glasses down, opened the whisky and poured a generous amount into each glass.

Jo thought if she made a toast, any sort of toast, she'd throw the drink into her face. Luckily, Allison didn't. She sat, lifted the glass and downed half in one swallow. 'No,' she said then, finally answering Jo's question. 'The police might not believe I didn't kill him.' She met Jo's gaze and frowned. 'I'm not sure why you wouldn't believe me, though; you've no reason to doubt me, no reason to believe me capable of such a thing. Unfortunately, the same isn't true of the police. They would have every reason to believe me capable.' She rolled the glass between her fingers before lifting it and emptying the contents. She stared into the empty glass and spoke, her voice barely above a whisper. 'Many years ago, I did something bad. There's no need to tell you the details, suffice to say it would make the police look at me with suspicious eyes if they knew I'd been on the platform that day. They'd never believe the real reason.'

Something bad? Was that how she saw what she'd done? Jo

didn't like whisky. She drank it anyway, throwing the entire contents back, choking and spluttering. 'Fuck!'

Allison reached for the bottle and refilled both glasses. 'Probably not a good idea to get blotto. I promised I'd bring back the passports when the money comes through.'

'It's not like you're planning on keeping your word to those monsters, is it?'

Allison looked surprised. 'I'll give them their passports back as I promised. That much I'll do. You never heard me promising I wouldn't tell the police, did you?'

'Is that what you're going to do?' Jo frowned.

Instead of answering, Allison picked up her glass and swirled the whisky, sniffing the aroma appreciatively. She put it down without drinking. 'Did you know that someone is reported missing every ninety seconds in the UK?'

They seemed to be wandering a long way from Allison's declaration that she hadn't pushed her husband under the train. Jo looked at her watch. Only ten o'clock. It was going to be a long morning. She'd let Allison ramble on. For the moment. 'No, I didn't know that.'

'Every ninety seconds. That's a lot of missing people. How many of them, d'you think, end up being victims of people like Stuart? I could easily have ended up one of those statistics.'

Jo sipped her whisky, quickly developing a taste for it. She looked at Allison, who seemed lost in her thoughts. Didn't she realise she'd never have been one of those awful statistics? Didn't she understand there was nobody who cared enough to report her missing? Her employer would simply assume she'd decided not to return following her bereavement. The human resources team might make a phone call or send an email but when they received no reply they'd tut, dismiss her as being rude, send off her P45 and never think of her again. That woman in her office, that Hazel, would move into her office, and the ripple of Allison's existence would become calm.

It was only in considering Allison's sad life that Jo acknowledged her own. Both women were haunted in different ways by something that had happened all those years before.

How incredibly sad.

73

Allison was lost in her thoughts. When Jo shuffled restlessly on her chair, she blinked. 'Sorry, have I been ignoring you? I was thinking about the woman before me. I think Portia stuck to the truth for convenience, or perhaps because she isn't a very imaginative woman, and the woman's name was Amy. Portia said she'd gone to the US just before we met. That would be about six months ago. I can give the police those details. They could get DNA from the room. Maybe put some poor family out of their misery.'

'And the terrible twosome would go down for her kidnap and murder?'

'Yes.' She pointed to Jo's watch. 'What time is it?'

'Ten thirty.'

Allison sighed. 'A long time to wait, still.'

'You need to eat something,' Jo said. She got to her feet and vanished into the kitchen.

Eating wasn't high on the list of things Allison wanted to do but she supposed she should; it would help to keep her wits about her. She'd need them. She was still puzzled about Jo's belief she'd pushed Peter under the train. Jo didn't know anything about her;

why would she think she'd be capable of such an awful thing? Was there something about Allison, after all these years, that made people look at her with suspicious eyes?

Her eyes were gritty from tiredness. She shut them, allowed herself to relax, to believe that all would be right in her crazy world. At last. A million pounds. It wasn't, as Jo had kindly pointed out, enough to buy this house. Such a shame. She'd been happier here than she'd ever been, it would have been nice to have stayed. Memories came rushing back. Peter laughing. Spinning her around. Kissing her. *Lying to her.* Her eyes snapped open.

'Food.' Jo came bustling through. 'You need to eat. How are you supposed to make decisions without sustenance?'

A plate of cheese and toast was put in front of Allison, each slice neatly cut into triangles to tempt her. She picked up one, nibbled the edge. It was surprisingly good. Within minutes, she'd eaten the lot. It was impossible not to laugh at the look of satisfaction on Jo's face. 'Yes, okay, you were right, I was hungry and feel a lot better now.' She wasn't lying; the food, or maybe the feeling of being cared for, had gone a long way to restoring her equilibrium.

'Well, are you going to tell me about what did happen on that platform and why you were there if not to kill your husband?'

That Jo would have thought Allison capable of such a deed still weighed heavily on her. There must be some sign, some mark. She shook the idea away. 'I told you Peter was stupidly excited about marking three months of being married. He was disappointed when I wasn't equally as enthusiastic, so I decided to make it up to him. I'd nagged him about being home on time for once and knew he wouldn't let me down.' Allison's hand trembled as she brushed toast crumbs from her mouth. Peter had been so stupidly, childishly excited about going out for dinner that night despite them eating out two or three nights a week.

'This is special,' he'd said, kissing her on the cheek. 'Three months married. Why shouldn't we celebrate?'

Allison shook her head at the memory. 'I felt guilty I hadn't made more of an effort, so I decided to do something special for him that day and planned to arrive on the platform and shout *surprise*.' She met Jo's eyes and smiled. 'He did love that kind of thing.' Allison's smile faded slowly as the event played out in her head.

'The platform was more crowded than I'd expected. I saw him, of course, he is... was... taller than average and he always stood in the same place on the platform. We are, most of us, creatures of habit. I saw him, but it was difficult to push through the mass of people. The crowd was unusually grumpy, everyone with long faces, a strange uneasy feeling in the air.

'The police told me later that there'd been a protest outside, and the station had been shut while it was dealt with, so I suppose that was it, everyone caught up in their own annoyance about being delayed. I tried to make my way to Peter's side.' She stopped speaking and looked across to meet Jo's gaze. 'At first, I thought he had seen me and was playing a joke on me by dropping out of sight. He was like that, you know, always playing silly games. It wasn't till someone screamed that I realised what had happened. I knew he was gone. It was odd, you know; I didn't see what happened, but it was as if suddenly a light had gone out. I didn't need to get closer to see. Didn't want to, anyway. Didn't want to see him like that, all crushed and broken.'

When silence stretched, Jo spoke, 'So, you went home?'

The memory of that horrendous day rendered Allison incapable of speaking. She nodded instead, the one jerky movement all she could manage.

She had scurried from the station. Only then, as she ran, did she realise that despite his flaws and archaic ideas, she'd loved

Peter. Only then. Not the months before. She'd thought of him as her ticket to a better life. A wealthy husband with a good job and a fancy house in a good part of London. It was ironic that none of what she'd wanted existed, and the one thing she didn't expect to want was the biggest loss.

Jo sniffed. 'You really expect me to believe me his death was an accident?'

'I don't really care what you think,' Allison said wearily. 'And I don't know why you'd find it so hard to believe me anyway. You think because you've followed me on Facebook and Instagram that you know me. You know nothing.' What did it take to convince Jo that Allison was telling the truth? Why did she care? 'The police are looking at all the CCTV footage to see if they can see anything untoward, but they won't. It was simply an accident.'

'Right.' Jo shrugged and took a sip of her drink.

'I didn't know I loved him until then. I'd told him I did, of course, the way you do. Meaningless words.' Would she have loved him if she'd known the truth about him? She didn't know; she'd like to have been given the opportunity to find out. 'I never really believed I was capable of love—'

'Because of what you did as a child?'

74

Allison stared at her, surprised. She was sure she'd said, *Many years ago, I did something bad*, not that she'd been a child... or had she? She'd blacked out earlier; had she done so again, perhaps a side effect of whatever drugs Portia had given her? Perhaps in one of those weak moments, she'd revealed a secret she'd kept for so many years.

Did it matter? Did anything matter any more?

'I'm going to have a shower and get dressed,' she said, getting to her feet so abruptly she surprised Jo, who seemed to be lost in thoughts of her own. Maybe she had her own problems and that's why she was acting strangely... or should that be more strangely. Allison had to keep reminding herself how little she knew about Jo, and what she thought she did know probably wasn't true.

A long shower didn't make her feel any brighter. She needed sleep: hours, or even better, days of it. Days without stress.

She pulled on jeans and a blue cotton shirt, pushed her damp hair behind her ears and opened her bedroom door. The sound of the electric shower in the main bathroom told her she had a few minutes peace without Jo's eyes following her.

Jo. She was a mystery. How did she know so much about Allison? Some, she'd already guessed, was from foolish Facebook posts, but not her address, not her secret. Did Jo really know this? It wasn't something Allison could ask, was it? *Do you know my dirty little secret?*

She was being foolish. Again. She needed to survive the day. Get the money. Get rid of Jo. Then... what?

In her exhausted state, she couldn't think. Downstairs again, she sat in the living room, rested her head on the back of the sofa and shut her eyes. She was so tired. Of everything. Of a lifetime spent paying for a mistake. Of never ever getting what she wanted.

She kept her eyes shut when she heard footsteps on the stairway. Wished she could keep them shut till it was all over.

'It's almost time.'

Reluctantly, Allison opened her eyes.

'Two minutes to one,' Jo said, as if Allison hadn't understood.

'Yes.' She shuffled to the edge of the sofa and got to her feet. 'I'll get my mobile.'

They sat in the dining room, on the same seats, staring at Allison's mobile as the last two minutes ticked slowly away.

Jo tapped the table with the flat of her hand. 'It's time.'

Allison nodded. Would the money be there? For the first time, were things going to go her way? Not the future she'd wanted but perhaps a contented alternative. Perhaps. She sighed loudly, drawing Jo's eyes from the phone to her. 'We'll wait till a minute past.'

For sixty seconds, neither of them moved. Allison wasn't sure they even breathed. 'Right, here goes.' She picked up the phone, tapped a few keys and stared at the screen.

'Well?' Jo's voice was sharp with impatience. 'Come on, is it there?'

'Not two million, no.'

'The bitch! How much?'

'Four.'

Jo reached a hand to grab the phone, missing as Allison reared back. 'Four... four hundred, is that all the miserable cow thinks your threat is worth?'

'No.' Allison held out the phone, turning it to show Jo the screen. 'She's sent four million.'

75

Before Allison or Jo had time to react to the four million pounds, the doorbell rang, their heads swivelling in unison to stare through the open door to the hall as if, any moment, the bell ringer was going to materialise.

'Ignore it,' Jo said, turning back to stare at the phone. 'Did Portia make a mistake? Or maybe she thought you were asking for two mil each?'

Allison had already considered and quickly discounted that idea. She'd never referenced giving money to anyone else. And nobody made such a colossal mistake. Portia was a lot of things; stupid wasn't one of them. The repeated chime broke into her thoughts and drove her to her feet. 'Hang on, I'll get rid of whoever it is.'

She had no reason to be wary of opening the door. The most irritating of her visitors was, after all, already inside. It might be the police, of course, with an update on the investigation into Peter's death. Opening the door with little interest, she wasn't expecting to be surprised, certainly wasn't expecting to be shocked.

She was both. Her first instinct was to shut the door in the woman's face.

'Wait, please!'

Allison wasn't interested in doing anything Portia said. A woman who'd lied to her, drugged her, locked her in that awful room. A woman who'd have stood by while her husband assaulted her. It was no thanks to her that it hadn't happened.

That was thanks to a different odd woman.

Allison was surrounded by them.

'Please.'

The pathetic one word worked where the demand hadn't. Allison, last of the suckers, sighed and opened the door wide enough to speak to the woman on her doorstep.

Portia. But looking less Portia-like than usual. Gone were the dark, arched eyebrows. The waves of lustrous black hair had been replaced by a short, steel-grey bob. The pallor on her cheeks wasn't due to her usual pale foundation, her skin patchy with age marks and sun damage. She wore lipstick but it was badly applied and leaked over the edges, giving her a sad, clown-like appearance.

And, equally odd, there was a large suitcase at her feet.

Allison didn't care, didn't want to know, but still found herself asking, 'You going somewhere?'

Portia raised a hand to her hair, a surprised look flashing across her face as she smoothed a hand over her short bob. 'I keep forgetting,' she said, almost to herself. She met Allison's gaze then with a faint smile. 'As far away as I can get. I need my passport to do that.'

Allison frowned. This wasn't in the script. It was too fast. If she handed over the passports, maybe the money would vanish as quickly as it had appeared. She didn't seem to have been left with an option. Opening the door wider, she stood back. 'You'd better come in.'

Jo was in the hallway behind. 'I heard voices.' She looked on in horror as Portia, a heavy suitcase dragging her down on one side, stepped into the hallway. 'What the fuck is she doing here?'

'She's come for her passport. Seems they're going away.'

Portia put the case down. 'Not they... just me.'

When all three women started to speak together, Jo's voice raucous, Portia's a sad mewl, Allison's demanding, she held a hand up to silence them all. 'Let's sit, then we can talk calmly.' She led the way back to the dining room. 'Sit,' she said, waving Portia to a chair. Jo sat in the seat she'd been in earlier and folded her arms across her chest, Allison mirroring her stance on the other side of the table.

She held up a hand to stop anyone speaking. 'Before we begin, I want to check that the money is still there.' It was. She nodded in satisfaction and put the mobile down. 'Looks like you have some explaining to do.'

'Are you complaining?'

It was Jo who jumped in to reply. 'Stop fucking with us, you nasty piece of work.'

'Ah,' Portia said, a smile curling her clownish lips. 'Am I to understand you're the friend who helped to rescue Allison?'

'That's it. I got her safely from your perverted clutches.'

'You did well. I hope she knows how much she owes you. Once she was in that room, her fate was pretty much set in stone.'

The memory of waking in that bed, naked and helpless, sent a shiver through Allison. 'Like all the women before me? How many were there?'

Portia shrugged. 'A few.'

'A few!' Jo slammed both hands on the table and glared. 'You don't remember, do you? What a disgusting piece of work you are. Seriously, you're depraved.'

Allison was trying to take it in. The money. Portia being there alone. 'You're leaving Stuart?'

'Yes.'

'Why?'

'Why?' Portia laughed, a harsh, unmusical sound. 'I wouldn't mind a drop of that whisky.'

Jo raised her eyes to the ceiling. 'Throw her out, Allison. We have the money; we don't need this crap.'

Ignoring her, Allison stood, went into the kitchen and returned with another glass. She filled it and put it in front of Portia before filling the other glasses. 'Now, we'd like some answers, please.'

Portia took a mouthful of her drink before replying. 'Okay. You want to know why I'm leaving Stuart. That isn't the question you should be asking, though; you should be asking why I stayed so long.'

76

Portia lifted the glass to her lips again and took a mouthful of the whisky, swirling it around her mouth before swallowing with a gulp. 'I met Stuart when I was sixteen and he was ten years older, a sophisticated, incredibly handsome, charming man who swept me off my feet. I was pretty, maybe even beautiful, but gawky, unsophisticated, clueless when it came to fashion. I was thrilled when he bought me stylish clothes, fancy handbags, high stilettos I could barely walk in. He took me for a haircut, told the stylist how he wanted me to look, bought me make-up, sent me for classes so I learnt how to apply it the way he liked. Sent me for a termination when I got pregnant because he didn't want a baby to spoil my figure. Something went wrong, though; they couldn't stop the bleeding and I had to have a hysterectomy.'

Allison met Jo's gaze across the table, saw the acknowledgement in her eyes. A malleable, gauche sixteen-year-old, an older, obviously wealthy man... coercive control might be relatively new terminology, but it was a very old concept.

Portia took a couple of quick sips of her drink. 'Apart from that, it was good in the early days. Stuart had sold an innovative tech •

company to Microsoft just before I met him, and he invested wisely over the years so there was never a shortage of money.'

Allison, watching Jo shuffle restlessly in her seat as the silence lingered, decided to ask a question before she made some caustic remark. 'Good in the early days... when did it start going wrong?'

'When I got my first grey hair, I think.' Portia ran a hand over her hair. 'I was only twenty-eight and it was only one, maybe two, but it repelled him. He started looking at me more closely, commenting on the little wrinkles that had started to appear around my eyes, criticising me if I put on weight, then more criticism if I grew too gaunt. I spent more money at the hairdresser, the beautician, the gym, bought that awful wig, had some cosmetic surgery. I had no more success than King Canute did holding back the tide.'

'You would have been better off to have left him,' Jo said.

'Leave him?' She drained the glass, held it out for more. 'No, I couldn't do that. By that stage, I no longer knew who I was without him.'

Allison would have liked to have slid the bottle down the table like a character in a bad Western. She might even have tried if the table hadn't been sticky from the earlier spillage. Instead, she picked it up, swung it gently by the neck till Portia caught it.

'Thanks.' She filled her glass and took a sip. 'It was probably a year or so later when he started cheating on me, spending nights in hotels with women he picked up at parties or in bars. In those days, there was always someone willing to make him happy. He was very generous. It was only in the last few years when it became more difficult.' She took another sip of the whisky, then stared into the glass. 'Unfortunately, although he got older, his taste remained the same. He liked them young, their skin soft and smooth.'

Jo sneered. 'So you started pimping for him.'

'Pimping, such a crude word, but sadly it's also apt.'

'Wait a minute,' Allison said. 'If he liked them young, why the hell was he interested in me?' What was it about her that this depraved man desired? Had he seen a kindred spirit, someone as monstrous at heart as he was? She needed to know the answer, dreaded hearing the truth. She wasn't sure she could handle any more.

Portia didn't rush to answer the question. She fiddled with her glass, tracing a circle on the table with the base. Around and around, the irritating grinding noise setting Allison's teeth on edge. She saw Jo struggling to stay quiet. This time, Allison wasn't going to stop her exploding.

Before either of them did, however, Portia spoke, 'By now, there was little love lost between us. I stayed because I couldn't leave; he stayed because he enjoyed controlling me. He took pleasure in it. Making me do things I didn't want to do.' She raised her eyes from the glass, looking at Allison with a smile. 'I never risked making friends. People ask too many questions. You, on the other hand, didn't. You were pleasant, unassuming and always just a little bit sad. I was drawn to you.'

And Allison had fallen for her scheming lies. 'Next you'll be telling me you really wanted to be friends.'

'I don't expect you to believe me, but yes, that's what I hoped.' Portia started her circling again. Round and round. She stopped, lifted the glass to her lips and swallowed the contents, coughing as the whisky hit her throat. 'I made a mistake, though; I should never have left the gym at the same time as you. Stuart was waiting.'

Jo laughed. 'Come on, don't tell me he saw Allison and became enamoured with her. No offence to you, Al, you're a nice-looking woman, but you're no Helen of Troy.'

Since it was what Allison was thinking, she merely nodded. 'Go on, Portia, explain.'

'He saw us together. I think I was laughing at something you said.' She moved the glass.

'Stop doing that, for fuck's sake,' Jo said, finally snapping.

Portia took her fingers away as if they'd been burnt. 'Sorry.'

'Ignore Ms Grumpy Arse,' Allison said. 'Go on with your story.'

'There isn't much more to tell. Stuart liked to be in control of everything, including what made me happy. Seeing me with you, it threatened his authority, his power over me.'

'Or maybe he was afraid a friendship with a successful woman might give you ideas,' Jo suggested.

Portia stared at her. 'Maybe you're right; I hadn't thought of it that way.'

'But you were still willing to drug me, lock me in that prison; you'd have let him rape me.' Allison had to remind herself what this woman was capable of. Had to keep reminding herself, to stop the wave of sympathy that was rising at the years of abuse this woman had suffered at the hands of that man.

Portia, who was still staring at Jo, turned her head slowly. 'No, I wouldn't have, actually.'

77

It wasn't the answer Allison had expected and rendered her temporarily speechless. It didn't have the same effect on Jo, who gave a cynical laugh before saying caustically, 'Yeah, right, easy to say that now, isn't it?'

Ignoring her, Portia kept her eyes on Allison. 'It's what I'd done before. Kept the woman subdued until she was forced to agree to the inevitable. Some did quicker than others, sex with Stuart being seen as preferable to being starved. When they realised he simply wanted them to lie there and accept his... attentions... they became more resigned.' She picked up her glass, realised it was empty and put it down again. 'Every time I conspired to drag another woman home, a little part of me died.'

Allison saw Jo raise her eyes to the ceiling and prayed she'd keep her mouth shut.

Portia kept her eyes on the glass she still held between her fingers. 'You did fall down several steps on the stairway, you know.' Lifting her eyes, she waved her index finger at Allison's face. 'It's where you got that and the rest of your bruises. I did say, but I wasn't sure you believed me.'

'I don't remember anything between drinking the spiked Prosecco and waking in that bed, covered in bruises and naked.'

'Naked, yes.' Portia sighed. 'It was Stuart's idea. He wanted to see your body and believed it heightened vulnerability and fear.'

Allison remembered the sense of dread, the panic. 'It worked.'

'I bet he had a good look, eh? A naked, helpless body. One he was going to get the opportunity to fuck at some point.' Jo shook her head. 'You make me sick.'

Allison held a hand up to stop Jo's rant. There was a memory haunting her; she needed to know if it was true or one of those hideous nightmares. 'He ran his hands over me, didn't he?'

'Yes.' Portia slid a hand across the table towards her. 'I wouldn't have let him do more, I swear.'

Allison laughed. 'Pardon me if I don't believe a word from your mouth.' She waited for Portia to say something more and when she didn't, she sneered. 'You expect me to believe you weren't going to help Stuart...' She couldn't bring herself to say the word.

'When you tripped on the stairway and landed in a heap on the landing, you lay there stunned, without moving. I thought, at first, you'd broken your neck or something. But then' – she looked at Allison with a strange smile, half admiration, half curiosity – 'you lifted your face, looked at me and said, *The wrong we do to others, it never stops haunting us.*'

Allison's laugh was forced. 'Really, I was battered and drugged, yet I managed to come out with some pseudo-profound crap.'

Portia shook her head. 'You said it so quietly, with such fervour, I know it meant something to you. After I left you in that room, the words kept swirling in my head. All the wrong I'd done to others suddenly overwhelmed me as it had never done before. I suppose you could call it my awakening.'

'Your awakening?' Jo shook her head as if unable to believe what she was hearing. 'You're seriously expecting us to believe that a few words said by a drugged woman made you re-examine your life choices?'

'When you put it like that, it does seem pretty unbelievable, yet it's what happened.' Portia shrugged. 'I don't know why. Maybe the self-hatred had been there all along, festering, just waiting for the scab to come off for it all to ooze out. I'm simply trying to explain why I had a change of heart.' She pointed to Allison's bruised face again. 'Stuart hates any kind of disfigurement. He was horrified when he saw the bruises. Every day, he'd ask me if they'd faded, and I'd lie, tell him they'd got worse, that you were a mess. When I told him you had broken ribs, he was disgusted.'

'Then you came home to find me gone,' Allison said, anxious to get Portia's tale finished. 'You must have been relieved.'

Portia reached for the whisky bottle and refilled her glass. 'Yes. Relieved and surprised. Stuart was incandescent with rage.' She got to her feet and, without a word, removed the cardigan she was wearing. Underneath, the sleeveless blouse exposed her arms. There was a multitude of bruises along their length. She pulled the bottom of the blouse up to show her belly and, with a slow turn, her back. There was hardly an inch that wasn't covered in various shades of purple and green. 'Usually, he's careful not to hurt me where bruises can be seen,' she said, dropping the blouse and reaching for her cardigan. 'I won't be able to go to the gym for a while.'

Allison felt that dart of sympathy again and fought against it. 'At least you've the sense to leave him this time; you should have done it years ago.' She knew the words were foolish. There had been enough information regarding domestic abuse for her to know it was never as simple as that, knew from reading about it, the horrors of coercive control. It had only been recognised as a crime recently but it had been going on forever.

But Allison had her own problems; she'd no room for Portia's. 'I'm surprised Stuart agreed to give us any money.'

'He didn't.' Portia's face tightened in satisfaction. 'He doesn't know a thing about it.'

Both Allison and Jo jerked back in their seats at this, each of them with their mouths open, both unusually lost for words.

It was left to Portia to fill the silence. 'Stuart always underestimated me. He thought his control was complete and I suppose it was, but I'd found ways, many years ago, to take a little back.'

'You squirrelled away some money?' Jo guessed.

'No, he'd have noticed.' Portia rested both hands on the table and mimed typing, her fingers tapping out a dull thud. 'He thought I spent my days at the gym or reading, but what he didn't know, what he never considered, was that I spent so much time on his office computer.' She sneered unpleasantly. 'He was so arrogant, so certain I was under his thumb, he used a password a child would have guessed. I spent hours looking through his files. It seems I have a natural affinity for numbers and before long I knew exactly where he hid every penny.' She met Allison's surprised gaze. 'I could have been an accountant had my life turned out differently.'

Jo waved a hand to get Portia's attention. 'So what did you do?'

'Do?' Portia lifted her glass and took a miniscule sip. 'I didn't do anything. Simply enjoyed knowing everything. Each time, when I'd finished, I deleted my browser search so he never knew.'

'But today,' Allison said, guessing she was on the right track, 'you were able to transfer the money to me.'

'That's it.'

Jo frowned. 'He doesn't know you've paid us off?'

Portia shook her head, a smile lurking. 'I transferred four million to you and two million to an account he doesn't know I have.'

Allison wasn't sure she could believe her. It couldn't be that simple, could it? 'Won't he simply stop it when he finds out?'

'Don't be silly. He's never going to find out.'

There was something in the way Portia said this, something about the look in her eyes that told Allison the woman's certainty wasn't based on mere wishful thinking. Did she want to know why Stuart was never going to find out? Sometimes it was better not to know the answer to everything. Looking across the table, she saw the same decision on Jo's face and nodded.

Allison looked back to Portia. 'Where are you going to go?'

'Paris first. After that, maybe Canada or New Zealand. I'm not quite sure.' She picked up the glass and drained the contents. 'I'm a bit scared of the freedom, to be honest.'

'It'll take some getting used to, I suppose.'

Portia got to her feet. 'I wish you well, Allison. I hope you manage to put those demons behind you some day.'

'As you will?'

'As I'll try to.'

'Wait a minute!' Jo glared. 'Is that it? We're supposed to simply let you and Stuart away with kidnapping, raping and murdering all those women?'

The back of the chair creaked in protest when Portia collapsed heavily onto the seat. 'What? Murder! Are you crazy? We never murdered anyone!'

Allison held a hand up to stop Jo speaking again. 'Amy, and the women before her. What happened to them?'

Portia looked genuinely puzzled. 'I told you Amy went to the US, about six months ago.' She looked from Jo to Allison in disbelief. 'You thought we killed them?' She sighed. 'I suppose I can understand, but I swear we didn't. When Stuart grew tired of them... and this happened quicker than you might expect, sometimes in only a matter of weeks... they were given a one-way ticket to wherever they wanted to go, and fifty thousand in cash.'

'No way,' Jo said. 'What was to stop them coming back and blackmailing you?'

'Because they didn't know where they'd been held, didn't know who we were. These were women on the edge of society. Not hardened drug addicts but women on that slippery slope. I'd take them for coffee and...'

'Drugged them.' Allison shook her head. So incredibly easy. Who'd have suspected Portia?

'Yes, and again before they left. They'd wake up confused and disorientated in the airport with a suitcase beside them and a letter explaining what to do. I'd watch from a distance, make sure they were safe, and when they were on their feet, I'd leave.'

'That's the craziest thing I've ever heard,' Jo said quietly.

Portia got to her feet again. 'Well, it's over now. Without me, Stuart won't be able to continue. He might try, but no woman is going to trust him.' She laughed at the expression on their faces. 'What? You thought I'd killed him? No, when I said he was never going to find out about the six million I took from his accounts, I meant just that. I've tied his finances up in such knots, it's going to take his accountants months to figure out what happened, if they ever do.' She smiled. 'Yes, I'm that bloody good. What a talent I wasted on him.' She took a step closer to Allison, reached out and laid a hand against her cheek. 'You never liked him, did you? You should trust your instincts more often.'

In the hallway, she pulled on her coat, put her hand in the pocket and pulled out her mobile phone. 'I'll ring for a taxi, if you don't mind. It shouldn't be long.' She ordered one, then hung up. 'Five minutes. Time to get my passport back and say goodbye.'

Goodbye! Allison shook her head. She was sure there was a lot more she should be saying than this one word... the thanks for saving her from Stuart's advances despite being responsible for her being there in the first place, the gratitude for the money, which would be enough to give her a more than comfortable future... enough money to get rid of Jo.

In the end, once Jo had handed over the passport, they stood in awkward silence until the toot of a horn alerted them to the taxi outside. Without another word, Portia took her suitcase and left.

Allison and Jo stood in the doorway and watched till the taxi pulled out and vanished down the street. Nobody raised a hand in farewell.

Jo left Allison standing in the doorway and went back to the dining room to collect the whisky bottle and the glasses. Back in the more comfortable living room, she put them on the coffee table and sank onto the sofa with a sigh. What a crazy day it had been. So far, she'd not been able to think about the money. She did now. Two million quid. Assuming Allison wasn't going to do a snaky slide out of their agreement.

Reaching for the bottle, she poured whisky into a glass and picked it up. No more cheap supermarket beer for her. She sipped, slouched down and rested her head against a cushion behind. Two million, and all she could think of buying was alcohol. How pathetic. She supposed she'd think of something better. An apartment, perhaps. Maybe in Portugal. She'd heard it was nice. She'd have to get a passport.

Allison was still at the door. Jo looked up from her whisky and wondered what she was thinking. Perhaps she was trying to calculate if she could afford, after all, to buy this house. It needed a lot of work so she might be able to do a deal for two million, but she'd have no money to do the renovations that were desperately needed. Of course, with four million, she'd have no problem. All she needed to do was to figure out how to keep it all.

Oddly, Jo felt no fear. Or was it that she didn't really care? Two million. She didn't really care about that either. So many years waiting for this opportunity. Allison was all hers now that Portia had left. It was time to finish what she'd started. Wasn't it? Or did she no longer care about that either?

Jo took another sip of the whisky. What was that expression... *in vino veritas...* was it equally appropriate to whisky? Because she was seeing the truth now. Or maybe she'd known it all along but had never faced it. She'd not been searching for Allison for revenge, hadn't been stalking her, waiting for her opportunity. Or maybe that was part of it, but it wasn't all. Nothing was ever that simple.

When Allison appeared in the living-room doorway, Jo emptied her glass in two swift gulps.

'I'm going to make some tea,' Allison said. 'Would you like a cup?'

'Sure, why not, I think the whisky is making me maudlin.'

'It can have that effect.'

Perhaps Jo should have waited for the tea but when time passed and it hadn't appeared, she reached for the bottle and poured another whisky. This time it was swallowed in one mouthful.

Allison returned moments later, a mug in each hand. She handed one to Jo before taking a seat opposite. 'What did you make of that?'

That? 'Do you mean Portia being abused by Stuart for years? Her not being such a pushover after all? That we really have four million quid, or that they never killed any of those women?'

'All of the above.'

'I think the longer I live, the more it is that nothing surprises me.' Jo lifted the mug to her lips, took a sip and lowered it. 'You aren't going to try to cheat me out of the two million, are you?' It was a silly question; if Allison were, she was hardly likely to admit it. Almost as silly as asking her if she'd put something dodgy in the tea.

Instead of answering, Allison sat back. 'How did you know my address here? I know I never told you.'

Jo nodded. Perhaps this was a day for revelations. Portia, now Jo.

'I followed you. I have been doing, on and off for years.' She thought Allison would look surprised, even shocked, but her expression didn't change.

'You know about me. About what I've done.' It wasn't a question.

'Yes.'

'How?'

She watched Allison as she tried to figure out how Jo could have known something that happened twenty years before. Something so few people knew. Strangely, now that it was time for her revelation, she was reluctant to release it. What would she do without this obsession? Replace it with money?

Perhaps, after all, she'd better drink this tea, hope it was poisoned, and die with her story untold. Wouldn't it be better? She'd escape a world that had never been good to her; Allison would get the life she appeared to want.

Jo saw something on Allison's face as she lifted the mug... a certain anticipation. Maybe even longing. *The tea.* Jo held the mug to her mouth and tilted it, swallowing almost convulsively as the liquid hit her throat, swallowed and swallowed until there was nothing left.

Nothing left. What a waste her life had been. It was better this way. She felt her eyelids grow heavy, a lassitude career along her veins. No pain. She was glad of that.

And so very, very relieved it was all over.

79

It had been a hell of a day. Allison wanted to go to her bedroom, shut the door behind her, and climb under the duvet to sleep for days. Instead, she sat staring at the woman opposite, whose dreadfully stretched face seemed incapable of portraying emotion but whose eyes were suddenly so terribly sad.

Allison didn't really want an answer to the question she'd asked, didn't want to know how this odd woman knew so much about her. She simply wanted her to finish the tea and be gone.

Her own tea was sitting untouched. With a sigh, she picked it up and sat back, hoping that seeing her drink it would spur Jo on to do the same. It seemed to work. Oddly, though, instead of drinking it slowly as she was doing, Jo emptied the mug in a series of violent swallows that had Allison widen her eyes in surprise. She met Jo's sad ones and for almost a minute neither stirred.

Allison wasn't sure either blinked, then, magically, she saw Jo's eyelids flutter, close for a nanosecond, snap open, then close again and stay shut.

Peace at last. Allison put her barely touched tea on the table, shuffled down in her seat and rested her head back. Within minutes, she was asleep.

* * *

Fear kept Allison's eyes shut when she woke. It had been that way for as long as she could remember. There were monsters in the world. She was one of them. Hiding in plain sight. Like so many other monsters. Like Stuart and Portia.

Being a monster, sadly, didn't take away the fear. In fact, it made it worse to know there really were monsters living among us, to know they looked like everyone else, that you simply couldn't tell... until they pounced.

She opened her eyes. The living room was in semi-darkness, lit only by the street lights that made strange shadows on the pale walls. Perhaps she should simply stay there, shut her eyes, try to sleep again. She was still so tired. Tomorrow would be time enough to face everything. She'd make an appointment with the solicitor, see if she could come to some arrangement with the RSPCA about money that would allow her to keep the house. Four million. She could do so much with that amount of money.

But tomorrow was a long way away. She'd still not finished with today. Getting to her feet, she crossed to Jo.

Allison had always been curious about her hair and, reaching down, she rubbed a strand between her fingers. *Real hair.* She pulled slightly, nodding when she saw movement over Jo's scalp. Real hair, but it was a wig. She stood looking down at her. Maybe it would be better to know the answers. Safer, perhaps.

'Wake up,' she said, shaking Jo's arm gently, a little more strenuously when there was no answer. 'Come on, you can't sleep there all night.'

'What?' Jo's eyes opened and stared directly into Allison's. 'You didn't poison me?'

'Poison you?' Allison reared back as if she'd been punched. 'Why would you say such a thing? Bloody hell, why would you even think such a thing?'

'Two million seemed a good motive to me.' Jo stretched. 'And I did go out like a light when I drank the tea you made me.'

'I think you'll find it was a surfeit of whisky that knocked you out. How many did you have? It's a lot stronger than that cheap beer you normally drink.' Allison sat on the sofa beside her. 'You really thought I was going to kill you?'

'Let's say it crossed my mind.'

'And you thought I'd pushed Peter under the train.'

'Yes.'

There was only one reason someone would believe such a thing of Allison, only one reason they'd go on thinking it. She'd asked Jo earlier; she asked her again. This time, she'd wait for an answer. 'You know what I did, don't you?'

'Yes, I do.'

80

Jo was so sure Allison had poisoned her... or had that been wishful thinking? Was she so tired of it all that death was preferable and she too damn cowardly to do the job herself? Had Allison really no idea? There was puzzlement in her eyes, in her furrowed forehead. Or maybe she was a good actress.

It was time. All these years waiting for this one moment. What a fucking anti-climax. She reached a hand up for her wig and tugged. It came away with little trouble and she tossed it onto the coffee table. She ran a hand over her head, lingering on the scars, scratching at a patch of irritated skin. 'I have some hair at the back of my head' – she turned to show the fine wisps – 'but it never grew again over the scars.'

'The wig is very good. You'd never know.'

'Yes, I think so too. It can be a bit hot, though. When I'm at home I don't bother with it.' Jo was tempted to keep this mundane conversation going. Tell Allison about the hideous wigs she'd had when she was younger. The teasing she'd got from schoolmates. The number of times someone, boys and girls, pulled it off and ran away with it, leaving her crouching down with her arms over her head, tears spilling down her cheeks until someone, usually a teacher, sometimes a guilty classmate, returned it to her. Then, she'd brush dust from the wig, or if it had been tossed into a puddle, she'd dry it with the end of her shirt before pulling it back on. She could have told sad stories for hours. Instead, she ran a finger down the scars on either side of her face.

'These scars used to be more visible. I had cosmetic surgery years ago to pull them further back so they could be hidden under the wig. It did the trick even if it means I look as if I've been trapped in a wind tunnel.' She wondered if Allison would lie, if she'd say *No, they did a great job* or if she'd agree her face was a mess. When she did neither, just sat there with that stupefied expression, Jo wanted to reach over and slap her to drag some reaction from her.

'When I first saw you, years ago, with your creamy, blemish-free, gorgeous skin, I hated you.'

This finally drew a reaction. Allison lifted a hand and smoothed fingers over her bruised cheek. 'I've always been lucky. My mother had beautiful skin; I guess I inherited it from her.'

Jo reached out and grabbed Allison's hand and, before she could pull it away, dragged it to her cheek. 'Feel my skin. Do you think I inherited this? Do you think I wasn't born with beautiful, smooth, silky skin like you?'

'Stop it!' Allison wrenched her hand away and got to her feet. 'Yes, all right, you do look like you got caught in a bloody wind tunnel and' – she tilted her head towards where the wig sat like a sleeping cat – 'that doesn't look remotely like real hair.'

Cruelty. Jo was used to it. It shouldn't bother her, shouldn't bring quick tears and a lump to her throat. Ignoring the woman who stood with her chest heaving as if searching for control, she reached for her wig, pulled it on and settled the strands around her face, patting it down until she was happy with it. Happy with it... she had really thought it looked okay, that she fitted in. Now she realised she'd been fooling herself for years.

'I'm sorry.'

Jo used one of the cushions from the sofa to wipe her eyes before looking up to where Allison hovered. 'People think saying sorry makes everything okay. It rarely does, you know.'

'How about I make it up to you?'

'The two million you're going to give me will help, don't worry.'

'No, I wasn't thinking about that.'

Jo was startled when Allison sat, reached out and touched her face. 'Better make-up would help.' She tugged at the wig. 'And there are much better wigs than this, honestly. We could go shopping for one together.'

Jo slapped the hand away with an involuntary cry of pain as the realisation hit her. This! This was what she'd been searching for! She pushed up from the seat, crossed the room to the window and clung to the sill, afraid to let go, afraid she'd turn and run back to Allison.

Fall at her feet and beg her to remember.

81

Allison didn't know what to make of Jo. Irritating, odd and annoying. But the woman had saved her. True, it looked as if Portia had had a change of heart... but Stuart may have persuaded her to change it back again. It had been Jo who'd got her out of the prison she'd been locked in. For that, Allison was willing to forgive her a lot, but it would be a hell of a lot easier if the stupid woman would stop thinking she'd tried to poison her and killed Peter.

It would also be a hell of a lot easier if Jo would answer her damn question. Third time lucky. 'How did you find out about me?'

It was a few seconds before Jo turned from the window with her usual unreadable expression.

'I've always known.' She reached up and straightened her wig. 'I suppose it's not surprising you don't recognise me. 1990 was a long time ago.'

1990. A year engraved in Allison's mind. The year she'd planned for her life to change... it had, but not the way she'd planned. It was the year the monster had escaped.

* * *

She'd planned it for months. Hours in her local library with encyclopaedias and research books, explaining to the staff that she was looking for information for a school project. They'd looked at her with indulgent smiles and told her to help herself. Not once did they ever investigate what the nine-year-old was reading. Just as well as no school project would have involved the best way to kill someone using whatever was available. She was searching for a simple, painless way for her parents to die, to make way for the adoptive parents who would adore her.

It was, in the end, her parents themselves who gave her the idea.

'I was so cold last night,' her mother complained to her father one morning. 'We should get a heater for our bedroom.' Their bedroom. Not Allison's room or those of her siblings.

'There's that old kerosene heater we used to use when we went camping. It's out in the garage rusting away; why don't you bring that in?'

Allison remembered her mother laughing and thumping her father's arm. 'Trying to kill me, are you? Don't be daft!'

That afternoon in the library, Allison read everything she could find on kerosene heaters. She took notes, covering page after page in her copybook with her neat writing, checking and double-checking that she had it right. When she returned home, she dropped her schoolbag on the floor and headed out to the garage.

A graveyard for redundant and broken household items... the electric mixer her mother had used once and decided she hated; a TV with a smashed screen; an old chair with three legs. Allison had to rummage through mountains of rubbish, brushing aside cobwebs and their leggy occupants with a grimace, focused and determined to find the heater.

And there it was, hidden beneath a moth-eaten rug. She picked it up and examined it. It looked similar to ones she'd seen in the library books.

Putting it on the floor, she tried the ignition. It was very old; it probably wouldn't work. But it did, first time. She looked at the flame with a growing smile, then switched it off. It was perfect.

There was no point in wasting time. With a look outside to make sure her mother was out of sight, she took the heater into the house and hurried up to her bedroom. It fitted neatly inside her small wardrobe.

Her plan was simple. Both her parents were heavy sleepers. Allison would stay awake, wait till an hour after they went to bed, then she'd turn the heater on, put it in their bedroom, and shut the door. A rolled-up towel at the bottom of the door would make sure all the carbon monoxide given off by the heater would stay inside.

In the morning, she'd take the towel away. Her parents would have died peacefully in their sleep. And Allison and her siblings would get the childhood they deserved.

Allison shook the thoughts away. They didn't go far, they never did, always ready to ooze out to haunt her when she least expected it, and every single time she thought she was putting her past firmly behind her.

Jo leaned back against the windowsill and folded her arms. 'You still have no idea who I am, do you?'

She could be any one of so many people Allison had dealt with at the time. Police constables, social workers, doctors, health professionals whose function she never knew.

'No.' She shrugged. 'There were so many people. After a while, I stopped trying to remember who was who.' It was a lie. Afterwards, when it was over and the monster had retreated, she'd been catatonic for weeks. The following years were spent in a succession of institutions before eventually she was housed in a series of foster homes that never, ever, came close to the dream she'd longed for.

She was weary of games. 'Who are you?'

Jo crossed and took her seat on the sofa beside Allison. 'Before the scars changed me, my name was Beth.'

82

Beth? Allison stared at Jo blankly. The years slipped away and Allison was pulled back to 1990, staring across the smoky landing to where her younger sister stood in the doorway, calling for her. Beth? What Jo was inferring was impossible. Beth was dead.

'You're thinking I'm too old, aren't you?' Jo huffed a laugh. 'You have to make allowances for the burns, for the years of pain, the agonising, searing anguish of skin grafts, the rounds of plastic surgery. I'm twenty-seven.'

'It's a lie.' Allison's face creased in anger. 'Beth's dead. I looked for her when I was old enough. They said she'd been adopted by a family who moved to Canada. They hadn't followed up on her once she'd left their jurisdiction, but they did have contact details and I rang...'

* * *

Allison remembered the call. She'd been nineteen, had been begging the social workers for years to allow her to contact her sister and they'd finally agreed.

She'd held her breath as the phone rang and when it was answered, by a woman with a surprisingly strong Yorkshire accent, she asked to speak to Beth.

'Who's speaking, please?'

'It's Allison.' The two words were released on a breath. 'Her sister.' She'd expected a word of surprise; instead, there was a deadly silence.

'I'm terribly sorry. I thought you'd have been told. Beth passed away about a year ago. A car accident. It was instant.'

* * *

Jo reached into her pocket and pulled out a photograph. 'ABC,' she said, putting it into Allison's unresisting fingers. 'I'll never understand why our mother thought it was amusing.'

Allison, Beth and Cassie. It was a worn photo, the faces of the three children softened out of focus by the years. But Allison would have recognised it anywhere.

'They lied to me.' The thought had never occurred to her. Why would it have done?

'I asked them to,' Jo admitted. 'I knew you'd come looking for me when you finally got out of whatever institute you finished up in. I didn't want to speak to you on your terms; I wanted to speak to you on mine.' She ran a finger over her face. 'Perhaps I'd hoped to look more normal by the time we met. It hasn't worked out that way, though, has it?'

Allison didn't want to look up from the photograph, didn't want to see what she'd done to the pretty child who'd sat cross-legged beside her on the back lawn of their house.

'It was taken late that summer, only three or four months before you burnt the house down.'

* * *

It wasn't me. It was the monster. My plan had been simple, but it had gone wrong. It had started all right. I'd pinched myself to keep awake as the house quietened around me. I waited till a minute past midnight. A new day for my new life. Then I took the kerosene heater out, turned it on and carried it carefully from my room. I had to put it down to open my parents' bedroom door, only a little, afraid they'd wake and see me, and my plan would have been destroyed. I was only nine, so perhaps my apprehension can be understood. But I hadn't taken it into account. Nor the fear-slippery hands that picked up the heater and passed it through the gap to put it down on their carpeted floor... the cheap carpet worn and rucked.

I shut the door quickly, so I didn't see the heater topple over, and when I came back with the rolled-up towel seconds later to lay it at the base of the door, I thought it was supposed to smell that way.

I was back in my bed within seconds, cuddling under my duvet, grinning at my success. It was several minutes before I heard the first crackle. I sat up, confused, and switched on the light. Wisps of smoke curling under my door startled me into clambering from my bed, frightened of what was happening the other side. I opened the door, my eyes widening to see the landing thick with smoke and a bright orange flame piercing the darkness. There wasn't supposed to be fire. Just carbon monoxide.

Something had gone terribly wrong.

I didn't know what to do. I was nine: old enough to have planned a crime, not old enough to know what to do when it all fell apart. I shut the door, got back into bed and pulled the duvet over my head, hoping it was all a dream. My silly plan. The crazy idea to get rid of my parents and replace them with more loving, caring ones. The unbelievably crazy idea to murder them.

When I started to cough, I risked peeking from under the covers.

Smoke swirled, hiding the edges of the room, making me cough even more and my eyes smart. I could hear louder crackles and now voices, shrill and loud. Impossible to know if they were coming from outside or inside.

I slipped from the bed. The air was clearer near the floor so I crawled to the door, sneaked a hand up for the handle and pulled it down. Moving backwards, I took the door with me. The crackling, the voices, all louder now, the voices shrill, filled with terror, pain, despair.

Fear kept me there, my eyes stinging. I wondered about trying for the stairway, but flames had sneaked along the cheap nylon carpet. I'd read about walking on hot flames. Could I do the same? Before I could decide, a door opened the other side of the landing and I saw my sister Beth's tear-stained, terrified face.

'Allison.' She called to me, her voice strangely distorted by the smoke. 'What should I do? I'm scared.'

I glanced towards my parents' door. Had they woken to find their room in flames? Were they crawling towards the door, hoping to get out to rescue their children? Or had they already succumbed to the smoke. I stared at their door, willing it to open, for them to come through, take control, save us. I promised I'd be a better daughter in future if they did, promised I'd never want to change them.

But no matter how many promises I made in the thick, choking, eye-watering smoke, their door stayed resolutely shut.

'Allison?'

I should have answered Beth. Should have tried to get to her but from behind me I heard a shout and, looking behind, I saw a light at my bedroom window and without another thought for my younger sisters, I turned around, shut the door, and rushed to be rescued.

* * *

'It was an accident.' How pathetic that sounded. It had been. Of course it had. Her plan hadn't been to burn the house down; she'd never intended to kill Cassie and injure Beth.

'An accident! I saw you that day, sneaking into the house with the heater. The same heater they found in our parents' bedroom. The one they blamed for it all.' Jo shuffled in her seat, crossing one chubby leg over the other. 'Between shock and the agony of my hideous burns, I was unable to answer questions for weeks, poor Cassie died in the fire, and you, well, you escaped too, didn't you? Catatonic.' She sniffed dismissively. 'By the time I was able to speak, they'd closed the investigation and never bothered me again.'

'They didn't need to,' Allison said. 'They found my old, scuffed leather schoolbag and all my notes about kerosene lamps and carbon monoxide poisoning. They knew it was me but, as you say, I escaped too, in a way.' She'd been under the age of criminal responsibility at the time so couldn't be tried for murder. It didn't matter; she spent the next several years in one institute after the other. She hadn't needed to be locked away to feel imprisoned... by the institutes, her memories, the name-calling, the hideous dreams of stinking smoke and wretched screams, the absolute failure to achieve the life she'd desperately searched for.

Allison looked at the photograph she held. The life she'd ended, the one she'd changed forever. 'I'd thought if I got rid of our parents, we would get better ones. Like Monica.' She looked up and met Jo's gaze. 'Remember her? The adopted girl in my class whose mother used to wait at the gate for her every day.' She wasn't surprised when Jo shook her head. It had been Allison's obsession. 'I was doing it for all of us. We'd have been happier.'

'I was happy, Allison. You took that away.' Jo's eyes filled, overflowed, tears trickling down her taut skin. 'I've never managed to find it again. My foster parents were kind, but to them I was a worthy cause to make them feel good about themselves, not a person to be loved.'

Allison heard the pain in the words. She'd done this too. Caused such pain. 'I'm sorry. It wasn't supposed to be like that. I'm a monster.'

Jo used the cushion again to wipe away the tears before tossing it aside. 'No, you're not. You were a foolish child. All these years, I thought I was searching for you to get revenge.' Her lips were perpetually tilted in a smile but now the smile reached her eyes. 'But when you offered to take me shopping, I realised this is what I had been searching for. My sister.'

Allison was stunned into silence. Didn't Jo remember? Allison had left her there, had shut the door on her entreaties and made her escape. Perhaps Jo had been spared that memory. Allison wished she had. She forced her lips into a smile. 'We've a lot of years to make up for but first, we need something to eat. Let me see what I can rustle up.'

83

Allison stood in the kitchen and tried to settle her thoughts. She *was* a monster. The catcalling from her younger years rang in her head. *Monster, monster, mon-ster.* Jo – Allison didn't know if she'd ever be able to call her Beth – didn't know what her sister was capable of. Her sister... perhaps if Allison had known about her earlier, things might have turned out differently. Perhaps. But in as much as leopards couldn't change their spots, she wasn't sure a monster could stop being monstrous.

Listlessly, she opened a cupboard and rummaged inside, shut it, opened the next, did the same. All she found, for her efforts, was pasta and a jar of sauce. There was Parmesan cheese in the fridge. It would have to suffice.

With the pasta simmering, she opened the jar, poured it into a glass jug and covered it in cling film to put into the microwave once the pasta was ready. She went back to the living room and stood in the doorway. Jo was sitting there staring into space, her hideous wig slightly askew. A tear had trickled down the taut skin of her cheek and had dried, leaving a slug-like shimmer in its wake.

She'd always been one to cry easily... a sharp word, a sad story, the day Allison had broken her favourite doll. Sometimes, she remembered with a twinge of regret, she'd set out to make the tears roll, fascinated even then by an ability she herself lacked.

Their differences were more apparent now, she taking her stature from their tall, thin father, Jo, obviously, from their shorter mother. Had their mother been stocky too? Allison couldn't remember.

Despite their differing physiques, would they have looked alike? The photograph Jo had shown her was too blurred with age to be sure. Perhaps they would have looked similar enough for strangers to pass comment. *You two have to be sisters!*

They wouldn't say that now.

Allison cleared her throat to draw Jo's attention. 'Pasta with a ragu sauce and Parmesan is the best I can do; that okay with you?'

'Sounds good. Can I help?'

'No, you're fine, it'll only be a minute.' She headed back into the kitchen and, this time, shut the door quietly behind her. The pasta was still simmering. Using a wooden spoon, she fished a single piece of penne out and, after a quick puff to cool it slightly, she sucked it into her mouth. It was almost done. She didn't have much time. Opening one of the cupboards again, she stood on her tippy-toes and stretched to reach into the furthest corner. Her fingertips touched the top of the bottle and closed over it to lift it free.

The bottle was small, slim. She held it up to the light. The contents looked so harmless. It could almost be water. Except if you swallowed this, you'd be dead in a couple of hours. It had been difficult to acquire but on the dark net, she had discovered, anything could be bought, and no questions asked. Even something as deadly as strychnine.

Poor Jo. Even when she was much younger, she'd always believed the stories Allison would spin, sometimes merely for their entertainment, sometimes as a cover for deeds she had done... the petty thieving, the rude words scrawled on the smooth surface of their house wall, the disappearance of plants their mother had painstakingly planted the day before. Jo would give a gap-toothed grin and believe anything her big sister told her.

As she'd believed Allison's story about surprising Peter. She huffed a laugh. Honestly, what a ridiculous tale and Jo had swallowed every single lying word.

Peter... Allison shook her head. They'd told her she was a monster and with what she'd done to her parents and sisters, it wasn't hard to believe. But she'd never allowed it to take control again. Not till he'd come into her life. All the elegant clothes, the highlights in her hair, the fancy designer bags and shoes had made her into the woman he loved. But the charade had been too difficult to maintain. And she'd been afraid – she could admit it now – that he'd hate the woman she really was. She could live without him, but she couldn't live without the life he'd shown her, and the home she loved.

So, she'd let the monster out and engineered his death. Someone had told her once that regrets were the currency of fools, and perhaps they were right. Discovering she'd truly loved Peter only after his death had been a shock. Finding out he'd been a lying bastard was devastating. If she'd only known... what a team they could have made together.

Too late, as most things were.

She'd bought the strychnine as a backup, in case something went wrong in the station. In case she'd chickened out at the last moment. Hadn't been able to give that final push. Hadn't really been able to kill her husband.

Mariticide. She'd looked up the word later. The word for killing a sister was already known to her: fratricide. There was no word for killing two. Allison had let the monster out; why not make use of it before burying it deep inside again? See it as payment for all the years she'd put up with that awful chanting that still rang in her ears. She could hear it even now over the bubbling pasta, that awful sing-song: *monster, monster, mons-ter.* Why not use it, when she needed to?

Without Jo, the money would be hers. Enough to buy the house, plenty left to do all that was needed to make it a home. Her home.

She put the jug of sauce into the microwave, drained the pasta and divided it between two shallow bowls. When the microwave pinged, she took the jug out and poured half the sauce over her pasta.

It was time. She twisted the cap on the small bottle, held it to her nose and sniffed. Not too unpleasant a smell. She touched the tip of her finger against the rim and put it on her tongue. Slightly acerbic but not too strong. The ragu sauce was quite spicy; Jo would never notice the addition. She took the Parmesan from the fridge and used a vegetable peeler to add shavings to each bowl.

All ready. She put both bowls on a tray. 'Here we go,' she said, placing the tray on the coffee table.

'That looks lovely!' Jo sniffed. 'And smells divine. I'm suddenly starving.'

'It's only pasta and ragu; I wouldn't get overly excited.' Allison handed her one of the serviettes she'd added to the tray. 'Enjoy.' She sat on the opposite sofa with her bowl in one hand, the fork poised in the fingers of her other. '*Buon appetito.*'

Jo looked at her, the smile still hovering. 'You did mean what you said, didn't you?'

Allison used her fork to stir the cheese through the pasta. What was Jo talking about? She'd said so many things. Some were even the truth. 'I'm sorry, I don't understand...'

Jo's smile faltered. 'About taking me to get a new wig, maybe better make-up... make me look, you know, a bit better.' She chuckled softly. 'Remember when you pinched some of Mum's make-up and did us both? We were like bloody clowns.'

No, Allison had forgotten. It came to her now, in full colour. Two giggling girls, mouths painted a garish red, eyes like pandas. Such fun... Allison could almost hear their laughter pealing through the years. It had ended suddenly when their mother appeared. The memory of what came next caused her eyes to widen and the hand holding the bowl to shake so badly a piece of pasta fell from the side of it to land on the sofa beside her, sauce spattering in a circle around it. 'You said it was you.' She met Jo's eyes. 'You took the blame. I remember Mum caught you by the arm and smacked you with the flat of her hand until she grew tired. You had tears pouring down your face, but you still didn't tell her it had been me.'

Jo shrugged. 'You were my big sister. You used to include me in everything, remember. I adored you.'

Allison remembered. Putting her plate down, she got to her feet abruptly. 'I'm sorry, it tastes like the cheese is off.' She held her hand out for Jo's plate. 'I can make some more; one thing we always have plenty of is jars of sauce and packets of pasta. It'll only take a few minutes. Maybe we can open a bottle of wine too, celebrate a new start for both of us; what d'you think?'

Jo handed over her plate without argument. Doing as Allison had told her all those years before.

In the kitchen, Allison used the toe of her shoe to open the pedal bin and scraped both meals inside. Despite what she'd done, as a child, as an adult, couldn't she even now change? Was it ever too late to make amends?

'I was thinking...' She stood in the living room doorway and smiled at her sister. 'Bugger cooking. If we're going to celebrate, let's do it in style. One of my favourite restaurants does delivery; I can order us a gourmet meal. What d'you think?'

Jo nodded emphatically, her wig slipping further askew.

Allison crossed to her side, bent down and straightened it. 'And maybe afterwards, we can start making plans for our future.'

'Our future...' Jo's voice wavered.

'No point in you paying London rent when this place is big enough for both of us, is there?' Allison tugged a strand of the wig gently. All these years of searching, she'd never found the life she'd wanted, the happy one she'd longed for as a child. Perhaps with this scarred woman, her sister, she could finally put the past behind her and put the monster to bed forever.

Maybe.

It was worth giving it a try.

ACKNOWLEDGMENTS

Book twenty-two – writing those words gives me an unbelievable thrill.

So many people deserve thanks for getting me this far.

Firstly, my amazing publisher, Boldwood Books. Such an amazing team: the CEO, Amanda Ridout; my supportive editor, Emily Ruston; copy editor, Becca Allen; proofreader, Shirley Khan; the sales and marketing team, Nia Beynon, Claire Fenby and Jenna Houston; and of course, the wonderful cover designers.

There are so many people in the writing community who deserve thanks for their support, but the following deserve a special mention – Leslie Bratspis, Pam Lecky, Lynda Checkley, Judith Baker, Anita Waller, Keri Beevis, Jim Ody, Donna Morfett, Beverley Ann Hopper, Helen Pryke Domi, Diane Saxon, Debbie Young, Helen Blenkinsop, Caroline Maston and Samantha Brownley.

Out on their own, of course, Jenny O'Brien – thanks again.

My family are always there for me – my eldest sister, Patricia Hudson, who reads an early draft and is always encouraging; my younger sister, Joyce Doyle, who reads and always has a question! I'm also lucky enough to have some wonderful nieces and nephews who are supportive – this book is dedicated to one, my niece, Niamh.

A huge thanks to my husband, Robert, who doesn't mind when I disappear for hours because I just have to write.

And every blogger and reader who reads, reviews, contacts me, helps to promote, thank you all so much. It means so much.

If you'd like to contact me – you can do so here:
Amazon: https://authorcentral.amazon.co.uk/gp/books
Facebook: https://www.facebook.com/valeriekeoghnovels
Twitter: https://twitter.com/ValerieKeogh1
Instagram: https://www.instagram.com/valeriekeogh2
BookBub: https://www.bookbub.com/authors/valerie-keogh

MORE FROM VALERIE KEOGH

We hope you enjoyed reading *The Widow*. If you did, please leave a review.

If you'd like to gift a copy, this book is also available as an ebook, digital audio download and audiobook CD.

Sign up to Valerie Keogh's mailing list for news, competitions and updates on future books.

https://bit.ly/ValerieKeoghNews

The Lodger, another gripping read from Valerie Keogh is available now.

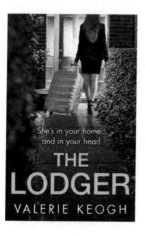

ABOUT THE AUTHOR

Valerie Keogh is the internationally bestselling author of several psychological thrillers and crime series, most recently published by Bloodhound. She originally comes from Dublin but now lives in Wiltshire and worked as a nurse for many years.

Follow Valerie on social media:

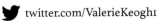 twitter.com/ValerieKeogh1
 facebook.com/valeriekeoghnovels
instagram.com/valeriekeogh2

THE

Murder

LIST

**THE MURDER LIST IS A NEWSLETTER
DEDICATED TO ALL THINGS CRIME AND
THRILLER FICTION!**

**SIGN UP TO MAKE SURE YOU'RE ON OUR
HIT LIST FOR GRIPPING PAGE-TURNERS
AND HEARTSTOPPING READS.**

SIGN UP TO OUR
NEWSLETTER

BIT.LY/THEMURDERLISTNEWS

Boldw**oo**d

Boldwood Books is an award-winning fiction publishing company seeking out the best stories from around the world.

Find out more at www.boldwoodbooks.com

Join our reader community for brilliant books, competitions and offers!

Follow us
@BoldwoodBooks
@BookandTonic

Sign up to our weekly
deals newsletter

https://bit.ly/BoldwoodBNewsletter